End of the River

End of the River

A Savannah Story

By

Robert David Martin

ISBN:9798722433190 (paperback)

This book is dedicated to Zaylee and Aria.

Table of Contents

The Beginning of the End

Ninety-three million miles away, the sun shines on the earth at the magical twenty-three-degree angle that creates the seasons and all of life. It hits the planet on this day along the river that courses through Georgia on its meanderings to embrace the world of a single young person. He knows nothing of the river's origins or course, but his life is entwined with its existence. In the world outside of Ricky Bateman, nature does its thing whether he knows it or not, whether he cares or not.

Yet the old Tugaloo and Chattooga Rivers still join and transform into the Savannah below the Hartwell Reservoir, then tumble down the unimpressive Calhoun Falls to find their regulator in the Clarks Hill Dam. It never completely recovers its old self but manages to regain its Savannah identity thereabouts; there is enough left to twist and turn past the Medical College of Georgia in Augusta, guaranteeing the Georgia border remains well marked by its sometimes turgid waters. Down, down in the forced Negro memory way, it courses past the cotton fields not too far from Egypt, a little town named by an old man that never knew more than that there were great pyramids somewhere in a country by that name. Savannah River run, run, run past the old cotton-gotten gin; flow, flow, flow speedily and swirlingly and smashingly against the banks where the Neegra folk (as the little barefoot white boys say) fling their lines for fish, dangling for lazy indefinite hours that hopeful string, not even caring if the catfish bite.

Your identity becomes more certain, Savannah River. No longer an "it." Now you are a living entity, embracing all that lives because of you bank to bank. You deserve to be personified, explained as a living entity, a body of water transformed into an element of existence for thousands.

Then turn, turn about your quieter, unpowerful waters and recorrect to seek your lemming paradise along the clay banks of your namesake town. Settle, settle, quiet yourself in the broad expanse of the Savannah cove beneath the Talmadge bridge. "Oglethorpe, Oglethorpe," you mutter and murmur within the opaque muddy slowing, thinking in your timeless way of the dirty cold-winded day in February when he landed on the banks with his load of criminals, Jews, and wide-eyed hopefuls grateful for his, the humanitarian's, largesse. Splash and splatter, soak into the land. Here old John Silver laid his murderous weapon against Robert Louis Stevenson's tavern fellow so fiercely that death entered the imagination of every youngster who dared to gaze through the darkened windows of the Pirates' House on old Broad Street, a breath from the wharf where the tall sailing ships once moored.

Your old, labored river waters, red, brown, green, gray, all mixed and stirred, all unbeautiful but so well known by the centuries of those of us who have walked along your banks and stared into only your surface reflection. We tried so to make you beautiful, to conjure poetry about you, but could not. Your effluvia nestles into the soggy edges beneath our feet, stirring the fiddler crabs, making them scurry scared into their holes, pulling after them their big oversized claw. Your long liquid wet decay now spreads itself widely over the marsh, soaking amid the tall thoughtless grasses, leaving, leaving, unconsidered, all the history that has been lived. The trilobites and other Jurassic creatures nevermore will crawl creepily in time with your currents and the way you condescend to merge with the Atlantic tides. What existences do you know without remembering? Gurgling, whirlpooling, idling, no-consequence river, you have little to show for yourself but archaic thoughts, white cotton, black refuse, evil white-hooded angries, and tattered emptiness. Slowly, so slowly, slowing down, water waffling, no crest waves, rippleless, currentless; still, you, the river, become quiet, soft, nearly motionless, then still again, lost without distinction in the estuaries that fold upon you. Day gives way to night. The robust, streaming necessity covered by the Southern sun reflecting on the mirrored waters is gone; night contains the visionless, formless, motionless wet. Forever you remain oozing in and out of the marsh mud, whispering against the salty sticks and muck, the silent tidal pools. Incessant mixing, mixing and mingling among the already been. Moist, quiet declarations move upward from your world. The waters have stopped yet you claim. Change ceases. There is nowhere to go, you say. Savannah is here and no longer moves, and nothing moves in it. Beyond this is the end of the world, the limitless

Atlantic. After Tybee, there is nothing worthy. Stop here, your motionless waters speak. Remain. Go no further. Remain. In this silent night conclusion, your impotent importance begins to sleep. "Remain," the breezes of the sunless warm clime sing. The sleepy night creatures languish in your savanna pools. "Remain." The sighs of your grass rustling hold on to the damp air and soothe the souls of those sleeping along your shores. "Remain," speak the sotto tones of the salty mists rising and spreading through the town squares and streets. Wafts of "remain" swirl around the tired and somnolent, holding them in a vibrantless life, floating for tomorrow without reflection. You, *terminatus terminal.* You, a final place You, living, resting river. You, capture, hold, keep, restrain those encompassed by your waters. Without waking, the thoughtless thousands of Savannah hear your call, detect your smell, feel the attraction of your Siren's message. Yes, they listen. They obey. They remain. Remaining is the compelling restraint. The misty dampness of the resting river surrounds the young man of the story.. Ricky awakens to another day.

CHAPTER 1

Ricky, an Introduction

THE SUN WAS not strong this morning of a Savannah awakening. Its power was blocked by the ever-present clouds, and today those clouds were particularly thickly gathered and blocked its rays. It was too cold for the vegetable and fruit pushcarts and their melodious owners calling out their meager offerings; it was too early for anything but the newspapers thrown onto the sidewalk as if the information they contained mattered. The eponymous river has settled in ponds, caressing the grasses but keeping itself far enough away from Ricky Bateman's house so that he doesn't consider its existence. Yet the water dominates the planned town and gives whatever of its coming and going is important to the idle, quiet, uncreative community that is Ricky's home.

It would surprise a lot of Yankees to know that the piercing cold of a snowless Savannah morning is more bitter to the body than the below-freezing temperatures of the North. The thirty degrees and the dampness in the air caused by the Savannah marshes make it all but impossible to push the covers away and prepare yourself for school.

There was no questioning: school had to be served. Attendance was a family requirement, and Ricky had learned that no amount of excuses would turn his parents demands' away. He took a deep breath, checked on the necessary positions of his tossed clothes from his place beneath the blankets. He noted exactly where his shoes were, saw his pants and yesterday's shirt draped over the chair, and calculated the amount of cold he had to accept and the distance involved. With sudden determination, he propelled himself toward them, pulling everything over his shivering body as quickly as he could. The vigorous process of getting dressed warmed him a little. Wondering for the hundredth time why his parents kept the house at the temperature of an igloo, he went through the mindless ritual of finishing his preparations for the day.

Breakfast was a hit-and-miss affair. Sometimes his mom would prepare something for him. Today it was Rice Krispies and milk simply left on the table. She saw him eat, then scurried back further into the house to wake his brothers. They were always less efficient than he was. At seven thirty, he was ready for almost nothing. He pulled his jacket around himself, held his books close, and waved to his mother, who, having waved back insouciantly, quickly and unceremoniously turned her back and closed the door. In this predictable and bland family fashion, he began his long walk to school.

Richard Bateman was not sure what he wanted to do about the most pressing topic preoccupying him. "I've really got to call her," he thought, and then immediately put the matter aside. "Thinking about Linkowitz is not going to get me to school." It was a gray-to-colorless, bitter, windy day in November; no day to walk the eighteen blocks to his destination, Savannah High School.

Linkowitz was the obsession that triggered his morning erections. His understanding of this was minimal. He didn't have the life experience to put his passion into a larger picture. He was blinded by the sexual and oblivious to the greater question of just who she was as a person. He could not reflect beyond his biological imperative.

Ricky was in the process of transformation. His intelligence and sensibilities had not yet embraced the realities of life. He was about to learn about all of that. At this moment, his thoughts were tossing about in his head: girls, Shakespeare class, seeing the school, getting to the school, and the cold.

He had not the slightest thought that this was going to be a year of dramatic transformations. Because he was merely seventeen, the future felt compelling. But this feeling was not translated into something he would consider. At the moment he could list his beliefs. His father was mean and unpredictable. Ricky was glad when the old guy was working and not around to yell at him. Girls were unapproachable and always right. He was a lonely person with few or no satisfying friends. He was Jewish in name but never felt the identity. His brother had had a bar mitzvah, and he hadn't. This happened because his father's attitudes toward religion amounted to heresy. The list continued. Ricky thought life was fair if you played by the rules, and, finally, and complete aside from the rest of the list, he couldn't decide if he was smart or dumb despite the persistence of his decent grades. He was a confused adolescent struggling to make sense out of it all. There was the ever pressing issue of Robin. Better not to think of her now. Better not to think. It was too cold anyway.

Once the girl of his fantasies was forcibly dismissed from his mind, his remaining preoccupation was blown into view by a cold wind. His father's car would have made his winter suffering unnecessary. It was not available. the patriarch cherished his car as if it were another son of whom he was proud. "He doesn't need it all day," Ricky argued to himself. The precious chariot was driven to the pawn shop on West Broad and parked; he would let no one touch it, least of all Ricky. From eight in the morning till nine at night, while managing the shop for Izzy, his employer of fifteen years, his father left him, his two brothers, and his mother to enjoy, guiltily, the pleasure of his absence. There would then be no fights, screams, or arguments. His father could not fight, yell, or scare his dependents if he was working. His occupation felt like a blessing to the entire family of five. They were all much happier when he wasn't there. But there was no car either.

He suffered the lack of car as he did anything else, shrugging it away with both shoulders, feeling himself an unfair object of life's roulette. He could not understand his father. He was a bother, a restriction. He never made sense. Why be a father if you couldn't act like one? Ricky felt only confused by it; he knew with certainty lonely that he didn't like Samuel Bateman. He saw him as a threat and a man who didn't care about his own family, least of all his oldest son. Ricky tried to put him and his rigid codes out of his mind. He never did it successfully. Mr. Bateman would always be the father Ricky wished he never had.

It wasn't that Sammy Bateman was a bad man, a man who hit, lied, or betrayed his family. He was honorable, responsible, and, from his point of view, financially supportive. From his point of view, coming straight out of the depression of the thirties, he did everything he was supposed to do. He was also difficult. Ricky felt the effects. His father's easy irritability and tendency to pick on his son over the years gave Ricky a hesitant, introspective style, a style filled with suspicious defensiveness.

Ricky's sensitivity, even a touch of paranoia, was acquired directly from the his father's behavior. His own personality was made problematic, leaving him with a hesitancy in social situations, a tendency to resent authority, and a quick wit in seeing the implicit hostility and unfairness that make up a lot of human discourse. For this reason, he was awkward and not popular. He felt the estrangement from others and often interrogated himself about his own personality. He wanted to change, to lighten up a bit, but couldn't. At least not yet. It was a struggle for him, this wish to have friends and the feeling of alienation his personality brought upon him. What else could he do but rationalize? "I'm not so bad," he would say. It was a hope, something he would tell himself whenever he felt slighted by someone. He was overly touchy about any criticism or friendly jibe.

The walk to high school seemed longer than it was. He felt the cold breaking through the barrier of his pants and swirling around all of his five feet eight inches, brown hair, and slightly stocky frame. The blocks were short, really, but the wind made his trip barely sufferable. He maintained a steady pace as he pulled his windbreaker up to his neck, crossing his arms so that his books were held to his chest. He didn't wear a hat, but his curly hair was protection enough. He could never comb it. His mother constantly yelled at him to learn to comb his hair. "You're getting big. You need a part in your hair," she nagged, standing with arms folded and eyes staring.

The hike was boring largely because the streets were empty and straight. There was nothing of much interest and no shortcuts. He had to take each block and make right angles for all turns. Savannah had been laid out in squares; even those streets extending from the original settlement followed the same pattern. The Reynolds route was no exception. There were only the imperceptibly gentle slopes, not even hills, which were strangely out of place in this flat world of partly covered marshland. In this sterile monotony, it was no surprise that his mind would wander.

"Robin, school, Mom, Dad, paper due…porch." It just popped into his head. There was no reason. He saw a porch. That was all. Why consider such a thing now as opposed to any other time? But there it was. The cold produced it. The cold and the porch. Completely contradictory. A contrast. His mind just reflected upon it. "*All* houses have porches," he told himself. Hardly a revelation. Was he surprised to find something new in what he saw every time he took the same streets to school? No matter how small the house was, whether of brick or wood, wide or narrow, there was a porch. "Why? They never use them." Even in the summer, he realized, the owners didn't use them. People would sit on the lawns, take walks, stand by the neighbor's steps talking over little more than subjects of trivial friendliness, but rarely would they linger on the porch. It was a piece of architecture from another place, or another time perhaps. "Maybe they use them in Mississippi or Alabama?" It was so Southern, the porch, a vestige of memories, of vistas long lost, something no one wanted to relinquish, however superfluous. What did it say? It was the symbol of Southern hospitality, a show of the gregariousness of the people, their affability. "Another false impression," Ricky thought. Savannah was always contradicting itself. "People are nice in Savannah." He pondered his own thought. "Well, they seem polite, but underneath, not so much."

"But Mrs. Larson uses her porch." The one exception he could think of. She lived two houses down from him. She always seemed to be there, like a monument, her gray hair in a bun coiffed by herself, atop her head like a stovepipe; her lean, underfed body in a blemished housedress, always sitting, pert, hands folded in her lap, going back and forth on her wide white wooden rocker, the only porch decoration. Seeing her there, alone on that moving chair wide enough for two, seeing her rock back and forth rhythmically as if to a silent Southern tune, was to see indeed that remaining Southern symbol, that more fortunate dame, an aged Scarlet O'Hara holdover from another South. She and the porch were a recalcitrant persistence, an historical remnant of yet another something the Southern spirit refused to put aside. It might be more of a fable, a romantic wannabe, but it persisted in the spirit of the Southern porch.

Ricky made his right-angle turn around the corner and could make out the vague outlines of the school. It was beyond the athletic field surrounded by the hatching of the hurricane fence, which obscured his view. Now he saw other kids coursing to the large brick three-story Greek-styled building where he was spending the last of his four high school years.

Ricky was Southern by birth. Ricky was Jewish by birth. He was troubled by both. He felt as if he were neither. He saw himself as a misplaced person, someone who refused to accept the accoutrements of his geography and his race. He was always taking exception to what others felt was proof of his affiliation, and he often enumerated his differences to himself. His brother, over whose birth he had never recovered from jealousy, had had a bar mitzvah, but Ricky hadn't. He absolutely did not have a Jewish name. His parents never celebrated the Jewish holidays. He never knew when it was Chanukah or Passover.

He also wanted to deny his Jewish nose. It was large and had that barely detectable but expected small hook at the end. This bothered him considerably. He had studied this Jewish characteristic in the mirror for some time and was despairing over it. To his pleasure, he'd recently become aware of the same nose on non-Jewish movie stars and was acquiring a new belief based on the popular media that he could dismiss the nose. Being in late adolescence, forming into adulthood, he didn't realize that he was merely exchanging one standard for another. Maybe someday the nose would have to be changed; for now, it was better to succumb to dismissing the problem.

After the nose came the next powerful impediment, the circumcision. He often heard his young Jewish contemporaries brag, "Only Jews are cut. Eight days after you're born. Nothing you can do about it. Ha ha. You can't fool anybody! Ha ha ha." For the longest time he felt stuck. "How do you dismiss a bris?" Then he read a novel that told how an Arab had escaped from an Israeli prisoner-of-war camp by showing he was indeed circumcised. He was amazed to learn that Muslims had the same ritual. "Those guys were wrong! They were just looking for something. Boy, did they get it wrong. If you don't know, you can be so easily misled. Somebody wasn't thinking. Why would you even bother to think if all you want to do is to put somebody down? It's anti-Semitism again." It wasn't the last occasion when he was impressed by ignorance.

But his quest for emancipation from his Jewish self could never be so simply accomplished. Two remaining obstacles stood before him, each like a leg of the Colossus of Rhodes: his father, one leg of the giant, and his *zeder*, who still lived at the age of ninety-two in New York, the other leg. Only a Jew would have a zeder. His zeder, his grandfather, his father's father, loomed as a Moses-like presence, insisting on his offsprings' allegiance. This grandfather, Ricky knew, or thought he knew, scorned Ricky's father. Zeder's son had defected from the sacred teachings of Judaism. He broke the rules of the Sabbath and committed untold other religious crimes. Then, in an inconsistency that Ricky kept silent within himself, the same errant father repeatedly lectured to Ricky that it was impossible to deny his origins. Zeder's son's words echoed in his Ricky's mind. "Remember," he would say in perfect New York English, shaking his forefinger like the iconic angry rabbi, "no matter what you think, you're still a Jew. If Hitler came here, you would be rounded up with all the others!"

There was no escape. He seemed stuck with what he was. He was not ashamed to be a Jew; he felt no hate for Jews. He simply never felt what he thought a Jew was supposed to feel. He lacked the awesome respect for God. He had no wish to help the UJA in its intense quest for supporting Israel, the supposed Zionist homeland, the newly formed emerging state. He felt no passionate drive to learn Hebrew or to study the Torah. He felt, well…nothing. Religion to him was a curiosity, perhaps an alien art form, a dance, a ballet he experienced as the work of a choreographer from an exotic world. When he did go to synagogue—an occasional necessity in a town with three to four thousand Jews, some of whom had children who were Ricky's contemporaries—then he would observe the dance with pensive detachment.

In the Shabbos ceremony Ricky rarely went to out of necessity, the rabbi moved solemnly to the songs of the cantor. Both of them seemed to be engulfed in their black robes. Their black-striped-white tallit swayed and flapped to the rhythm of the shifting bodies. The bending and bowing to the unintelligible Hebrew chanting seemed designed more for a celestial observer than the minions in the pews. Ricky let his imagination go. "Yes, I am here with the rabbis, the priests, on a plateau in an unnamed territory. There are no boundaries, no cities, no demarcations to make me feel familiar or comfortable. Their arms are holding the Torah, calling to Yahweh repetitively and yearningly." For what seemed like an endless expanse of time, the davening, singing, and subvocalizing to God would continue. "I am somehow a part of this, but I am the unbelieving sinner. The ritual is not for me. I don't believe. I am alone, frightened. There is a horde around the rabbis. Everyone sways and sings in unison except me. I'm a pretender, a reject without credentials beyond my birth. Fear." They kissed the Torah over and over. The clouds parted. A celestial hand stayed the lightning meant for the one who didn't belong, leaving the alienated unrepentant to feel only misery. The crowd cheered, grateful, joyous. He, the sinner, was spared with them, though only a fellow traveler included by the error of being in the congregation. Nevertheless, he was grateful, though confused. "Maybe I will be Jewish?"

Then, the singing and swaying completed, he was jerked back from his imagination, bored with the tedium of the real ceremony. He asked himself, "What *am* I doing here?"

Religion was important to Ricky in spite of his alienation. He wanted so much to resolve the battle between what he was born to be and what he should indeed be. He felt in his core that the solution would have major repercussions in his life, though he could not explain why. His mind gripped with confused claws onto the issue and would not let it go.

But it took second place in his repertoire of concerns: sex and science. Religion, as serious as it was to him, withered by comparison. He was seventeen, almost eighteen. He thought about sex more than about religion, more than about science. He could get passionate about both, though there seemed to be absolutely no connection between the two. Science was grand, it was mental, it was the future. With science the mind rose into deified intellectual harmonies with the firmament. If Yahweh wasn't there, then Einstein certainly was. It was a prepossessing subject. To him it was, indeed, mind music.

Sex? Different. Below the waist. He felt it. It rose in him. It held him. Nothing rational, nothing clear thinking about it. It simply was.

"A person doesn't consider sex, he does something about it. Sex is natural," he argued, though his virginal biology remained mystified. "It's in the Bible, even in the Koran. It's everywhere, in everything. It's part of religion." He seemed certain while understanding nothing. Sex was an exotic animal that held him, but he had no idea why. He was merely part of the reproductive-animal world, and he did not, could not, see his place in the natural scheme of things. Sex was a part of him he had yet to understand. He could put it up there next to religion. He could make sense of neither.

He was not equipped to observe his argument, to decide upon its reasonableness. He didn't want to. While Ricky's interest in science was limitless, widespread, and there was no corner of that subject into which he did not look, think about, or taste of its wonderful and endless diversity, his interest in sex had a limited, specific, singular goal: Robin Linkowitz.

At that moment, Ricky turned the corner. He was in the same block as the school. He didn't know, but could easily assume on reflection, that Robin Linkowitz was already in class. In fact, she was in homeroom. She was not in his homeroom, because he was assigned to a different one. He knew she was sitting in Mrs. Bonton's class, talking with other Jewish girls. The girls Ricky's age were cliquish and careful to congregate within their ethnic class. They would be reluctant to talk with the Christians.

Robin was attractive, but not terrifically so, not beautiful. She was brunette, a dark-haired, sultry, bewitching Jewess. He saw her with her tender complexion and flowing hair as an enticing goddess. He missed the hidden, mysterious, nocturnal presence that always shadowed the inner female aggressiveness. No matter—she spoke in a soprano voice with a recognizable Southern slur at the end of her words. Her breasts were not large, but with the stiff material of the pointed bras that created the conical form, the two orbs penetrated the air, piercing a great distance approaching Ricky's imagined touch.

That moment in his approach to school, his obsession with Robin and sex was reaching a crescendo. She was already seated in class, completely engrossed in conversation. Not the din of the other students in the room, not the voice over the loudspeaker nor the calling of the teacher for order, could interrupt her bibulous infatuation with her friends. These were engrossed, Savannah teenager Jewish girls. The topic was certainly nothing weighty, nothing of moment. There were no allusions to Eisenhower's nuclear strategy, nor concern over the problem with Nasser in Egypt. To them there was something of more immediate concern. The young Southern girl of that moment was intrigued by crinoline and blouses. Leaning…leaning backward over rear of her desk chair, in a huddle with two others, she was immersed in her dialogue. Her hair was held back with a broad white headband. The lipstick she wore was especially red and dark. If she weren't Jewish, her brown-and-white saddle shoes would have marked her as a bobby-soxer; there were always some who believed it was impossible to be both a bobby-soxer and Jewish. The contemporary females of Savannah, whatever their persuasion, were, well…contemporary.

"I just bought it at Levy's on Broughton, you know the place. Nine ninety-nine. That's all it cost."

Robin's voice, to any normal mortal, would have been ordinary, perhaps a little charming. Ricky thought it mellifluous.

"Really!" Lyla, her sometimes friend, answered. "Why, I heard you could get the same thing for eight ninety-nine at Penney's. It's really the exact same brand."

"I wouldn't buy anything at Penney's. I don't even like to go into that store. Why do you go there, Lyla?"

There was an edge to Robin's voice, a slight tone of disdain. Becky, the third girl, picked up on it and hurried to Lyla's defense.

"Oh, I don't think Penney's is so bad. They have woonderfulll baargins." Her accent was the thickest of the three.

Chatter chatter. The three friends went on like this, talking of daily living, the costs of fabrics, dresses, scarves, shoes. Their world was much removed from his. They had no concerns with religion, politics, or science. There was hardly any common ground between them and a boy like Ricky.

No. There was one. They shared the same concern as did he with sex. Though they might never display their interest to the boys around them until later in their lives, their preoccupation was no less. All the gabbing was to heighten their communal sense of what it took to make one sexually attractive. A boy like Ricky might look with disdain on such a conversation were he able, in the unlikely event, to hear it. But he would be wrong, for they and he thought alike in truth. Below the waist they were all as one.

These were the friends of the girl of Ricky's dream. This was Robin's milieu. The conversation went on like this for quite a while. Nothing more of substance entered their world. The essence of the Southern belles revealed. They were young, reasonably pretty, and as empty headed as could be imagined. Crinolines, dresses, parties, the fundamental demands of school—just enough to get the respectable C—made up their world. They joked that college was for the MRS degree. Learning? Not for this group.

So why did Ricky think of nothing but Robin? Why was she the sole solution to his sexual needs? They were young, attractive, and living close together. It would be easy to see them as an appealing young couple. Beyond that and the clear sexual vibrations, there was more.

Ricky and Robin were truly star crossed. Regardless of one's beliefs in astrology, no one could deny that they both were born on the same day, at the same time, at the same hospital, Telfair, on the same floor, and were first deposited in nearby rooms. His mother used to joke that the nurse had brought Robin to her first and then realized she had made a mistake. And now, in what to some might seem like another complete coincidence, Robin's family lived on the same block as Ricky's did.

He had always admired Robin's house. It was two stories tall, white framed, with a gabled window in the front. He always thought her family had more money than his. He saw that rich home every day and wondered about its insides. He never knew whether the gabled front window was Robin's or not, but he let himself believe it was. His modest home was eight houses away, almost at the other end of the street, but still on the same side, just before where the paving disappeared onto dirt. It was impossible for him not to pass what must have been the entrance to her bedroom every time he went to school. He wanted to stop and stare but was afraid a Linkowitz would come and ask him what he was doing. This fear was unfounded, because in all the years of living on the same street, he never remembered seeing, except for one little birthday party, Robin or any of her family. He felt a kind of mystery persisted about the single gabled edifice, a mystery encompassing an uncertainty about someone who seemed like a sister, an erstwhile sexual fantasy, but who in the real-world scheme of things was only a neighbor.

For years Robin was of no importance to him. Aside from the silence seemingly emanating from her house, nothing about her caught his attention. Only recently she, the girl behind the window, began to intrigue him. He could not explain this emerging obsession, this interest in her, but he didn't care. She became his imagined Aphrodite, the fulfilling of his youthful sexual passion. She was the girl he thought about if he released himself in an onanistic moment. It would have been impossible for him to consider that she could transform into something other than engrossing. He could never think of her as someone punishing, someone like a Lilith.

From sixteen on Robin noticed Ricky's interest, his staring up at her window, his seeming attentiveness. She made herself believe he was completely unimportant. She knew he was viewed by the other kids as somewhat of an oddball. Though she saw him often at parties, she could never understand why he was invited. She noticed he wasn't ugly, but her slight attraction to him never overcame her sense of what was socially right. Her mother would ask her sometimes why she didn't date him. "Mom, he's too much into his books. The other girls don't like him either. He's OK, really, but I just don't think we'd get along."

Ricky was not popular among the other Jewish kids, certainly not a date that Robin's friends would envy. He was just *there*, as far as she was concerned. As her awareness of his interest in her increased, she came to see him more and more as an inconvenience, though his attentions did offer her an ounce of pleasure. Once in a while, she would consider him with an inner smile, a sort of a joke to herself:

"He thinks just because we have the same birthday and all, we've got something together. Huh!"

Ricky remembered her eighth birthday party. He knew he was invited by her mother, who arranged the whole thing with his mother. They must have thought it was cute and about time. He, nevertheless, kept mostly to himself. Then the two mothers insisted he join Robin to blow out the candles together. Being forcibly joined to celebrate that day, the day they were both born at the same time, created a bond of sorts, and he felt even more attached to her. He did not know her mother had forced the invitation upon her. "You've got to ask him, honey. He lives on the same block. Besides, I don't want to offend his mom. She was very sweet about it."

He had all these feelings and other unconscious, ineffable considerations. He could not put everything together into meaningful form in his mind. They all worked together to glue Ricky's thoughts to Robin the person.

Anything but glue was working for her side. At the moment that this infatuation was unfolding, the astrological significance of being star crossed with Ricky meant danger for her. She believed intensely in astrology. She had learned it from her grandmother. The shtetl-born wizened old woman had a hump in her arthritic back and a mild-mannered peasant perspective in her mind. Immigration to the modern world of America had done nothing to alter her natural convictions about the stars, an absolute belief beyond argument about their permutations, acquired from her mother and other women of her village when she was a little girl in Eastern Europe. Before she died at the age of eighty-six, she left with her favorite granddaughter the belief that stars had an overbearing influence on her life. "Day must be taken seriously," she said with a trembling extended forefinger. Though Robin long rejected the idea of Ricky, finding it usually distasteful to hold her name and his in her mind simultaneously, the astrological power of the connection was not lost upon her. Whatever her feelings, in the primitive and unthinking world of star magic, anything could happen.

Over the past year, as his adolescent sexuality imposed itself on his intellect, Ricky decided to pursue his presumed love despite her clearly demonstrated persistent disinterest. Try as he wished (as great as his desire was, his pain upon being rejected was almost its equal), he found himself unable to distract himself from her many enveloping attributes: her breasts, her narrow waist, her ebony hair atop her lush Jewish body, all reminding him again of Aphrodite, or, more appropriately, of Ivanhoe's Rebecca. He came easily by his literary allusions and enjoyed comparing his love with anyone that seemed exotic and beautiful enough.

He might be able to put her out of his mind as a literary allusion, but he had no control over the morning erections. His passion repeatedly rose with the sun, and he was driven to telephone her for a date. Many times Robin, like the imagined literary Rebecca, said no to the best, most impressive, most beckoning voice he could muster. He would hang up the phone with a feeling of despair and self-recrimination. Once he recovered, his desire to make out with her intensified. (It would never occur to him to even consider going all the way.).

Ordinarily, perhaps, his rational scientific mind would have put her image into a petri dish and stored it successfully in the refrigerator. He would have recognized her reluctance and dismissed her as not worthy of his effort. But there was no stemming the force of his nature. The potent addition of the repeated charges of his groin and the sunrise of his mental image of her gave him little alternative than to succumb to the inevitable.

This was the state of the virgin's romantic life as he turned the corner and walked toward the school.

CHAPTER 2

School

THE SPRAWLING BRICK building was suddenly before him. It was always like that. One moment he was feeling his way along the early-morning desert of empty streets, and the next thing he knew, the massive building came upon him like an elephant on the African plains. The athletic field with its bordering chain-link fence seemed to prevent the building from attacking him. Now, passing the field, he became filled with all memories of his failures as an athlete. "What choice?" The same question every time. Like a lab rat, the football turf stoked his disappointments, his memories of having not made the team. "Why did I even try?" It was his forsaken football turf. The same obsessive ideas emerged. "I could be there working out for the game, but I screwed up. So…I'm not a jock." His inner voice sounded plaintive, designed to heal. He remembered how diligently he'd pursued his goal. He never missed an afternoon practice. He always came early. When the coach called, he jumped with an eagerness that suggested football was the only thing he loved.

"Why didn't I make it?" The answer was all too simple. Despite his yearning, his heart was not into getting mauled. He saw those guys running toward him looking for his blood, which not coincidentally, he knew, happened to be Jewish blood. He saw their Southern Christian white eyes speak: "Smash him! Pulverize him!" He felt the threat, the guarantee that if he stayed in this sport, these massive tanks were going to annihilate him. When the gargantuan human instruments of his destruction came toward him, he wanted to cry out, "Look, I'm not really Jewish. I wasn't even bar mitzvahed!" Though he never spoke these words, he hesitated, he feinted when he should have run forward into the mass, and his tendentious enthusiasm in scrimmage easily came to the coach's attention. Ricky did not even make second string. These often-repeated thoughts caused him to sigh to himself. "So I'm not a member of the football team. There are compensations. At least I won't have to have spinal surgery at nineteen." With that pleasant thought, he walked by, finally, the remaining symbol of what he had relinquished in his lost football, and was, in face-full, staring momentarily before ascending, the steps of the of the school.

The huge supine H-shaped brick building with its two token white Doric columns at the doorway loomed before him as he began walking sprightly up its sixteen steps.

"Hey, Ricky…licky dicky! Hey, hey, Ricky. Licky doo dicky! Hey…you *mastur-bate man*?!" There were three of them cackling, laughing, and swaggering at him, but only Bill Williams sang the song. Ricky felt the anger that always welled up in him when he was being insulted. There was, too, the expected despair. It was a despair built on the belief that there was nothing he could do. Bill Williams glared at him, slick and white, his cigarette lip with its two-and-a-half-inch appendage dangling James Dean style from his mouth. His grin was sinister, and he was working hard to exhibit ruthless disdain toward his noncombative adversary. His white T-shirt, leather jacket with shiny silver buttons agape, his deep black wop of hair greased down to his flat-topped skull, his teeth reflecting the morning sunlight bouncing off the white school columns: he was the epitome of the envious angry punk. But Ricky did not know that. To him, Bill Williams was pure intimidation, Any reasonable retort was hopeless. The two like-dressed comrades who paraded about joining the chiding dance gave a group-ritual quality to the moment of cheap, low-class triumph. Bill might be hanging on to high school by a thread, suspension could be just a few days away, but "Boy," Ricky thought, "he sure knows how to get to me!" Ricky walked by him, making as if the musical words and choreography were of no consequence. The three necromancers joined as if rehearsed with their sneering, but Ricky was now through the door and grateful that he couldn't hear them. As he entered and turned his head for a look, he saw Bill giving him the finger, thrusting his hand repeatedly upward in a gesture as obscene as any evil witch doctor could contrive.

Bill Williams. Two first names, he thought. Funny how these hates build up. All from a stupid, unimportant incident. The feelings couldn't come just from that. These feelings had their roots deep inside Bill's world, a world exotic to Ricky. But the incident certainly fueled the fire, and the flames resisted any forgetting.

Ricky and Bill had a history beyond high school taunting. When they were little, they had been neighbors. Friends, even.

CHAPTER 3

An Important Digression

BILL AND RICKY had been friends at play. As with so many pre-teenagers, they didn't know the soon to be defined issues of discrimination and hate. They had not yet been taught.

Bill had lived a mere five or six houses away on the opposite side of Duffy Street from the Batemans This story happened before they moved to Fifty-Seventh Street, the richer block where Robin lived. The location change was all an accident, an incidental relocation, with nothing to do with the following tale of Ricky and Bill. The family merely went slightly economically upward. That was what they thought. That was how they wanted to see it.

These were the days of Ricky's pre-high-school childhood. To Ricky home was home, and the economics of it meant nothing. The reality was different. The houses were on a dirt road of minimum wages. While Ricky lived down the road from his then friend, his family's perspective was for a better economic future. Bill's family was stuck with no prospects out of the deprived present. It was a period when stories would be remembered.

Bill's house was diagonal from Ricky's, the apex of an acute angle. The old dirt street had rocks, hills and valleys that demanded attention. the town having not yet paved that far away from its urban center. Ricky was number seven, and Bill was twelve.

During the early part of their friendship, Bill liked to come over to Ricky's backyard because of the very large pecan tree there, a tree that would forever be a fond memory. It had huge branches extending low to the ground, perfect for climbing and sitting. The kids spent a lot of time cowboy shooting make-believe at each other using the tree as a western mountain hideaway.

One day, Bill got something more inviting in his yard: a raccoon. He possessed it. It was his treasure tied by a light rope to a small magnolia tree trunk. Ricky would go over those first few weeks after the raccoon arrived and play in Bill's backyard. There, the animal replaced the other usual pastime of throwing stones into an oversized mud puddle that substituted for a pond.

Ricky remembered that Sunday as if it were the same day he walked into the school after being taunted. In fact, it was the very image he had as he walked away from the tormenting trio. He could then see Bill from his house and remembered sauntering over. When he arrived, he expected, as always, to dodge the splashes from the rocks Bill threw.

This time he discovered his friend with another boy, Oscar, playing with the animal. The two were so engrossed with the mask-eyed critter that they failed to acknowledge Ricky's presence. Ricky felt a natural cautiousness and stayed back, watching Bill and Oscar tease the new pet with a carrot. Ricky slowly walked nearer and noticed a thin rope around the creature's neck, clearly meant to keep it from running away. The raccoon would pull at his leash as he desperately tried to grab and eat the carrot, held just beyond the limit of the rope. There was no way to bite it. After watching awhile, Ricky was convinced he had become a member of the group and asked, "Can I touch him?" He was ignored. The raccoon took advantage of the now extended play of the string and ran away to the puddle. He dipped his paws in the water and, while sitting on his hindquarters, rubbed them together. Ricky stood silently. The other two boys, wearied of their entertainment, took and tied the now frustrated animal to the backyard swing. They never gave the carrot to him; Bill stuck the vegetable in his back pocket. The two moved over to the seesaw made of old building plank and a cut tree trunk.

Ricky saw the animal was unattended. He felt more confident and walked over, picked up a rusty can with water, and placed it within reach of the raccoon, wondering how it would react. Bill called out in a harsh tone, "What're you doin'?!" Ricky, startled, stepped back abruptly. "You leave my raccoon alone. Get away from here, you Jew bastard!"

Ricky, though very surprised, answered instinctively, "You can't call me that. I let you play with my airplane, and you climbed my pecan tree."

Bill laughed. "Who cares about your dumb old airplane. It ain't an animal, is it? I don't like your pecan tree, anyway, it's too easy!" Oscar joined him in the derisive glee, laughing in a kind of snicker.

"Anyway, you can't talk to me that way!" Rick yelled back with a confidence and rage that surprised himself. His shock and anger gave way to fear as Bill and Oscar began picking up small rocks and throwing them. Though Ricky did not fully understand the words he heard, he knew exactly what the rocks meant. Throwing the rocks and watching Ricky run across the furrowed street, the two assailants warmed to their entertainment. "Stay off my property," Bill yelled, happily now some distance away. Ricky picked up a large stone, larger than any sent his way, and threatened to heave it at his two adversaries. The stone rested on his palm, held up to his shoulder like he was a disc thrower. He stared at his new enemies across the wide boundary of the dirt street.

His nemeses decided it would be better to stand their ground and not pursue their now offensive quarry. The street became the new great divide between their sense of self-righteousness and the presumed loathsomeness of the contaminating Jew boy. Safe upon their sacred land, across from the execrable antagonist they'd created, they shouted over and over, "Jew bastard, Jew bastard!" They were impressed with how effectively appropriate their words sounded. Somehow the entire scene in which their performance took place seemed right to them.

To Ricky, the new situation certainly felt serious, even though he could not explain the feeling to himself. Moreover, why it had happened was a complete mystery.

Ricky waited that night for dinner to be finished and for his father to retire to the large, cushioned chair reserved by the family for his primary use. He sat across from him, staring at the *Savannah Morning News*, which hid the man entirely from view. Ricky took a breath and spoke.

"Daddy, can I ask you something?" He put the question hesitantly to his father. He decided to be vague. He was afraid of telling the entire story, because he was not sure whether he was somehow at fault.

"What?" his father responded, putting down his newspaper in a rare moment of receptive paternal concern.

"Well, you know Bill Williams?" His father nodded that he did. "Today he called me a Jew bastard. I don't know why. I didn't do anything to him. At least I thought I didn't."

His father became attentive, and for a moment the room filled with silence.

Ricky waited for the recrimination, but instead of admonishing him, his father sat erect and took on a very serious expression. "Who said that?"

Ricky was puzzled by a question he had already answered; but the repetition, which made it sound as if it was his young adversaries who were on the block, increased his confidence. He continued. "I told you, Bill Williams."

The father surprised him by not pursuing the details. The father's expression became very serious. The father became the judge in court. "Ricky, there are some Christians, not all of them, who hate Jews. They have not thought about it very much. They are stupid and ignorant. We know we are smarter. They have to call names at Jews to make themselves feel better. Stay away from this boy. He is bad. If he does this again, let me know. I am sure he is trash anyway. Now you know what it is to be a Jew. Now you understand!"

Ricky didn't at all understand what his father was alluding to. He did know that there was something special about him, but it was a specialness beyond his comprehension. As far as he could tell, he was exactly like Bill and Oscar. But perhaps he wasn't? At least his father said he wasn't. The confusion, in any case, did not keep him awake that night. He just made up his mind that he would give Bill and his friends a wide berth. He never played with them again.

This story framed his relationship with Bill from that time forward. Over the years Ricky heard the whispered word "Jew" coming from Bill whenever he came near. This episode now at the high school entrance was nothing new, but it stung, nevertheless. As usual, as on the many other occasions, he hung his head low, stared at the floor in front of him, and quickly stepped away from the jeering. The acrid soiunds disappeared as the swinging doors closed behind him.

Again, as he passed through these high school doors, Ricky remembered the entirety of the story of the raccoon. Remembering, he had now learned, was something the persecuted did well. He remembered the details. He recalled their clothing; the early remorse over being denied friendship; the disappointment at being denied the right to play with a friendly creature; and the entire sordid meaning of Bill and his friend. Back in the present, inside the entrance of the school, the exact emotion came back but more intensely. He wanted to fight, to rage against their taunts. Instead, he walked away without saying a word. He felt like the same coward that had failed at football. His opponents were the victors. His silence gave every indication that he tolerated their abuse.

Then he quickly decided against this momentary conclusion. He was not a coward. He was practical. He knew he left the offal with a feeling of victory and himself with a mortifying sense of cowardly weakness. They had won nothing, however. He knew they were still cavorting and singing, "Ricky Bateman, masturbater." He didn't care. He remembered what his father said. Bill Williams and his like were living from ignorance and fear. They knew nothing. "They probably masturbate, too," he thought, laughed to himself, and walked on.

Two girls Ricky didn't know passed him in the doorway, giggling, and it was clear they had heard his assailant's song and were sharing in the fun of his adversaries. They were the same, feeling the same harshness, having the same wish to hurt. It didn't matter what sex they were. Their giggles identified them. They were the same as Bill and company. Their souls reveled in the abuse inflicted on him by the others. Staring back through the doorway at the cackling ex-friends who'd begun the assault the girls now enjoyed, he felt the confident grins of these three sleazy alligators hissing at his heals. He continued at a rapid pace into the school, pushing himself further and further into an embarrassed distant retreat, making his way into the waiting crowded channels of the cool school halls.

Room 324. That was his room. He had to pass Robin's homeroom to get to it. He was in luck. Her door was open. He slowed his pace. There she was, talking to her girlfriends. He thought he sensed her looking beckoningly toward him. He felt the urge to go through the wrong doorway to her.

Then he saw she was engrossed in something other than him, something seemingly important. Though, through her chattering, he felt she was looking straight at him as he passed. She gave absolutely no indication that she saw him. He wanted to say something to her, but he didn't dare suffer another embarrassment that morning. He walked past, wondering if she had really noticed him. Was it his imagination? Would she say yes if he called? Maybe, yes, she would. The thought exulted him. In his happiness he felt, the dulling pain from Bill Williams began to dissipate. A charmed peace encompassed him as he entered his homeroom.

CHAPTER 4

Shakespeare Class

THE INCONGRUITY NEVER left Ricky when he considered the contrast between Miss Johns, the wan, anemic, spinster English teacher with whom Ricky was forced to suffer, and the rich-lived and always trenchant Shakespeare. She was the twelfth-grade teacher he hated most. As this class began, he found within himself the usual mixture of pleasure over the material and anxiety and distaste with the media in which it was placed. Miss Geraldine Johns had the beginning of a good name. Ricky wondered whether she'd lopped off the "-ton" as the suffix for her last name for some malignant reason. Perhaps in Grecian or Renaissance times, she would have been applauded for having the svelte figure of an alabaster nereid, but today she seemed more like a sinister antediluvian witch-goddess disguised as a pert, irritable English teacher. Never was there anyone so inappropriate to teach the subject. Her approach was narrow in scope, shallow in depth, and empty of reflection. She made it clear to everyone, even the most conforming Southern student, that she feared sex, love, aggression, any emotional intensity, or philosophical questioning, but, most of all, any challenge to her evidently pitiful understanding of the material before her. She feared the essence, the intricacy of life that literature, at its best, is supposed to spread upon the pallet of existence.

Perhaps later in life, when Ricky was more settled in his understanding of the variegated nature of human beings, he might have forgiven his last high school English teacher. He might have appreciated the social demands upon a Southern woman in the sixth decade of the twentieth century; he may have seen that in the eyes of the school system or her principal, she was a superior individual, someone who could with absolute safety be presented before the community. No scandal would ever emanate from this woman's class. And—God forbid! —no rebellious behavior would ever be displayed. But in his senior year, in his inchoate departure for college and the wide world outside the mind of this woman, Ricky was going to forgive nothing. He felt he was in a dark and sinister narwhal's classroom, frozen there not by his will but by the demands of the senior year schedule.

He was in a dilemma. He could not forgive her stupidity, but he could not be outspoken either. She was the general in the classroom. With a surprising ease, she could inflict damage upon him from which he would not recover. There would be no chance of winning an out-and-out battle in front of her or any other teacher, for that matter. He had to be careful to disguise his disgust. Each day he smoldered beneath her banal observations, her trivial, meaningless comments about whatever was in front of the class. Ricky tried very hard to control himself. He was usually successful.

Today the subject was Macbeth. Miss Johns taught *Macbeth* by not teaching it. For explanation she substituted class reading. By making whatever observations popped into her head at the moment a student struggled with the seventeenth-century text, she was able to avoid preparing at home, reviewing critics' thoughts, or reexamining what was on the printed page in any way. For her it was an easy day. For Ricky it was agony.

Many of the students could hardly read. Some would ponder endlessly over a single word while she sat high on her desk, behind spectacles, waiting insouciantly, though patiently, for the pre-graduate to sweat. She offered no assistance, apparently believing that by the time someone achieved twelfth-grade status, he or she should be able to prespire without help. It was only time for independent study without guidance.

Ricky was relieved when he knew his turn to read out loud was coming. At least he would not be bored out of his mind. He could read quickly, insensitive to his fellow classmates' dismay, rationalizing that it didn't matter, as they probably wouldn't understand what was in the play even if he read slowly. As he mused superciliously over this fact, his pleasure was tempered by the realization that he would surely be interrupted. Whenever he and a few of the other good readers took their part in the play, Miss Johns became more attentive. She would transform into a scrutinizing vulture and give every appearance, at least, of pondering meaning.

It was clear to Ricky, having already gone through *Romeo and Juliet*, that his button-topped teacher, with her blouse secured about her neck schoolmarm fashion, would not tolerate any allusions to text sex (as he liked to call it), even in the great Shakespeare. Every time a line suggested the hidden body parts, Miss Johns would say, "Go to the speech by Duncan at the bottom of the page." Or, "Let's continue reading at line seventy-two." Or the like. She never said what her mind must have spoken—"Avoid the dirty filthy sex lines coming up"—but her meaning left no question.

As he expected, she called on him. Bateman followed Anderston. It was all so nicely laid down. The alphabet exerted its tyranny. Neither adversary could escape what the order of the world predicted. He was prepared to go along today. He hated her and did not want her to know it. Did she know? The inflexible bitch! From her desk she stared at him with her stygian smile. It was if he were transparent gossamer. She didn't see him, Richard Bateman, person, student, someone with a complexity, a story. No, she saw the wall, the book, the task to be completed before her. She did not even see his barely disguised attitude, his scream to escape from her imposed control. He wondered. Maybe she did see it?

"Mr. Bateman, do you know where we left *Macbeth*?"

"Yes, ma'am. It was act 1, scene 5." Did he impress her? No. There was no reaction, only the anemia, the pallor of her mind and skin, her lack of concern for him as a person.

"Good. You read today."

"Yes, ma'am."

The battle lines were drawn. Rick himself didn't know the storm he was about to stir. The trumpet blared for the battle to begin. The Baptist and the Jew squared off. The Effete Phobic gripped the weapon against the Presumed Intellectual. The Empty Isolate stared blankly at the Emerging Explorer. It was (Ricky had told himself later) Ignorance against Knowledge.

Ricky's Prospero placed his hands upon the wrong edition, which had slipped into the school. It was the unabridged version, forced on his adversary because the usual texts had been ruined in a flood in the basement the summer before. He began to swirl the brew with pleasure.

In truth, he had not begun to enjoy the genius of Shakespeare that much. It was hard to read and often confusing. He was just getting an inkling of the drama of the play and began to read with perhaps more excitement than the lines demanded.

As he read, he began to feel like the unseen observer watching a crime about to be committed. Duncan is coming to Inverness. Lady Macbeth knows of the prophesy. She is excited by the prospects. She has just been told that Duncan is to stay with her and Macbeth that night. She speaks:

"The raven himself is hoarse that croaks the fatal entrance of Duncan under my battlements. Come, you spirits that tend on mortal thoughts, unsex—"
"That's enough, Mr. Bateman. You may go on to line 59 on the top of the next page. This is the place where Macbeth enters and says, 'My dearest love.'"

He had to admit, she was deft at this kind of interruption. He marveled at the bland, indifferent way she protected the class from the almost-released smut of the text. The class was not fooled, however. The girls, especially, tittered and giggled. One boy anonymously let out a grunt, and everyone laughed in group safety. In spite of himself, Ricky felt a bristle of anger. "She cut off one of the most dramatic speeches in English literature," he thought. "She doesn't care about the play, or Lady Macbeth's reflections. The essence of the play be damned! All she can do is avoid sex!"

"Why? Miss Johns." He would have to admit to himself that now he'd let the cat out of the bag. His anger was obvious. The class heard him too. His fellow students became abruptly silent. It was a confrontation. The sudden hush scared him. He tried to control himself. He wanted to retreat.

"What is that, Mr. Bateman?" It was a pretension, and he knew it. She had heard him perfectly well.

"Ah, nothing."

"Go on then." She had won the first round. He reconnoitered and felt retreat the safest course. He could feel the class relax. He did as he was bid, continuing through scene 5 and into 6.

There were no more interruptions. He forgot the battle, let down his guard, and began enjoying himself. In scene 7 the two married collaborators finally make it clear that they intend to kill the very person who has been so grand and good to Macbeth. What treachery! But Macbeth has second thoughts. Lady Macbeth upbraids him: "Others have done well by themselves, does their fitness now unmake you? I have given suck—"

"Mr. Bateman, go to the line where Macbeth says, 'If we should fail—'"

"—and know how tender 'tis to love the babe that milks me."

"Mr. Bateman, do you hear me!?" Her voice began to have a shrill. It was as if her house were being blown down. The Great Zephyr swelled his cheeks with yet another attack:

> "I would, while it was smiling in my face, have plucked my nipple from his boneless gums—"

"Mr. Bateman! I demand that you listen to me!" The lean, mean, dark witch of Hansel and Gretel was standing, now asking Hansel why indeed he would not stick out his finger from his cage. She glared at him with a surfeit of rage. The entire class was staring at him. He was gazing fixedly at the text. He had no intention of looking up.

"*—and dashed the brains out—*" Rick shouted in the sound vacuum of the classroom.

"*Mister Bateman!*" she shouted back at him. She wanted to grab him and shove him into the burning oven. At the very least, she wished Mephistopheles would whisk him off to the netherworld. He should burn in hell, simmer in hot oil; he should suffer all the tortures and torments of heathens who demystify the *Ave Maria*. Her aggression knew no bounds. She felt the full moment of tragedy of this 1957. She could do only what she could do. What frustration!

"—had I so sworn as you have done to this." He actually whispered the last line. The effect was wonderful, he thought to himself. The ravenous ambition of Lady Macbeth and the angry rebellion of Ricky Bateman were one. He stopped.

"Should I go on, Miss Johns?" He stared at her angelically, his heart palpitating gladly at his feeling of victory.

"Why didn't you stop when I told you to?" There was a plaintiveness to her tone which surprised him. Was there a note of sadness in her voice as well?

"Miss Johns." He paused and took a breath. "I couldn't stop. The speech was too important. There really is nothing that I could skip. It *is* important."

"In the future, Mr. Bateman, you will do as I say. Your grade in this class is based on participation and decorum, not only on test papers. Do you understand?"

What a brief, sweet victory he had had, but no more. He was victorious and defeated simultaneously. The "grade" got to him. He knew she would take her revenge on him through the grade. He could not win. He couldn't change teachers in January. If he brought his "problem" to the principal, it would be a mess. How could he bring together this threatened woman, this dangerous viper whose very essence was threatened by forbidden words, with his parents in a confrontation? Impossible.

He sensed the class was angry at him. What was he trying to do, anyway? It was just a crummy English course with a dumb play. They hated every moment in the classroom; why did he have to make it worse? What difference did it make if they skipped parts? The whole thing was so boring anyway. This was what their glowering eyes said to him. It would be better to shut up and sink down into his desk chair. He felt alone, angry, and sapped of his rebellious energies.

"Yes, ma'am."

Edward Blaker was told to continue reading. The class period ended with the stuttering enunciation of the reader who made the cries of alarm over the death of Duncan sound like the directions to the third floor toilets. But in Ricky's still-reeling mind, the death of Duncan was exciting because in the king's place he put Miss Johns. He smiled quietly as he imagined the general applause at the insertion of the daggers into her prim white bodice. The fantasy salved his irritation and despair as he rose with his classmates to leave the room. He slunk out, expecting the still-alive Medusa to keep him after class, transforming him into a stone of compliance. She did not. Apparently, he thought, his suppliant "yes, ma'am" was sufficiently obeisant for her to not push matters further. Besides, she was probably glad to be rid of him for the day. As he entered the hall, he took in a deep breath of resignation.

"I thought you were right; she was no phantom of delight," a clever new voice said in a sardonic tone from very close behind him. Ricky spun around to see who it was.

Standing just behind and to the right was Wally Streeter, a tall blond-haired Protestant whom Ricky had long observed while wandering in the stacks of the library but never met. Wally often sat by himself reading, He had intrigued Ricky, but never enough for him to introduce himself. He concluded that Wally was a little odd, a little aloof, and a little too mysterious. Meeting him might bring to Ricky a world he would probably be better off avoiding.

"The speech was essentially right just the way it was written. It develops the idea that Lady Macbeth was more interested in killing Duncan than Macbeth was. I don't know why Miss Johns is so upset about it."

"She's afraid of sex, that's why." He looked gratefully at his new, instantly made friend. Perhaps he was too intense. He immediately regretted the strength of his response. Wally seemed to pull back. A sudden shyness enveloped him.

"Maybe. Anyway, I thought you were right." There was no agreement, and yet there remained complete agreement. The two souls suddenly saw that they were in the same universe.

"Thanks."

What is it that unites people? Sentiments? Shared views? It was these two melodies that instantly sparked interest in these two dissimilar boys. Whether such moments would unite others was a matter for each to find. Certainly these two were quite different on the surface, one a Christian from a broken family, the other a Jew trying to escape from the sentimental bonds of his people and his Savannah. Nothing seemed to draw them together, if an agreement about literature could be considered nothing. Yet they were quickly and forever united, even in the penultimate months of departure from the town in which they met.

These two vastly different people strangely found themselves in the same orb. Wally was too quiet, too Southern, clearly Christian. He seemed to fold into the school walls, dressed in nondescript shabby clothes. Ricky saw a lack of masculinity. His character appeared more than a little effeminate. He never spoke in English class and usually spent the period writing for himself. It was as if he had decided to bide his time and only to eventually finish the English requirement by merely attending class. Ricky always considered him insignificant, an idler possessed of little thought, just another poor Southern boy surviving school. It came as a surprise to Ricky that Wally was not only clearly aware of the text of *Macbeth* but had a considerable understanding of it.

As Wally left him walking down the hall, Ricky observed his blue work shirt and khaki pants held up by a narrow old belt. There was not an ounce of fat on that lean Savannah body. Ricky could not help but envy the lanky, insouciant look.

No one would ever consider his new friend handsome. A Yankee would have easily decided Wally was a redneck farm boy. He would be unwilling to accept the fact that Wally had never been near a barn.

Rick did not know it then, but Wally was to become one of the most important friends in his life, and it never would have occurred to him that he was more a soul mate than most of his Jewish acquaintances. Wally was a turning point in Rick's barely emerging view of the world. From Wally he learned that it was not true that the Jewish diaspora was exclusively for Jews, a special place of the privileged Old Testament descendants. Wally was to teach him that the world was a sea of variegated humanity. No one had a monopoly on wisdom or decency. Myths were an impediment to wisdom.

CHAPTER 5

His Father's City

MOST PEOPLE WHO were born in Savannah, lived, and died in Savannah. Ricky was born there, but he knew he wouldn't die there. Before he met Wally Streeter, he dreamed of leaving, of going to the big city. It wasn't Gotham, the dark town of Batman; nor Metropolis, the bright high skyscraper city of Superman. It wasn't nearby Atlanta, either. It was New York, New York, the brassy beckoning world of all books and movies. He was nurtured by images of this great city. It seemed to be the only place that anyone thought important in the movies Ricky saw. Fantasy, legend, reality—it seemed to have everything. But first, before these reasonable considerations, before he could even discuss this wonderful place, he learned to fly over it.

"Tall buildings in a single bound. Is it a bird? Is it a plane?" Superman was above everything. Invincible and commanding of the space over the tallest buildings in the world, Ricky played the role of his greatest hero. He was a five-year-old in the guise of the most wonderful of men. He would stand on the steps of his house with his brother's baby blanket tied around his neck. In those wonderfully grandiose moments, he placed himself on the highest step, five dizzying units above the earth below. In that singularly anticipated ecstatic second, his hands reached high above his head into heavenly imagination. Very slightly he would bend his knees, so slightly, just a little, so that he knew the gesture was imperceptible. Then suddenly his thrilling cry would possess his entire body with his encompassing sense of vivid reality: *"It's Superman!"* And with that call into the generative preadult universe of wonderment, he thrust himself into the Metropolis firmament. He became magically transformed into more than what he was. He floated, he made curves and arcs, he pierced clouds, he sailed, all the while keeping a keen eye on the good health and demanding welfare of the magnificently important people of the bustling city below. This was Ricky's first true vision of New York.

In his adolescent eye, the cold, damp, drab mossy grayness of Savannah seemed unlit and unexciting. The past-summer azaleas and leafy live oaks with their Spanish moss made no meaningful impression. From the movies and books, it was clear: New York was the place to be. Not only was Superman there, so was everything else.

It was also his father's hometown. He'd once visited his zeder there. He was eleven. Everybody gathered at Aunt Frieda's apartment to acknowledge the visit of the transplanted Southern Jews. He remembered the clutter of cousins, the cacophony of all those children. Captain Video was on the television, an innovation in media that had not yet come to Savannah. Aunt Frieda's cleaver made the penetrating sound of the rhythmic chop, chop, chopping of her determination to prepare the gefilte fish for the multitude. He begged to go out and see the December holiday snow. Its whiteness beckoned him like the diamond sparkles of a make-believe land. Giving in to his entreaties, his mother finally allowed him outside. Completely over bundled in his thick coat, he emerged from his aunt's Williamsburg apartment on South Street to discover the congealed flaky ice from the sky.

Savannah never had snow. There, lying on the asphalt ground, was that magical white stuff, that peculiar northern America accumulation of sky-scrapped flakes. It was mixed with dirt and grime, the detritus of a traffic-ridden city. He looked at it and smelled the cold air as if he were on an exotic planet in a different part of the solar system. The streets were crowded with people avoiding puddles, crossing and dodging the cars and carts, entering into and emerging from the subway, watching their steps to avoid slipping or, worse yet, bouncing into another New Yorker. Ricky wondered why they didn't stop to admire the snow. He held some in his hand. His gloved thumb pushed a little dollop around in the palm. The grains were thick and clumpy. He concentrated intently, trying to make the clumps into smaller and smaller grains. He knew from a book in school that snow was supposed to have crystals. It was these flakes he wanted. He wanted to see the crystalline structure in its symmetrical variety. "Where are the crystals?" the boy from Savannah asked. He looked. He picked up new snow and looked again. There was nothing but melt and wet gloves for all his hopeful expectations.

Memories tend to mist over details. On another day, paired, the oldest son and his tutorial-spirited dad left the family milieu together. They were going somewhere. He felt the vibrations coming from his father who he sensed was eager to teach his first born about his world, the important things from his own childhood. That much he knew and it made him feel excited and gay and observing. The bustle, the excitement, "the busyness," as Aunt Frieda would complain. Everyone was running, walking fast, talking fast, talking more loudly than even the noise of the city demanded. There were so many instantaneous happenings, too many to examine and meaningfully take in.

A New Yorker doesn't take a slow bus ride unless they must. They use the subway. Storefronts beckon everywhere. Things to see that have never been seen before. Again, another train. Standing amid the touching crowd and holding tightly to the pole, he could barely make out the long, black, multiwindowed bread shapes racing through the dark tunnels, blinking their lights on and off, making the steel-against-steel screech and rattle, warning of a dark and scary netherworld. Within their protective coverings sat stone-faced people controlled by forces beyond their own awareness. Ricky saw them leave the cars and, in newly animated form, push and run through the crowds to a place of seemingly special disappearance. To him, their merging with the hundreds of people in the train station was the same as if one of life's mysterious forces had simply swallowed him. The train opened its maw and received him and his father at the connection to move anew into the tunnels. He felt robotic, becoming someone strangely controlled by an outside series of mechanical forces. He imagined his will disappearing. He was no less a machine than his container, the long, black, steel, baguette-shaped car. He fought. He wouldn't let it happen. No force would manage him. He would manage it. He began the psychic struggle. Would he win? Just as his child's war began, he abruptly no longer had to fight. The train came to a stop and filled with light. His father told him that they had to get off. It was their final destination. They exited at Radio City Music Hall.

There were rippling rainbows everywhere. From the darkness of the subterranean world of magical robots, he had entered the serene mysticism of arching colors. As he looked at the hues semi-circled so high above his head, he felt a peculiar dizziness. He marveled at the fact that he was still below the earth and then wondered for a flash the whereabouts of Superman.

"What you are going to see are the greatest dancers."

His father was exceedingly enthusiastic and expected Ricky to feel the same. The man holding his hand was experiencing again his own childhood, looking at his son for reassurance that his memories were not fabrications lost to him from his own memories. After finding their seats in the massive arching auditorium, the excited father-man-child could hardly contain himself. "They are always *exactly* together. Watch. Do you see anybody out of step?"

Ricky looked carefully and thought he did see a wrongly positioned leg. "How about that one, Daddy? The one on the right side. See her over there." He pointed with a sense of victory, his finger outstretched.

His father's fantasy and excitement had to dominate; memories had to be preserved. "No, she's all right. Just watch."

The show was a spectacle, a dazzling display of New York glitz. When it ended, some people in the audience stood and applauded. Ricky's father didn't, but he seemed very pleased. Ricky followed his father's lead and enjoyed the social rebellion. They remained in their seats, patiently waiting for the film his father said would come. It came and went quickly without leaving any impression; and, in what seemed like the least important moment of the night, the two life consorts found themselves outside on Sixth Avenue. The darkness refulgently lit by marquees and billboards made the overworld of the underworld seem everywhere.

Whenever Ricky thought of his father, these memories formed a backdrop. There were always these persistent, vague feelings against the expiring ground of his last year of high school. But what powerful feelings they were. His urge to travel, to leave, was so palpable, yet uncertain and, at the same moment, ineffable. He knew he had to go to New York to materialize them, to bring new reality to replace the old memory. He wanted to transcend the mere child observer and become a living part of the hustle, a cog in the wheel of moving minds, someone with his finger on the button of life. He wanted to go to Broadway shows; talk about music, all kinds of music; discuss art; and be a complete New Yorker. When he thought of it, his pulse became rapid; there was this inner excitement. As if talking to an unseen adversary, he shook his head at the lifelong prospect of seeing Savannah's Broad Street as the Great White Way, of playing golf on the weekends, of being dulled by the monotonous, repetitive waves along the dark sand of the Tybee beach shore. He saw his future stay-at-home alternative to a Yankee town citizen. He would be a bored, tired, un-informed, slow-witted, jailed spirit, gradually becoming so mentally compromised that no new thoughts entered his mind. New York was life in its most scintillating, varied, and stimulating form; Savannah was creaking invalidism. He knew he would leave. He had to.

CHAPTER 6

Who Is Wally Streeter?

WALLY WAS A godsend for Ricky. In the split moment when Wally spoke as a whisper behind his back, he felt he had found an ally against all his protagonists in life. "The speech was essentially right just the way it was written. I don't know why Miss Johns was so upset by it." Ricky often thought of that meeting. It bolstered his spirits many times over the ensuing years.

Though he felt a closeness, a sense of being a partner in life, with his new and serendipitous friend, the same could not be said of Wally. Wally always seemed unreachable, a temptation dangling before him, carrying Ricky along a winding trail he could never complete, a carrot he could never savor. Ricky tried to bring Wally closer, to make him an intimate. But there seemed always to be that hiatus, that peculiar gap separating the pleasure in some shared feelings from the complete realization of a joining of minds with the special sense of compatibility between them.

Wally always treated him civilly; Wally was always polite. Whenever they saw each other, Ricky felt that barely allowed sympathetic sense of comradery emanating from his new friend. This at least was acknowledged. More important, whenever they were in class together, Ricky tried to be clever and watched happily out of the corner of his eye to be sure his contribution was appreciated. It mattered nothing whether the teacher noticed; it was aimed at his new friend. He wanted to solidify what had begun, reaching out for that pithy comment or simulating observation that would seal the relationship and make the unbreakable grand impression. He was sensitive to Wally's reactions, and, after making any comment, he would furtively and greedily grasp as his reward any change of expression from his friend. Often, no reaction could be detected, and he found himself responding to his presumptions of Wally's thoughts.

He began to try hard to come up with original and interesting ideas to create a sense of feeling never witnessed on his friend's placid face. It was irrelevant that the teacher did not recognize the wit, the cleverness, the brilliance of the offering. Wally was there. If, on that rare occasion, Wally perked up, seemed slightly affected by Ricky's comments, or, most wonderful of all, added his own ideas to Ricky's, he felt a surge of ecstasy. It confirmed again the exclusive bond between them.

Then why, Ricky wondered, would Wally rarely acknowledge him in the lunchroom? When Ricky joined him at the lunch table, where he was usually sitting by himself, Wally seemed inward, unexpressive, removed, even aloof. It was sometimes uncomfortable just sitting there. Ricky had to create conversation so that Wally would be forced to answer, struggling for the illusion of a dialogue.

In spite of this needed effort, Ricky refused to give up. He felt there was always a glimmer of interest. Wally did seem to feel his presence was important. "Peculiar" was the working word that defined their relationship.

The essence of what they were to each other was beyond any full explanation. Ricky persisted; he embraced his attraction and felt affection. He could not dispel that special feeling between himself and Wally. He had hundreds of experiences that he thought of as meaningful contacts. In the hall Wally would give him a knowing nod as they passed one another. Sometimes they seemed to accidentally meet in the bathroom, where both would choose a stall over the exposed seatless toilet and listen silently to each other's body water. He would see Wally on the opposite side of the street with his books in his arms, his head turned slightly toward Ricky, staring at him without even a nod, yet acknowledging him and the world they both inhabited. Though Ricky knew there was a special connection, even an ever-strengthening bond, he knew too that Wally wanted no overt declaration of its presence.

Ricky wondered often about this strange situation, especially the religious difference. Wally was Christian. Maybe he was anti-Semitic. Did Wally hear of how Ricky was insulted by Bill Williams, and did he perhaps feel the same way? Sometimes, Ricky knew, he could be obnoxious. He thought of the way he wanted to exert his intellectual dominance in the classroom. Did Wally find this too unpleasant? These thoughts would often enter Ricky's mind, pushing other thoughts out, troubling him, demanding that he resolve the uncertainty.

All doubts aside, Ricky that was convinced he had found a friend. This was a real friend, someone he knew shared his interests, someone who felt the emptiness and the fullness of the world as he did. He knew Wally was someone who saw things the way he did. Life was a paradox in which this wish to live was juxtaposed with insistent death. Wally understood his soul. Why was he not willing to link arms with him? They might walk side by side, sharing the same world, sharing the same views and sense of this world. But they remained unlinked, disconnected by Wally's insistent separation. The answer to why Wally continued to be so distant eluded Ricky. The answer remained in the depths of Wally himself.

In spite of Ricky's being a Jew, even if in name only, in spite of his shortcomings as a personality, Wally stayed his distance. It may not have been for any religious reasons, or reasons relating to Ricky's style. His behavior may have had nothing to do with Ricky. There may have been reasons Ricky had not even considered.

He perhaps stayed away because he did not know how to come close, because he was uncomfortable with intimacy. Wally's love was his mother. His was a childhood romance that continued throughout his life. This all-embracing original union made in the bowels of his particular misery was always to be the source of his only complete and safe companionship. Ricky did not know this in the senior year of high school, but he knew vaguely that there was something in his friend that kept him removed and apart. This gaping psychological consideration was outside of Ricky's teenage understanding. The idea that a person's behavior could be related more to his developmental history than to something in the here and now, whatever it was, was not a part of Ricky's repertoire of understanding. During the next six months, this fact of life would intrude on his beliefs, changing him forever; but at the time of developing his friendship with remote Wally, the ideas simply were not in his head.

C H A P T E R 7

Wally's World

SCREEEEEHEEEEN! IT WAS the siren, no doubt about it. It was old Jethro Taylor in his police car, grabbing another out-of-towner. "Ludowici is one hell of a town for car drivers," Wally Sr. chuckled to himself on another hot day that baked upon the red Georgia dust as it drifted downward lugubriously in the air. "That old Jethro put this town on the map, but I'm not sure it's such a good thing," he continued aloud to Carl, his bedraggled helper at the gas station. He saw Jethro standing next to the red-clay dusted car that was unknowingly cursed by displaying its New York license plate. He was chewing on something, one hand in his belt, the other on the open window of the car door. "Lemme see your license, mister!" he said in his coarse Georgia accent.

Wally Sr. stood by his pumps, looking and absorbing a scene he had witnessed many times before. The spot before his gas station was the favorite place for this display of the South again asserting itself against the brazen descendants of General Sherman. Jethro may have been pushing sixty, but he was the prototype of the Georgia cop: big, tough, harsh, mean, and determined. Wally Sr. knew the Yankee would cough up the inflated fee of fifty dollars, curse under his breath, and drive away. There was nothing else anyone could do with Jethro. You might as well fight with a Brer Rabbit's tar baby.

This was the world of Ricky's Wally. Born in Ludowici, a town some distance from Savannah, known primarily and exclusively for its one outstanding feature. It was a feature that had made it notorious. Why, it was once the subject of an editorial for the *New York Times*. The Ludowicians were really angry with the infamous article: "Georgia Speed Trap, Like Nowhere Else." They may have been upset with the notoriety, but they knew the article was true.

A person couldn't drive too slowly in Ludowici. In fact, the speed you drove through this town didn't matter at all. Tickets were given at random, for all rates of velocity. Nobody who lived there bothered much about the town's reputation. Jethro had helped bring in the revenues that built the school and the sidewalks. Let those Northerners think whatever they wanted. The speed trap was there to stay, even if not a source of pride for the little town.

Wally Sr. didn't care about the town's reputation either. He was a simple man, having grown up completely within the ten square miles of the hamlet, mostly spending his time at the gas station. Because he early on became an expert in repairing tractors, he could claim he was the main reason for the station's solvency.

He knew Mary Tearth all his life. No one was surprised when they married. The attraction was entirely physical. Whatever Wally Sr. knew about tractors, it did not transfer over to women. Mary wanted security and love. He wanted comfort and a place to plant his pressing adolescent cravings. Sex was his primary recreation, after beer drinking and the Georgia Bulldogs. He had been stung once by Susanne Frank and barely escaped having to marry her at sixteen. He never knew whether the pregnancy didn't hold because that was "the way of things," as he told his friends. Maybe it was because Susanne did something to release the two of them from eternal bondage. In any case, his fundamentalist Baptist parents were so harsh (his father gave him one of his many beatings, but this time it was special—he used a section of a discarded truck tire), the impression was made. He honored Mary's condition. He did not want another beating by the man he had grown to hate. This was the spirit in which he and Mary, a girl he had known all his life, wed.

It must be admitted, the tall, lanky, yellow-haired Southern boy who ostensibly agreed with everything the hard, coarse road cop Jethro Taylor represented married the demure, soft-spoken, easily subjugated alternative girl. She was the one he didn't "fall in love with."

The two of them had lived in Ludowici all their lives and were planning to continue doing the same. For them life was an ongoing, unplanned experience. They possessed no philosophy, no reflections upon the future, no aspirations, no awareness that there was anything like an aspiration. Life was a given thing; it was like receiving a present you didn't really want, but you might as well make use of it. While using it, they gave more life to two children, Wally Jr. and Sally. Mary came up with the names. She felt Wally's name would please her husband (it did, very much), and she liked Sally for reasons unknown to her. If anyone suggested it sounded roughly like Susanne, she would have been amazed.

It wasn't a bad life in Ludowici, Georgia. Wally Sr. often had a long lunch, either eating at home with Mary or having a sandwich at Galtry's bar and grill. Though the workday was long, from seven in the morning till eight or nine at night, the lunch and other natural breaks made it easily tolerated. He and Mary would often make love in the afternoon.

Their income was small but just adequate, exactly equal to the severity of their economic demands. With their parents' help, the young couple was able to buy a small house near the main highway. Maybe because of Jethro, it wasn't very busy anyway. The kids grew up sharing the second bedroom.

What small events change a lifetime? This ordinary family would have easily played out their quiet lives in this undemanding setting had not the owner of the gas station, Conrad Owens, gotten sick. Conrad had, in many ways, been as responsible for Wally Sr.'s upbringing as his parents, giving him his job at such an early age and letting him manage himself and the station, more or less. In return, Wally Sr. was completely devoted. Conrad was best man at the wedding. Conrad was at the christening of both children. He was brother, father, friend, protector. "God gives and God takes away," Wally Sr. said in a moment of angry reflection, "but why the hell did God have to take Conrad?!"

The doctors at the medical school in Augusta could not, at first, figure out was going on. First they thought it was in Conrad's mind. After all, the symptoms made no sense. What do you do with the complaint of "out of sorts" anyway? Conrad's lassitude persisted and forced a second round of "blood tests, X-rays, and poking around," as Wally Sr. later explained it to Mary. "Those doctors found something, but it won't do no good."

Within five months, during which Wally Sr. was in complete control of every detail of the gas station, Conrad was dead, right in the arms of a helpless medical student. The doctors announced that they had missed the diagnosis because the cancer was hidden behind the kidney, but it would have made no difference. It was highly malignant.

Pursuant to Conrad's wishes, Wally Sr. was able to sell the station to Wilfred Chase just before Conrad's death. They were drinking buddies at Gutlers and Wally Sr. was buoyed by the idea that Wilfred was an all right guy and an amiable friend. Wilfred was the second-best thing after buying the station himself. He had tried. Conrad's widow wanted to sell it to him. He just couldn't get the loan from the bank without any collateral. Wally Sr. had never felt poor before, but for the first time he realized what the lack of money could mean.

In the sale contract, Conrad had specified that Wally Sr. was to be guaranteed a job at no less wages than he was already receiving, with the stipulation that the wages would be increased by over 2 percent or more each year. It was a generous gesture by his dearest friend. Wilfred accepted it without question. Wally Sr. felt secure. Everyone was at Conrad's funeral. There was a pervasive Baptist reverence, all with their hands folded or clasping while crying.

Wilfred changed. He transformed and revealed a bad side Wally Sr. had never considered possible. He became an impossible boss, an impossible owner, and a disaster for business. The station began losing money. He was stubborn and refused to listen to Wally Sr. Their long-standing, amiable friendship dissolved quickly. Wilfred put strict hours on Wally Sr.; he argued with regular customers and refused to perform the little extra favors they had come to take for granted. Fewer people came by, going five miles farther out of town for their repairs.

It was the end for Wally Sr. He had to get away. Now Ludowici seemed confining and unpleasant. He and Mary began fighting. His drinking became a problem. The loving couple became estranged. Mary drew her children closer to her for comfort, giving them the portion of affection previously available more exclusively to her husband.

Wally Jr. was her favorite. He had a winsome disposition. She would hug his little body as if it were a teddy bear and spend time watching him read his little books. Her husband would call her smallish boy a sissy and warn her she was ruining him. Wally Sr. felt the lack of affection; his wife's devotion to this little, quiet, not-mechanically-gifted boy only increased his rage.

One of the guys at Gutlers mentioned an ad in the paper looking for men to work at the Union Bag and Paper Corporation near Savannah. Being a piler and sorter, Wally Sr. knew, was heavy, hard work, but it paid well. For the first time in many months, he put his unfinished drink down and went home to tell Mary.

Wally Sr. walked away from Wilfred and Ludowici on a Friday night without a word to his onetime friend. There was only a note left on the cash register: "Send my pay if you have a mind. Good-bye." An address was added to the bottom. He and Mary, Wally Jr., and Sally got into their pickup truck and drove away. Wally Sr. saw Jethro and another New York motorist on the side of the road with the police lights glowering. Jethro waved to them as they passed.

The family moved to a rented apartment in Savannah. Their income was better, the drinking was less, but permanent harm had been done to the family. Mary held back. She often touched the gold-plated cross around her neck, inwardly sighing desperately because of the neglect and growing indifference of her husband. Her warmth and receptiveness had lessened.

Wally Sr. felt this and made his adjustments. He spent more and more hours away from the apartment. He felt angry and bitter that his wife had not supported him while he labored with great aggravation under Wilfred Chase. He could not see his drinking and irritability, his increasing time at Gutlers before they left, as a factor. As far as he was concerned, his high school romance was over. She became a bitter pill to swallow, and he would do the best he could.

It never occurred to Wally Sr. to divorce his wife. He simply moved further and further away from her in his mind. She became a secondary consideration. "If I cover my bases," he thought, "she'll have nothing to complain about." Mary saw him sullen at meals and breathed a sigh of relief when he found an excuse to spend the night out. With his new income, he was able to buy a small house for his family. Rather than this being the foundation of a new solidarity, it proved merely to be the solution only he felt. He still held on to his guilt. His saw his family well ensconced. It was time for him to leave.

Wally Sr. did not go far away but simply into a different neighborhood. While he shared enough money to allow his family to live poorly but comfortably, he moved in with a black woman on the Abercorn extension. It was a scandal absorbed by the separate communities of the town. Mary's friends whispered about it. Wally Sr.'s friends laughed about it. But neither connected, and so the gossip became encapsulated. The situation was tacitly accepted. The town was big enough, just big enough, to allow the unexpected and the unaccepted to continue on the surface of poorly communicative society.

Wally Jr. understood little of this. He felt sorely the loss of his father but was afraid to ask his mother about what had happened. He had no idea that his mother's attitude toward him was part of the problem. Deep within was a little satisfaction that all the attention was toward him (and a little for his sister). He thought only that his father had left because of fights with his mother. So Wally's world became socially narrower, and he enfolded himself within the protective skirts of his mother, feeling her comfort and adoration, enjoying the conflict-free silence of his books and his increasingly autonomous sense of his own importance and his own confusion.

By the time Ricky heard Wally's voice speak to him those life-confirming words in the school hall, these events were five years in the past. Wally Sr. was with his Emily in the Negro section of town. Mary was barely keeping things going on Duffy Street, where the house was being maintained by her still-husband's steady economic support. Sally was entering Savannah High School, the same school where her brother was in his senior year. Though there was a persistent gloom over the Streeter home, there was also a warm, intimate symbiosis that softened Mary's cloying manner. Humor was a rare and alien visitor, but despair was not its alternative.

Wally loved books. In them, he found solace from the pain and sadness he saw in his mother's face. Out of the mystery of his family's changed fortune, he tried to fathom an explanation, drawing from all his reading. The mystery remained, and he developed a sense of perplexity and acceptance of the futility of the real world. The works of the East, Hinduism, Buddhism, the teachings of the Tao, became his discoveries and his friends. He slowly acquired a passive acceptance of whatever life had to offer. Questioning was a disturbing and unnecessary alternative to acceptance. His naturally shy nature digested these complex readings in an unexpected manner. He developed from them a sweet, accepting philosophy that proved the antithesis of Ricky's struggle to find a solution in everything.

Ricky did not know that he had met someone with a sensibility similar to his but with a perspective that was far different. He did not realize that whereas they both could feel the sense of the grandeur in Shakespeare, they grabbed hold of it in totally different ways. There was a magnetism between them, but inherent in it was the source of discord. One was a boy who wanted to conquer, to master, and the other was one who wanted with all his heart and being to accept the what-is of the world. Despite the closeness the two would feel toward each other all their lives, they both would also sense the abrasive impossibility of a completely salutary compatibility.

Ricky approached Wally as a Christian and compared himself on religious terms. As he gradually began to realize this was not a reasonable way of thinking of his friend, he felt confused. Wally had developed a personal religion that didn't compare easily to Ricky's obsession with being Jewish. The religious uncertainty of Wally's feelings became a stumbling block for Ricky's acceptance. He had long reduced the world into two parts. Now he was confronted with a perspective that worked against the dichotomy of Jews and Christians. He didn't know what to do with it.

CHAPTER 8

Ricky's Savannah

RICKY WAS EMERGING from his cocoon of adolescence. He was finding himself. Wally Streeter beckoned partly because he synchronized with Ricky's sensitivities, his love of books, but partly, too, because he represented a palpable strangeness also possessed by the South. Both had their silence, their mystery, their complicatedness. Wally, the person, and the South, the place, they both had a song. The two uttered melodic poetry; their musical notes led to the enchanted siren call. You could be seduced by them, if susceptible. There was always the danger. Tied to the mast like Ulysses, you would experience the near useless resistance to the South Sirens and their death-inducing beckoning.

Inside Ricky, Wally and the South created an aura, a formless though captivating orchestration filled with color and shifting uncertainty. It was impossible to be close without feeling something, no matter how ineffable. This indescribable thing was confining, captivating, and powerful; it was almost as powerful as Robin Linkowitz.

Ricky didn't see it, but Robin Linkowitz was his Jewish side. The enigma of Robin was whether she would ever pay attention to him. This preoccupation was not associated with the South. It was the antithesis of antebellum—the hoopskirt, mint juleps, plantations, and demure probity. Her dark eyes, dark hair, and darkened inaccessibility brought to Ricky's postpubescent mind the sands of the deserts drifting into the waters of the Mediterranean Sea. Her hair, her eyes, her astrology were the cabala, the Ptolemaic orbs, the universal harmonies, the unknown territories that persisted against attack and contrived the history of her race, *his* race. He was attracted with a magnetism he could not understand; in his emergence from childhood, it was an understanding the importance of which he did not even know.

These two preoccupations were mixed, outside of his awareness and concern, with his Savannah. He would always remember them when he considered his home, his origin, his time of youth, himself. This paradox of feeling that attracted him to them and alienated him from them stirred in his mental brew. His town of birth, his chrysalis, Savannah, was poured into the pot of this consideration. He could not deny having been a part of his hometown for seventeen years. He felt he knew the choreography so well and for so long. It wasn't that he did not know the steps; he did indeed. No one would have found him faltering. Was it right that he lived there? He never thought it was a place he didn't belong. Yet he felt his inner self to be different, and he continued to sense his separateness, this separateness that made him ask who he essentially was, in idea, in future. He saw himself in the town. He felt he, indeed, did not belong. Yet it was his birthplace. It had its molding effect. He would not be recognized as a New Yorker. Did he ooze the Southern way? He hoped not. He thought not. He did not like Savannah.

Whatever Ricky did mattered little to other Savannahians. They went along with their beliefs and lives regardless of his struggle and his opinions. No one in the moss-covered oaks and the park-squared landscape cared about his ongoing transformation. He was enamored of the Greeks. He saw Savannah as the ancient Athenians saw Sparta: dry, mechanical, empty. He wanted to be Greek and dreamed that he could fulfill a role like that of Socrates. No, Socrates was too old. But he could at least be one of his pupils. How old was Crito, anyway? Yes, he preferred to be Athenian more than Savannahian.

No Savannahian cared for his dream. No one felt the inner criticism of the young man of the agora, his complaints, his discontents. He was ignored in his new inner disguise, the disguise that merged with his wish to go to the greatest agora of them all, New York. That he had become a person in the spirit of the golden age of Greece concerned the people of Savannah not at all.

Ricky may have had his dreams and imaginings, but little or nothing seemed to change around him. Savannah continued to be Savannah. Though the town's quiet and stillness contrasted and conflicted with his eruptive inner self, there was much that pleased him, even despite his yearnings for the metropolis.

The mornings were the best. The black women in 1957 still came around carrying large hemp baskets on their heads, singing and singing for the sale of their wares. It was beautiful. Better than *Porgy and Bess*. There seemed to be one in particular with the talent of an opera diva well within her coloratura range. You could hear "Scrawwwwwberrieeees! Scrawwwwwwberrrries!" Or,"StriiiingbeAns annd turrrrnnnip greeEEeeens…stAriiiinnngbeeans and tuRRRRnnnip grEEeeeens!" The actual words of strawberries, string beans, and turnip greens might be lost to the inexperienced ear, but what a beautiful and captivating song it was. Many times, in the too-early-but-not-too-cold mornings, he would awaken and feel annoyed. They would come around long before school started, long before it was necessary to wake up. Irritated, his first impulse was to shout out of the window for the women to shut up, but he never did. The song captured him, so melodious, possessing a kind of tenderness, seeming to gesture to him an understanding of his unwanted alertness, his continued sleepiness. He listened, though he tried not to. Lingering in bed, he would raise his head onto his hand and lean on his right elbow. He would stare out his bedroom window and soak up the memory and the sound and the specialness of the moment. It was a moment he did not know would someday become a craving, a grieving sense of loss as the modern pace of the town's development would warrant that it disappear. Her pace in the now of Ricky's moment matched her rhythm and melody. She was tattered, clearly poor, and probably lived in one of those gray-slatted wooden shacks. She was probably wearing one of the smiles that Ricky and his father often saw as they drove by on Sunday on the way to get bagels at the delicatessen.

As Ricky leaned on his elbow and watched, he thought about going out and talking to her. No. It wasn't done. And why it wasn't done remained an unanswered question. If, as often happened earlier in his life, his mother told him to buy some string beans for her, he would race out, quickly place the money in the Negro woman's hand, and race back with a fear tickling him. He didn't understand at all this peculiar anxiety he had about the colored folk. He would always be ashamed of it, and the feeling of this dishonor would always linger, a trickle of guilt. But from the distance of his bedroom window, safely nestled, he would gaze at this miracle of sentiment in time. The rest of his life he would remember this song, this beauty of the South contained in the ragged, the dirty, the poor, the downtrodden, and the beautiful.

It wasn't easy to be Greek when you were enchanted by the food vendor's melodies. The Greeks had no Negroes to appreciate or hate. Yes, they had slaves, but that was a very different situation. You couldn't compare the coloreds of Savannah of 1957 with the slaves of Greece in 400 BC. Besides, Ricky didn't want to think of the Greeks as slave owners and denied himself the truth of that fact. There are truths you can't face until you agree it's time to face them. To him Greeks were saintly men wearing robes, all looking like Socrates, all listening to one another as they talked. He saw them all nodding their heads in wise understanding, and all willing to die for an idea.

He did not know he was confused about all of this. On the contrary, he was certain about almost everything. His certainty was a disguise for confusion. He lived an adolescent naivety, denying in his overconcern with himself, the history of the current world, the horrors of Stalin and Hitler, and saw only what was a part of his immediate experience. He didn't even know of his own blind side, his own denials.

He did not know that he loved this town of his. He thought he hated it, seeing it as boring, tedious, and torpid. He yearned to leave it, never realizing that many years later he would want to talk of nothing else, keeping his silence only out of embarrassment.

It was a town with sunny days and frequently misty nights. There was no fog exactly, but merely this encompassing and obscuring mist. The mist surrounded moss-laden trees, enveloped stately houses on Washington Boulevard, hid everything from the keenest eye on Factors Walk near the river, and enhanced the sense of the past held in the opaque present. Only the feel of the cobblestones beneath the feet and the smell of the waterside were left.

The spread of this unalterable night grayness enhanced the sense of mystery, the feeling of moldy historical death, and the palpable perception that time was not truly formless, elusive, but rather a substance, a thing that oppressed the mind. It might not come immediately to the thoughts of the walker of this old city, but ineluctably, intensely, any explorer, even an idle tourist, would slowly come to feel, like Ricky, with each step upon an ancient cobblestone, the past. Oozing about him were the memories. The landing of Oglethorpe with his eighteenth-century debtors; then the courageous Revolutionary War, followed too soon by the disheartening and miserable Civil War with its Yankee invasion. Should he be glad Sherman had spared his town?

Challenging any romance was the modern Union Bag and Paper Corporation.

It felt closer to Ricky's home than it really was. It rested busily along the dirty old Savannah River, pouring its chemical byproducts into the waters and air of the town. Ricky had visited it only once with his class from school. The trip was titled "The Great Savannah Paper Mill Visit" on the form sent home for parental signatures. There was, strangely, mainly a civic awe and respect for this venerable institution. The company representative proudly escorted the class around the "largest paper mill in the world" with an air of superciliousness that belied the profligate moneymaking of the massive assemblage of pulp tanks, paper rollers, and chemical processors, the labyrinthine trails of pipes, the trucks and piles of wood, the mashers, squeezers, holders, and the like. It was then that Ricky learned the origin of that particular smell he had known all his life. Even within the potent atmosphere of the enclosed plant, he could tolerate the smell. It was unmistakably pungent, with a lingering peculiar and unpleasant sweetness. This was a unique smell, a smell of and in Savannah, special for the old hometown. It was a smell that might have emanated from any paper mill anywhere. But when mixed with the odors of the dirty meandering river, when stirred into the damp marsh air and touched by the hanging Spanish moss in the aging live oak trees, it became the special Savannah smell.

This excrescence of industry would come and go. Wind shifts would sometimes carry it toward Hilton Head, across the river, into South Carolina, or toward Atlanta, two hundred miles northwest. When conditions were right, the wind and the dampness and production combined in just the right proportions, and it would then descend upon the village like a plague of locusts, irresistible, familiar, expected, strangely reassuring, accepted, and embraced. People would complain how bad the odor was, but no one suggested it be eliminated. It was in the fiber of the community, a part of the comfort of the identity of the place, strangely consoling. Street talk referred to the smell affectionately: "Looks like the Union Bag is givin' us dat smell again." "Yep, pretty bad, ain't it?"

This recurring effluvium mixing with the people, their clothes, their ideas, and their reactions, typified that Southern passivity that has been so much a part of them since the Civil War was lost. In fact, they were proud of their town's smell. These people of Savannah arrogantly possessed the largest paper mill in the world, and it felt exclusive. Just as Christ carried his cross to a greater glory, Savannahians carried their smell to a greater distinction than they would were they to realize the truth about it. The Union Bag smell was presented as if it were a prize relic in their home, something every visiting guest should experience.

Ricky knew this smell was no badge of honor, but he also knew it was useless to tell anyone that the familiar wafting from up the riverbank was a putrid, pestilential result of an irresponsible industrial hegemony. He knew they would only turn their heads and make a gesture as if to say, "What c'n we do 'bout it?" Secretly they would be proud and deny the pollution, the irritating odor, the danger to health. They would deny the skeleton in the closet of the town to which they had committed their lives. Not only would they deny it, but they would enjoy the mill's presence and let no one outside the Savannah family make a criticism against it. This passivity was the way of the people of Savannah. This was the Southern way.

In the winter months, sometimes, the mist, the aroma of the mill, and the dampness would descend at once, seeping into the atmosphere and beginning the rot that was the essential evidence of the persistent aging of the town. During this bleak, often sunless time, cold would be added, and the aged citizens felt the beckoning of the cemeteries. Ricky would occasionally ride his bike past the most frightening of them all, the Old Colonial Cemetery along Abercorn Street.

This decaying remnant of the American Revolution was a reminder of the violence and disruption, now entirely dormant but once very much a part of the town's life. The graves were all aboveground, built in the form of little brick houses standing six feet above the damp, sparse, scattered tufts of grass.

He would remember how he used to play here when he was five or six. Climbing up to the top of the "houses," he felt like a conqueror, a hero of a war he could not possibly know anything about. He felt energetic, youthful, agile, confident, in a way that dispelled the reality of the death below. Once he saw a crack through the cement-plastered roof. He stared hesitatingly into the impermeable darkness. "What's in there?" he remembered asking himself. "Death and Savannah. Savannah and death." He was too young. What did he know about death? But the words always seemed matched when he thought of his grave-climbing.

Death and Savannah formed an inextricable bond. He would always associate them. Stillness murmuring silently. Stillness, no movement. Stillness and darkness. He knew *something* was there. Like the mist, death bound the past, present, and future, rendering the triumvirate singular, the singular of monotony. The town and history were forgotten in this bed of death that sent a shudder into him every time he rode by the graveyard. The graveyard in the town was the graveyard in the colony. The town would always be a colony, a colony for the lost who knew that even with success, the metaphor of the cemetery house would capture the soul of the inhabitants again and again. "Monotony," the small summer breeze of that childhood experience, blew yet another word through his ears.

Ricky was now trying ardently to deny the hold of this place upon him. He knew the dark crack through the roof of the death house was calling him to confess to his alliance with the spirit of the town. He wanted to run. He would fight off the beckoning. He would not let the stale, monotonous, entrenched hopelessness that permeated the worst that was his seedbed bury him. He would not become a tenant of the eternally silent old cemetery's brick-cement houses. He would wrest himself from the image of the lost flesh of the now forgotten skeleton. He would leave this indolent acceptance of whatever there already was. He would make his way to a life that denied this reality. If he was to have this moment in demise, it would have to be somewhere else, somewhere the ghosts were more compatible.

The cemetery always beckoned. He liked to play there when he was younger, but now he avoided it.

CHAPTER 9

George McGregor

THE FAMILY STOOD outside the doors of Morrison's Cafeteria, about to commit an act of Jewish betrayal. They knew it, and Samuel Bateman was going to see to it that, despite the laws of the Sabbath, they were going to walk into Savannah's *traif* institution. Ricky's lifetime of silent protest against his unyielding father was again being fought in the contrived quiet rebellions of the Bateman family. An orthodox Jew would have been horrified. It was Friday night, a usual evening meal for the Batemans, but walking into the restaurant would be against the Torah for anyone observant of the kosher laws, not to mention the rules honoring God. Ricky was hungry and looking forward to satisfying his appetite. His two brothers, thirteen and eight, were giving evidence of their need to eat by fighting each other over who was going to get to stand in the cafeteria line first. Sam raised his voice:

"Both of you, *stop*! Keep this up and there's no dessert!" The authoritative growl immediately proved effective.

Their obedient silence achieved, he and his two oldest boys took their first steps into the restaurant. Sarah followed, holding Jerry's hand.

The five Batemans may have flaunted the laws of their ancestors, but they were welcomed as frequent customers. The smiling staff consisted mostly of Negroes working the lines. One man came over dressed in a black jacket, bow tie, and black pants, handed Samuel a tray, and welcomed him to his place in the line.

"Nice to see you again, Mr. Sam."

"Nice to see you, George."

The ritual continued for each member of the family, even the smallest, who wasn't allowed to carry his own tray. George McGregor, decked out as usual in his pseudotuxedo, pushed it along the track for him, telling him what foods he might choose while steadily glancing over at the mother to be sure no choices were out of line.

As they pushed their trays from one serving station to another, they were greeted by white-aproned Negro women who smiled and made food suggestions.

"Yes'm, that's a might fine choice," responding to the mother's finger pointing at the tray as the food was spooned onto a plate. "Sure you don't want some collard greens, too, or this fine cooked chicken with cream?"

Ricky's mother looked up and smiled politely. "Not today, Betsy…been eating a little too much lately."

Betsy giggled. "Yes'm."

Jerry barked, "Can I have some grits, Mom?"

"Mary-Lou, would you give some grits to Jerry?" A plate appeared, filled with hot grits topped by butter.

Morrison's was for families, mainly of the Christian faith. Since Jews were rarely, if ever, customers, the Batemans would never be revealed to the larger Jewish community. Samuel Bateman could feed his family there with impunity, suffering none of the opprobrium a more closely knit community might impose. Ricky was aware of this peculiar nonconforming behavior of his father but didn't know what to do with it. He always enjoyed the restaurant while also feeling a member of the outside. He knew that his father wore the badge of eating here with a strange pride.

The dining room was a large rectangle with many tables. The staff stood in their black-and-white attire in a line anticipating the customers arriving with their trays at the cash register. After the customers paid and got their slip, followed by a nod from the white cashier, the next Negro in line would move up to get the family's trays.

"I'll take it for the Batemans." George McGregor intervened in front of his colleagues, who acquiesced in deference to the understood connection between the family and the waiter. The Batemans had known George for nearly the ten years he had worked on the line. A kind of homage on either side of the racial divide had built up. The family and he felt a special comfort with each other.

The Batemans moved along to their table. Just behind them George and another Negro helping him brought their food and placed it before them. The family sat and waited as the two spread five starched white napkins onto their laps. Ricky observed the napkins and the fact that there were only white customers in the entire place; but all the staff, except the cashier and the owners, were black. It was understood by the Negro community that you didn't walk into Morrison's and expect to be served. On this particular evening, for the first time, it occurred to Ricky that there was something strange about all this, but he kept this thought to himself.

As the Negroes were about to leave them to their meal, Sam pulled out two dollars and handed it to McGregor. It was a bountiful tip, and the tall Negro accepted it with a bow.

"Thank you, sir. Thank you, Mr. Bateman. I sure do appreciate it. You Batemans have a nice meal now, ya hear?"

"You be well, George. Nice seeing you again."

It was a big tip by the usual standards, and George communicated his awareness of it. Most of the tips were meager, but the staff seemed happy for the work. At least, that was the impression they left for the whites.

Despite all this conviviality, the Batemans were not the best behaved of customers. The three boys, especially the youngest two, fought over almost everything and anything. Sam Bateman would rage at them, often taking one forcefully outside to stem the loud yelling indicating a sibling conflict, ostensibly for nothing. Through it all, Morrison's tolerated them and welcomed them as steady customers. The Negro waiters, especially George, would often come over to offer their help since they knew the boys well. "C'mon, Mr. Jerry. Let me show you somethin' over here." Jerry would suddenly quiet down at the nonfamily intervention. The two would walk away with Jerry's little boy's white hand nestled softly into the dark-skinned one. They ambled away toward whatever had been invented to show the child. The result was a now quiet and rescued table minus a complete loss of temper by Sam.

The two worlds, that of the Negro and that of the whites, worked comfortably together. One subservient by necessity, the other adaptive as whites in the South. The Batemans played their superior role without feeling particularly superior, accepting the Jim Crow situation as it was presented to them. If you asked a Negro Savannahian if she felt anger at the arrangement, she probably would have said, "It's the way it is." If you asked a white, the answer likely would have been, "We don't have trouble. They know their place around here." The two colors lived juxtaposed between slavery and tomorrow.

This was the latency period of race relations. It was the time before Negro self-consciousness about what the Negro deserved. Painful memories of slavery and its mind-gripping reality was weakening. The Negro as a human being was becoming a truth in the suffering Negro mind. It was just before that moment in history when the Negro was accepting the status quo and the inchoate revelation of the simmering rage against it. The wronged human was just emerging from its chrysalis but had not yet dried and spread its wings to fly.

The Ku Klux Klan persisted, but its power was diminishing. Most whites, especially the Jewish whites of Savannah, were weary and critical of the Klan. Its operations had waned. There was no overbearing feeling that the Klan would ride into town to harm the Negro. Certainly, the white hoods remained a threat. There was, indeed, the Klan, but its activities were not as ever present as before the war. It was not referenced in the *Savannah Morning News* and was treated by the predominant and non-Jewish whites as something in bad taste. For most of Ricky's childhood, there seemed a moratorium on murdering Negroes wantonly. To all perception, the relations between Negroes and whites were cordial and polite, a postwar adjustment waiting its time.

Ricky grew up with little thought of the Negro. He felt that warm feeling a child feels toward his mother's maid who treated him as if he were her child. He was oblivious of the complex racial currents in his town. He was emotionally colorblind. Because of this, his thoughts turned mostly inward, trying to understand himself, not another human being of different skin coloring. Except for Uncle Remus.

Song of the South was released when Ricky was just old enough to see it and be dumbstruck. The Disney film blew him into another dimension. Just at the time he was suffering the sudden disciplinary rages of his father as a little boy, and feeling alone in his despair, the movie introduced him to its iconic character, the old Uncle Remus. Elementary school Ricky missed entirely the fact that the storyteller of the film was a slave now allowed by his master to while away his final days in his humble cabin on the plantation. Ricky was Bobby Driscoll's Johnny, sitting at the rocking chair of the ancient story-maker taking a draw from his corncob pipe, absorbed in the tales of Brer Rabbit and his enemies.

This spinner of tales was larger than life, a grandfather, a caring man whose color and situation did not even enter the boy's mind. Ricky was Brer Rabbit, and as the wily rodent outfoxed the fox, so did Ricky think he could be clever and find his way in life. Ricky learned to love his briar patch just as the rabbit did. The film was real to him, and its fantasy spinnings imbued the world spirit of the Negro as a people who were kind, imaginative, thoughtful, and caring. Other than the marginal contacts with Morrison's personnel, his mother's indulgent and soft-handed maid, and Uncle Remus, he hardly knew the truth about the Negro's world. This changed when he met George McGregor.

During the time George McGregor was an employee of Morrison's, the Batemans knew him well, and, of course, he knew the Batemans. Sam used to joke out loud to the tolerant Negro that he was the only black Scotsman on the planet.

"Yassah, Mr. Bateman. You is right there. It's a long tale, and when you got the time, maybe I'll tell it to ya." The two men would laugh as the table was set before the family. George would amble off, laughing out loud and creating calm in the busy space. Afterward, Sam would lean into the table and whisper, "Slavery." Ricky's mother would nod, and they would begin their dinner. This would happen nearly every time George brought their trays. George never told his story to the family. He did one day tell it to Ricky.

When he told Ricky, it was an unexpected occasion, an accident unforetold. It occurred about a week or two after the last Morrison's Cafeteria meal during the emerging spring. Ricky was on his bicycle, his favorite form of everyday transportation. The bicycle took him everywhere in traffic-lazy Savannah. Even on the busiest days, there was not enough vehicular congestion to matter. Besides, Ricky could weave in and out of cars with a surprising agility.

On this particular after-school exploration, he was looking for the hobby store, where he could buy an F4D Skyray modal jet to build. It would turn out to be the last hobby model he would invest in, and it wasn't necessary he have it on this trip. He had saved the money by working at the pawn shop on Saturdays, and, as his mother liked to say, it was burning a hole in his pocket. He, too, was having mixed feelings about spending this rare money on hand for a somewhat frivolous elementary school hobby. He loved airplanes and flight and found himself in an indulgent mood. He could have been waylaid from his plans easily if something interesting showed up to grab his attention. It did.

As he pedaled toward East Broad, he decided not to ride straight but to go down a side street from the currently busy Paulson Extension. There was no reason to it; he just felt a sudden curiosity about a turn he had never before made into a part of town he had never visited. Pedaling fast, he went a block or two onto the now unpaved road to find himself in what the whites called Negro Town. The houses were small, street-level, slightly deteriorating bungalows, each with the standard Southern porch. All were slightly different but neatly arrayed along the unpaved street, each with a small lawn. He noticed at once that there were no whites in the area. He saw a mere handful of blacks. He became self-conscious. This was not his usual world but a new one in the middle of an afternoon. He felt a little tinge of tension. He was in the midst of another culture where he had never been before.

Suddenly a familiar voice called, "Yo! Hey, Master Ricky. Ho!"

The call came to the right of a house Ricky had just sped past. He put on his bicycle brake, came to a stop on the dusty, rocky road, looked around, and there was George McGregor leaning over his mechanical lawn mower, smiling and waving at him.

"C'mon over here and let me see you. You have grown. Are you near twenty?"

Ricky laughed and answered him as he would any elder. "No, sir, I'm only seventeen. Wish I were twenty."

McGregor looked at him, grinning. "Well, don't rush things, son. You-all get there soon enough. What ya doin' 'round here? You lost?"

Ricky answered, "No, sir, just exploring. Made a turn I don't usually make. I was just going to buy a model plane and decided to see what was up this block. Is this where you live?"

"Yassah, Master Bateman. Dis is where I lives." McGregor began walking toward the back of the house with his lawnmower and at the same time beckoned Ricky to follow him. "If you've got the time, son, I'd be glad to share a Coca-Cola with you. You wanna come in, sit down, and talk awhile?"

Ricky was pleased at the invitation and accepted with a clear expression of pleasure. McGregor leaned the mower handle against the side of the house and led him into the kitchen just beyond the three outside steps. He motioned to Ricky to sit down at one of the table's folding chairs. He got two Cokes from the small refrigerator and quickly prepared them with a flick of his bottle opener. He handed one across the table and sat down.

"Nice to see you, son. Welcome to my home."

"Thank you, sir. It's nice to be here."

"My woman is out working today. Thank goodness she's earnin'. No way we could afford this house with Morrison pay. I wouldn't be here if I was working, but I'm not goin' into Morrison's until six. Thought I'd mow some lawn, get some work done. What you grinning so strong for, son? You's got a smile from ear to ear. What you thinkin'?"

"Well, sir. I hope you don't mind my saying, but I'm thinking that you remind me of Uncle Remus."

George's smile turned serious and questioning, and he rubbed his graying beard just as the old retired plantation man would have done.

"Ricky, isn't that the slave old man who tells stories in that Disney movie *Song of the South*? I hope you don't mind, but I feel a might uncomfortable thinkin' about myself as a slave, or even an ex-slave. It's hard enough being a free man these days and making ends meet. Thinkin' myself as a slave is just ornery."

"Did you see it, Mr. McGregor? I thought the old man was pretty wonderful. I didn't think you would object to him."

"No, son. I didn't see it. I can't spend my money on tomfoolery, but I heard about it. You's got to understand, son. Slave is slave. There ain't no getting' around it."

"I'm so, so sorry, Mr. McGregor. I never thought of the comparison that way. I thought of Uncle Remus like a kind and loving grandfather. That's what you made me think of. The slave part was far from my thinking. Please accept my sincere apologies."

"All right, son. No harm done. It's just that I've been through a world war, fought side by side with a lot of prejudiced white men, and I'm a might sensitive about any association with slavery. Now, I just realized you're only seventeen years old. How much do you knows about the Negro man's history?"

Ricky was flummoxed. For the first time in his life he realized, what a dolt he was. He knew nothing about the Negro's history. He knew there was a civil war, but he didn't understand it. He was educated in the South. It was as if a whole section of world history was deleted.

"Mr. McGregor, sir, I know nothing. Not a thing. Uncle Remus just seemed like a good man to me. I thought it was a compliment comparing him to you. The slavery thing didn't enter my mind. I'm truly sorry. I hope you'll forgive me for the dumb teenager I am."

"No, Master Ricky. You ain't no dumb teenager. You is a smart one because you is willing to learn. I'm going to teach you if you'll let me."

"Sure, Mr. McGregor. I'm always willing to learn. Sure. Please."

The pleading in Ricky's voice pleased the old man. He leaned back in his chair authoritatively and began his story.

"It was fifty-somethin' years ago when I was born outside Pembroke, Georgia. My parents were tenant farmers. They'd growed the land. Ever pick cotton, Ricky?"

"No, sir."

"It's backbreakin' work. Wouldn't recommend it to nobody. It was just one of the little crops my folks could manage. It was a tough one.

"They could barely make ends meet with the little share Mr. White let them keep. That's not his real name, but it will do for now. It kind of tells it all about him. I gotta say, as a child I was treated pretty good, but we were so poor that my brother and sister died of bad feeding. I don't know the all the cause, but my momma said it had something to do with food not being kept properly. In those days there was no refrigerator. Now I gotta tell you, you gotta understand, my mommy and my pappy were the children of slaves."

"Slaves?" A word Ricky rarely heard or used, and it surprised him.

"Yassah. Slaves. My grammy was a slave raped by a Mr. McGregor. My daddy was her child. Now you know where ma name comes from. Nobody ever thought of changin' it. My daddy's mammy told him that she barely escaped the rape with her life. Mr. McGregor, my grandfather, used a knife to scare the bejiggers out of her and made her cooperate while he did his business. He let her keep the child he gave her because he was a self-serving son of a bitch who was a proud bastard who loved to hell his animal skills. With all, my daddy said Mr. McGregor was taken with him. Somepin' charming about my daddy even when he was a kid, I think. So, Mr. White loved my father and hated parting with him after the Civil War done past a bit. But my grandmother hated Mr. McGregor so much that even with her freedom, she could not abide to stay on the plantation for pay. She hated the sight of that man.

"Grandma left the white man as soon as she could rustle up my father and his sister into a wagon. She was helped by the Negro who was the father of the girl. My father only had Mr. White to call his own, and the way my grammy told it, 'White' was a name never to be spoken. I don't know what it was like to be brought up thinkin' your daddy was evil. My father never talked about it. But I could see the pain in his eyes ever' time anyone told any tales, fancy or ordinary, about his daddy.

"My mother never talked about her parents except to go on about never letting anybody bein' made slave again. She acted like the only person that she cared about was my daddy. It was a love match, and everybody knew it.

"So I just figure all my family came from bein' ex-slaves, and that was that."

Ricky was riveted to story but only vaguely appreciated its implications. Everything he heard was new to him and needed to be digested for the rest of his life.

McGregor went on. His Coca-Cola was only half full, whereas Ricky's had been consumed.

"My life on the tenant farm was not bad. I had no run-ins with white folk to speak of. Once I saw the Klan ride into town, but they rode right out again and paid no mind to me. My mother was holding my hand at the time, and I reckon as she almost squeezed the water out of it like as if it were a rag.

"There wasn't much schoolin'. Still, some luck was on me. There was just enough for me to learn to read and write. I don't know why, but my parents pushed learnin'. I gotta be grateful to them two. They give as much as they could."

Ricky was immersed in the world McGregor was describing. "So, you never suffered discrimination from white people?"

McGregor looked at him with honest eyes. He knew the word, thought a moment, and said, "Not as a young'un. I lived in the world of Negroes, and it was for the most part a quiet place fo' me. The I grew up and joined the war. I became a sergeant in the Seventh Army Battalion." McGregor gave a little salute sitting in the chair.

"I was in the army now. There's where you learned about badass whites. There are whites, Ricky, who love slavery in any form."

Ricky interjected, "But slavery was banished, wasn't it?"

"Slavery comes in many forms. When one people wants to kill or rule over another people, it's a kind of slavery. White-only water fountains, white-only bathrooms, bars where Negroes can't come in, the hate you feel if you're a Negro talking to a white woman who's lookin at you like you goin to hurt her in some way, schools that are no good for any Negro child. Low wages for the colored. It's all a kind of goin' on of slavery. You ain't a human bein' when you's a Negro, Ricky. You just a tolerated brown animal. You know that at any time, dat toleration can turn. Any time."

Imploringly, Ricky looked at George McGregor and asked, "What happened in the army?"

"I feels pain to tell this story, but I'm goin' to tell you, because you seem to want to learn. Also, a Negro needs any white friend he can get, and I think you can be a white friend."

Ricky winced inside at the new responsibility he felt.

"John Brown was the lieutenant's name. You're smiling, Ricky. I am not making a joke. The man was as white as an alabaster stone just like the Harper Ferry's John Brown. This guy was opposite of that old abolitionist, but, still, that was his name. Life is full of ironies. Anyway, he had it in for me. He couldn't understand how I'd made sergeant. He once said to me, 'How can somebody from an inferior race become an NCO over us whites. We are your superiors from the womb? Who do you think you are? You lead whites? Fuck that. You are black trash. Here I am by the grace of God forced to be your officer, and, by the army rules, you have to work for me as my sergeant. I'm still in charge of you and don't you forget it. I can't change what is in this war, but I will do everything I can to screw you. You'd better watch yourself, nigger. Do you understand me?'"

McGregor paused for a moment, swallowed, and said, "I couldn't believe the outright meanness of this man. I had lived without getting much of this kind of treatment. Here I was. I had to say, 'Yes, sir' and walk away. You can only imagine the anger in my heart.

"I lived with this coyote for one year before we were shipped to Germany. He insulted me whenever the chance came in, right in front of my men. The white ones snickered; the Negroes fumed but didn't show anythin'. The treatment brought me closer to my brothers. I tell you the truth, Ricky. I could feel this man from Alabama was different. I swear on my mammy's life. But I did not let my hate for this white officer man make me hate all white people. I knew there was somethin' raw and bad about this one. I just took it in my heart he was KKK.

"In Germany, the platoon was kept together, and I was still sergeant. I kept my rank. I's still proud of dat. I don't know how I did it, as this character did all he did to hurt me. More than once he sent my platoon into fire. I think to this day he wanted to see me killed jus' so he could enjoy the show. I can swear the man just had a fundamental hate for Negroes. He would send me out on forwards with my brothers, but the bullets always missed me. There I was wid this KKK man trying his best to get me killed. No white man was wid me.

"I don't know how I survived, but I did. I get no pleasure sayin' he did not. A German sniper got him running from his foxhole toward the enemy. He was not a coward, just not a good man. A brave piece of shit. I saw him fall and quick-like crawled beside him to look. I stared into his white eyes. I felt sorry for the early end of his life. I also felt he deserved what he got. I felt just a little bit mo' safe. I know then there was a great divide in the world. It would be a rare white man who could understand what the Negro feels."

This was not an Uncle Remus story. There were no twittering bluebirds. This was what George McGregor lived every day, every time he showed his dark face to a white one. Ricky understood why McGregor responded as he had to his Remus reference. The boy becoming a man felt ashamed and lucky at the same time.

"You must be angry when my father makes a joke about your Scotch name. Is he the kind of white man who doesn't understand?" Ricky expected the answer that would confirm the question.

"Your father's a special man, Ricky. He understands everythin' I've told you. His joke is not so much a joke as a signal between two knowing men. You don't know him, Ricky. When he makes that joke about my name, it ain't just a joke. The sound of his voice and the kindness in his voice tell me he understands. He knows the history of Negro folk. Another white man could have made the same words and it would be hurt me. Your father is complimenting me. He's saying that he respects what my grandmother went through and what it means to me to have a Scottish name. He understands the Negroes' misery, the discrimination, the unfair world they suffer, the hate for no reason besides their color. You can be proud of your father, Ricky. He's one of a kind.

"I don't rightly know why the white man has to subjugate the darky. He needs to believe we're inferior to boost himself. He thinks he has no worth, otherwise why put down the Negro? Why put down anybody? The trouble is that some Negroes have go along wid this. They live poor lives because they think they don't deserve better. The Negro accepts he's an inferior being."

McGregor turned away from Ricky. He reached for a framed photo on a nearby mantel.

"Dat's why I keep Frederick Douglass's picture here." McGregor picked up the photograph of the bearded, well-dressed Negro and showed it to Ricky. "Do you know Frederick Douglass, Ricky?"

Ricky thought for a moment out of respect and was forced to answer, "No, I never heard of him."

"That's OK, that's all right. You don't have to know. There's a lot of colored history. You don't gotta know everything. Frederick Douglass was a special man to us. He was a runaway slave. Story is, he was forced to pay for his freedom after he was grown up. Can you imagine? After he's free, he has to buy himself free. Why is dat? Because there were laws sayin' that any runaway slave could be captured and sold again. He kinda bought himself 'cause of dis law. He taught himself to read and write. He wrote lots a stuff. He became a famous speaker for the Negro people. Because of Douglass, recruiting Negroes for the North during the Civil War turned out successful. During the war, he met with President Lincoln. He stood up for the colored cause. He wrote many books and was famous. We Negroes bring up Douglass because he represents the truth that we ain't a race of fools. Ricky, ain't nothin' inferior about us. Douglass is the stuff we is made of."

The afternoon was running into twilight. Ricky knew riding his bike after dark was not a good idea. Yet he was so taken by the intelligence of George McGregor, the plight his brown skin brought him, and the enormous ignorance he felt in himself about the Negro situation. He could not get up from his chair.

"Well, son. Thanks for listening to my woes about me and my people. I gotta say, you are your father's son and a good listener. I look forward to bringin' yo' tray to you and yo' family at Morrison's. I see it's getting dark, and yo' better git goin'. I hope we can have another Coca-Cola sometime. Thank ya, Ricky Bateman. Thank ya."

"I thank you, sir. It has been great! I need to think about what you said, and it does make me think a lot. I'm sorry I have to get home. Sorry to leave you."

"Tha's OK, son. I know you's got to go. My wife's comin' soon. Besides, I gotta get dressed for Morrison's. They's openin' right soon."

McGregor seemed thankful to Ricky, and Ricky felt transformed. His world again changed. This moment would be burned in his mind forever. There was nothing inferior about the Negro. To think about Negroes as a group as inferior or stupid was wrong.

The bike was in motion. The planet was in motion. The mind of Ricky was in motion. Nothing was as it was. Ricky pedaled home a different person.

Chapter 10

A Father's Intervention

He was driving alone at night, in a hurry to get to Horace's house. He was picking up Alan and was late. He heard that Horace was having a soiree, offering wine, music, and talk about literature, current affairs, and other topics reserved for the bookish crowd. Ricky didn't like wine, but he looked forward to the party because he enjoyed the lively intellectual banter, however pretentious. At least he could talk freely without anyone calling him too intellectual. He thought Horace to be a strange fellow in his costume of smoking jacket, pipe, and moustache, all contained in a lean frame, always making affected accents and trying to be some special type of completely unfamiliar person. He might not fit the bill of Noel Coward, but at least he was smart. What he had to say always seemed interesting if, admittedly, frequently annoyingly unctuous. Ricky was looking forward to the experience despite the fact that it gave him more than a twinge of social discomfort. Distracted then with these thoughts of Horace, he was forced to reduce his speed suddenly because of the car in front.

Reducing his speed was all he could do. He was on Abercorn with its island in the middle, and the car before him was in the center of his one-way lane. Cars parked on the side made it impossible to pass. The other car was moving quite slowly. He could see a man was driving, with a woman sitting beside him. An opening in the road appeared where no cars were parked. Ricky increased his speed to pass, but the car ahead moved in the same direction to impede his movement. All he could do was to move back into line, angry. He decided to blow his horn, believing that possibly the guy didn't see him and all that was happening was unintentional. Maybe the driver wasn't paying attention and had moved to the left unaware that Ricky wanted to pass, he thought. He pressed on the steering wheel gently, a slight hoot just to alert the source of his trouble still in front.

Ricky was sure that his obstacle went even slower. "Damn! What the hell is he trying to do?" Without thinking, he blew the horn again, loudly. At that, right in the middle of Abercorn Street, at eight thirty at night, the man stopped his car, and Ricky was forced to stop behind him. He was considering what to do. It was dark, and the two cars were the only vehicles to be seen. In retrospect it seemed peculiar that he had no fear, only anger. He was going to give this guy a piece of his mind. "What the hell is he doing?" he thought again.

He saw this tall, football-lineman figure emerge from the other car and come toward him. The imposing, lumbering shadow was at least five eleven, walked like a prosimian, and quickly crossed the space between the two cars. Ricky knew he could outtalk any orangutan and had already planned his choice words. He felt unjustly treated and was angry that he was being made later for the party. There was no nervousness, no worry, because Ricky felt intellectually superior. He would have no trouble putting this bastard in his place.

Now at the door of the Oldsmobile, the menace glowered at Ricky, who opened his window and his mouth at the same time. Both were exposed. The were the unwitting objects of rage, an unexpected rage from this Godzilla of the South.

Abruptly, something solid and overpowering smashed into Ricky's open oral cavity. He felt this shock of nonverbal dominance and in an instant realized that he was not going to say anything. As the fist crashed reality into his jaw and his adolescent mind, he knew in a flash that he had been defeated by his own pre-smashed-into-the-face worldview. As he bounced back into the new space between the human cudgel and his bleeding head, he felt he'd been the dupe of his presumed sense of security. He knew that he had left part of childhood and entered the territory of the adult. In this new domain, in the matured view, anything could happen. That night, the anything happened, and Ricky grew quickly into a new sobering truth: don't blow your horn at bigger guys with who might know only aggression as a way to settle arguments. As quickly as the leviathan's prideful appendage did its damage with the single punch, the guy said, "Who do you think you're blowing your horn at, you little fuck! Don't you ever do that to me again, or next time I'll do worse." Whereupon the atavist turned on his heels and walked back to his car.

Stunned, Ricky gently felt his lip and noted that a piece of skin was hanging. Because his father always yelled at him to take a handkerchief, he had one to press against his mouth to stop the bleeding. His car lights were on, and he had a moment to see the other car's rear license plate and make. He repeated the number in his mind over and over while pressing his wound firmly with his left hand. With his right he leaned over, opened the glove compartment, and found a piece of paper and a pencil. He awkwardly scribbled what he needed.

He decided the best next move was to go home. There was blood on his shirt. He was shaken. He needed some time to consider the event. He drove back with only his right hand on the wheel until only a few blocks away from his house. He noticed the bleeding had stopped, and he entered the driveway with a swollen, red, injured face, an outer flag of the inner change. His father saw the flag first.

"What happened to you?

"Nothing," he answered with a shrug.

"What do you mean nothing? Margie!" his father called to his mother. "Look at this!"

"What happened to you?" his mother demanded.

His father scowled. "Don't give me this 'nothing' business, Ricky. You tell me what happened."

Ricky felt not only the depth of his father's concern, but also his recrimination. Refusing to tell the story would result in a terrible scene with his father screaming, stomping about, and throwing things around the house. Ricky was in no mood for a major confrontation and elected to tell the story. It also pleased him to pour out his sense of righteousness as the victim, hiding his shame; for Ricky knew he should not have blown his horn so intensely at anyone. He was afraid his father would pounce on that fact and attack him in his misery.

"Sammy, let the boy wash himself, he's all full of blood," his mother said before he could begin his tale. Just a moment before, she had been asking the same question. As if turning on a dime, she had now decided that Ricky should clean himself up first.

"A guy hit me," Ricky piped up.

"What guy? Why did he hit you?" his father pushed.

"There was this guy in front of me in the car. He was going so slow that I couldn't get around him. You know how it is on Abercorn if cars are parked. When I tried to get around him, he swerved to block me. I blew my horn. He stopped his car and came out. Then I opened my window to say something, but before I could, he hit me."

His father stood there in the foyer of the modest three-bedroom ranch house, wearing an open white dress shirt with gray slacks held up by a wide belt. His right arm hung along his side, his right hand holding the remains of an unlit cigar. His face had an intense, powerful look. He was genuinely worried about his son, but Ricky only saw a scowling, critical father, one that could burst into rage at any moment.

"Do you know who this man is? Have you ever seen him before?"

"No, but I have his license plate, and he was driving a '55 Chevrolet."

"You got his license plate after he hit you?" his mother said with surprise and apparent pride. "With all this bleeding and pain, you were able to get his license plate?" Ricky felt her glow for just a moment. The implicit approval was wonderful. He relaxed with the realization, bestowed upon him by his gentle and usually clueless mother, that he had done something special.

"Yeah, Mom. I wrote it on a piece of paper I found in the glove compartment."

"Let me see that piece of paper," his father insisted. Ricky handed it to him obediently, his usual defiance noticeably absent. For the moment there was a unity between two rival forces, a harmony that disarmed them both. The family was joined.

"Ricky, go wash yourself, and lie down for a few minutes. Which way were you going on Abercorn?" his father asked.

"Toward the Savannah River. Toward downtown."

His father stood still in concentration.

"Go on, Ricky. Wash yourself. You'll feel better." His mother gave him a little push on the shoulder. "Go on."

"OK, but afterward I still want to go to Horace's house. He's having a party. It's still early." Neither parent answered.

Ricky went to the bathroom, took off his shirt, and looked in the mirror. His lip was filled with blood on the left side, the skin split open by the impact. He gingerly patted the area clean with a damp washrag. The swelling was obvious, and he knew he would get a lot of questions from his friends. He went to his bedroom, took out a clean shirt, dressed himself, and came out to tell his parents he was leaving.

He found his mother sitting at the kitchen table reading the *Savannah Morning News*, even though it was well into the night. She never finished the newspaper.

It was available through the entire day as a salve or distraction whenever needed. She looked relaxed and at ease, with her cigarette on the ashtray and both elbows on the table as she looked down at some insignificant item of news. It could just as well have been an ad.

She wore her usual housedress emblazoned with large, brightly colored flowers. Her still-dark brunette hair was cut shorter than when she married. It fell just above her shoulders. Her posture, the attitude of her face and body, expressed an insouciance that belied the violence of the event Ricky just brought home. To her it was as if nothing happened. Within Margie Bateman, the world would always be a nonmoving place of calmness and quiet, only slightly altered by the occasional ripples of life. "What is there to be bothered about? No one died," she often said.

Ricky looked at her with his usual mild disdain. "Mom, I'm going to Horace's now. Where's Dad?"

"What do you want to go to that peculiar boy's house for? He's not for you. Your father went out."

"What! He took the car? I need the car. Where did he go? I told you both I wanted to go out again. Why did he do that?" Ricky expressed considerable anguish, completely avoiding his mother's comments about Horace. She always criticized Horace. He accepted the fact that she didn't like him. More important now was the fact that the Olds had disappeared with his father. Without the car, he couldn't go anywhere.

"He went out. I think he's looking for the man that hit you. He said something about going to the Savannah Theatre. He thought that since the man was going in that direction with his girlfriend, he was probably going to the movies. At least that was what he said."

Ricky's mother related all of this with the same attitude she would have had she been explaining why she bought grade A eggs instead of grade AA. Ricky's response was being flabbergasted. He laughed to himself that his father would never be able to find the guilty single car with the right license plate in the dark, but he was amazed that his father had gone to try. It quickly occurred to him that his father could be hit too. That bothered him more than he could explain. He found himself worrying. As he worried, his irritation returned.

"What am I going to do? Damn!"

"Stop it, Ricky. Your father will be back soon. It's early. There is still time to go. I don't know why you want to. Go read a book."

Ricky sat at the kitchen table with his mother instead. The two of them had spent many hours doing just that. She seemed never to tire of the gossip concerning his life. He had once enjoyed her eager investigations. She asked him the most trivial questions. She almost clapped her hands in glee with his placid answers. He never failed to be impressed with the happiness this gave her.

She would want to know what dress the girl wore, what kind of music the band played, where they went afterward, and were her parents nice to him. She would ask about decorations in the dance hall, whom he danced with, and were certain kids there that she knew. The motherly grilling was especially intense during junior high school. It was the only real bond between mother and son.

The past year or so, Ricky had grown impatient with this, feeling the intrusiveness of her need to be fed from the trough of his life. He had yet to grow up enough to appreciate her, her care, her complete devotion. Instead, he found himself staying away from what he felt were her intrusions into his private life. Her questions forced him to doubt himself. Why didn't he have a date? Why wasn't he invited to a party to which others were invited? It was impossible for him to answer these existential questions. Without realizing it, he began avoiding Mom and the kitchen table.

Here he was again. In spite of himself, he had to admit to himself that he felt the need for family warmth and comfort. Here he was with his mother, repeating the same story he had told in the foyer just minutes ago. She wanted to know if the man was tall or short, did he seem angry, did the girl come out of the car, how did he get the license number if it was so dark, why was there no one else around?

If there were a purpose to her questions, she would have seemed like the greatest detective, but there was no purpose. Or the purpose was inherent in the act of asking questions. She simply wanted to be in her son's life, bask in his youth, and enjoy her connection to him. He could not understand this and resented her probing imposition joined with her almost uncaring serenity about everything.

Only later would her style become a fundamental part of him, and he would find its like described in books concerned with the Eastern philosophies of Lao Tzu or Buddha. She had no inkling of being so profound; but nevertheless, as with those ideas, she was part of the flow of existence, suggested she felt merely a part of nature's flow, and wanted, metaphorically, nothing more than merely to be part of the wind.

They both heard a car in the driveway.

"It's your father," she said. He didn't even wince at her always annoying declaration of the obvious.

Together they went to the front door to let him in.

"What happened?" his mother asked, expecting the entire evening to be summarized before he crossed the threshold.

"Ricky, was he a tall boy with dark hair, wearing sneakers?"

"You found him!? He wasn't a boy. I don't know about the sneakers. How did you find him?" Ricky rattled on in respectful awe.

"I was right. He went to the movies. I walked around the blocks by the movie theater, and I found the car. I got a policeman and showed him the number on your piece of paper, and it matched that of the car. It was a '55 Chevrolet, all right. The policeman then went into the theater and had the usher make an announcement. The guy came out thinking his car was in trouble. The policeman arrested him on the spot."

"Arrested him!" Ricky could not believe what he heard. He was astounded again. His father did this for him. The man he had hated, wished dead, fought severely with, this man had run out at night and found his assailant and had him arrested. Ricky grew again. Life was not what it seemed.

"Yes. He took him to night court," his father continued. "He didn't have to stay in jail. They let him out. But he was charged! We only have to go to court when his case comes to trial in two or three months, the policeman said. We'll get a notice about the exact time. At least he won't hit innocent kids again!"

Sammy Bateman was emphatic. He had interpreted his son's injury in a way that Ricky could never have expected. He did not even hear the part about Ricky blowing his horn. He only saw his son's injury and became angry in his heart. This boy, this firstborn, cherished product of his dreams, could not be attacked. His New York street smarts took over. No one would do this to his son and get away with it, no matter how much he was provoked. These were the father's sentiments, and this was what Ricky felt.

Wally was not someone Ricky could easily understand. His meaning as a person eluded him. Now his father altered forever the idea that he was merely a threatening and scary patriarch. Savannah was beloved and deplored at the same time. What were the best values to have? What did the world have to offer in the form of certainty? Things were increasingly unclassifiable, undecidable, as this precollege year progressed. You could almost see the alterations in Ricky's brain. He had started this year with convictions of an unthinking dependent who saw people only as simple categories. He was ending it with a transformative sense of reality called his life.

CHAPTER 11

Walpurgis Nacht at Horace's

"Do you happen to know what's playing at the Savannah Theatre tonight?" Horace asked after hearing Ricky give his explanation of his freshly cut lower lip.

"No, what?" Ricky answered, having left his mother less than a half hour ago against her entreaties to stay home. Now he deliciously awaited the response.

"*Julius Caesar*, with James Mason and Marlon Brando."

"Really?" Ricky responded in sincere surprise.

"Yesss." Horace was now at his affected best. He stood like his avatar, Noel Coward, a regal presence before his own distinguished court of presumed admirers. He postured in what was clearly meant to appear like supreme confidence while his audience, Fred, Ricky, and Hubert, gawked. He wore a dinner jacket, the first Ricky had seen off TV. In his hand was a long cigarette holder containing a Camel, a brand that must have some kind of unique quality. Ricky knew nothing about cigarettes. He just assumed that Horace would only have the best. His erstwhile friend's thick oily hair stayed obediently in place, and his thin, freshly minted, pencil lined moustache seemed to snarl with each word.

"Yesss. Can you imagine?" An unbelievable sound came from Horace. It was a high-pitched feminine sound, the kind of sound that contradicted the presence of Noel Coward and suggested a fictitious Tallulah Bankhead pretending to be regal. "This oaf hit you without cause and then took his pretty girlfriend to see *Julius Caesar*. Oafs simply don't see *Julius Caesar*. Life can certainly reveal the very unexpected." His arm came down in a debonair sweep, ending, at just the right moment, poised above an ashtray. The pseudosocialite delicately flicked his ashes with his two fingers upon the cigarette holder's shaft, allowing them to drop quietly but distinctly into the patiently waiting ashtray held so delicately in his other hand. The cinders rested there to everyone's morbid wonderment, the detritus of his thought.

"Maybe he had to go for a college course?" Fred offered.

"Why, Fred, would he go with his girlfriend? Well, I suppose," Horace said, answering his own question, "he might have fulfilled a requirement, but certainly without absorbing its substance. Or perhaps he went to see Hollywood's version of Roman martial arts." Utterance completed, he gave a wan smile to his audience and took another demonstrative puff of his cigarette. Everyone but Ricky laughed in a whimpering sort of way, more like a swallowed snicker.

"I think it's so ironic that a crude jerk with no sense of restraint would go to see Shakespeare," Hubert, the sycophant, responded, chuckling. "It's a terrible contradiction. How can a man behave so badly and yet possess any culture?"

"I did blow my horn. I guess I shouldn't have."

"Oh, don't be silly, Rick. The man assaulted you. He deserves to go to jail. He could have killed you. Your horn is not important. He was wrong in any case," Horace went on seriously.

"Rick did provoke him," Hubert interjected. The short and slightly rotund Hubert gave an exaggerated look of distaste. He and Ricky had always had a not-so-subtle dislike for each other. Ricky felt the source for the mutual distaste was with Hubert. Ricky had always admired Hubert's apparent culture, especially his love for classical music. It was Hubert who'd introduced him to music altogether. Before Hubert, he had not even heard of Beethoven. Hubert had such self-confidence, giving him an imperviousness to criticism to which Ricky knowingly aspired. Ricky also envied the fact that Hubert's family had money and were able to send him to Country Day School, a private prep school totally inaccessible to Ricky's middle-economic-class status. With acknowledged envy, he did not understand Hubert's enmity and felt a peculiar shiver whenever he sensed the usual coldness blown toward him. "Is it me or my money?" Ricky often asked himself.

"Yesss. But he didn't mean to provoke him. After all, the man was blocking the road and going very slowly." Horace was coming to the defense, and Ricky was impressed. He became silent, drank his Coke, which he insisted on having over the offered cognac, and listened.

"I agree the man had no right to hit Ricky, but he certainly was provoked. I think Ricky has to take part of the responsibility for what happened." Hubert was taking the opposing side of the argument to heart and wasn't going to let the issue pass into social pleasantries. It seemed for a moment that the discussion was going to get heated. This could not be allowed in Horace's hallowed halls.

Horace took control. "Pooh! What does it matter? We're here for some fun, and besides, Ricky is injured and needs some comforting." With that he went over to the upright piano in his parents' modest Oglethorpe Street apartment and began playing from a piece of sheet music. That anybody could sit and play the piano was a mystery for Ricky. Every time he tried, however much he desired it, however much he knew the melody, he was able to twist out of the keys only the simplest of sounds. "Three Blind Mice" enchanted him. Yet here was Horace, with all his unreal and inflated egoism, performing wizardry and creating music magic from notes on a page and finger tapping on a piano. Horace was the priest who knew the secrets of the instrument. He knowledge allowed him to enter the temple of music. Ricky could only stay outside and wonder in awe.

"Have you heard this? It's a big hit in New York." He sang as he played. "'With a little bit o' luck, with a little bit o' luck…'"

Ricky read from the music sheet *My Fair Lady*. He was frustrated that he had not heard of it. He was not a member of this group either, really. There was a charm in all this forced sophistication. He felt drawn but could not embrace the accoutrements of the style. With Horacfine and Hubert, he always felt uncomfortable while intrigued. Now, taken in by Horace's performance, all he could do was to stand by the piano in discomfort. He saw Hubert, all smiles, beginning to sing along with Horace in knowledgeable, self-conscious abandon. Fred, always wanting to be a member of anything at any cost, tried unsuccessfully to catch the tune, botching the euphonious sound of the two Broadway savants as they illustrated their mordant sophistication.

"Would you like to hear the record? It's wonderful!" Before anyone could reply, as if anyone would want to be contrary, Horace had it playing on the phonograph. Ricky tried to follow the tunes but couldn't. He felt dismayed that the language and melodic style eluded him like New York itself. He couldn't conceive of what a Broadway show was like and could not visualize the context in which the characters would be saying whatever it was coming from the recording. He was completely outclassed by Horace and Hubert. They were ostentatiously enjoying the lyrics immensely.

Horace was prancing, lifting his legs in the mimic of a show horse. He held his arms out as if in a circle of dancers. He showed the arrogance of his assumed superiority. Spinning himself with arms outstretched, he was unwittingly immersed in an incantation of some Sufi whirling dervish ritual. Ricky felt something primal, uncontrollable, and yet infantile about the gyrating and gamboling. As Horace high stepped around the small apartment, he sang out the memorized words of the show.

"'The rain in Spain falls mainly on the plain…I think she's got it…I think she's got it.'" Horace played each character. Hubert, who also appeared to have memorized the entire show, then forcefully chimed in. The two were having a wonderful time. Fred and Ricky looked on, the first yearningly, the second increasingly angrily. Ricky saw in his mind's eye that he had been given a scarlet letter emblazoned on his shirt, an S for stupid. He was the unjust outcast, the one that didn't fit in.

Fred's being excluded as well meant nothing. Fred was forever the misfit who didn't know he was excluded. He seemed never to suffer the truth of his place in the group. Fred always tried, always failed, but always expressed a satisfaction in just being there. He was swept up with the ebullience of the moment.

Ricky knew what Fred denied. He realized he was ignorant of the world of sophistication that Horace and Hubert represented. He should not have felt troubled, for later he would learn that real sophistication was never exhibited or bloated. Having knowledge of the arts was a gift of humanity, not something to demonstrate like the medals on a general's shirt or the dazzling epaulets of an African potentate. He had started to learn, started to read, but he had yet missed something. Despite the fact that he had been with his father to Radio City Music Hall, he never realized there was a Broadway. "Theater" meant movies only. A musical like *My Fair Lady* was alien ignorance.

Ricky couldn't fathom why Horace and Hubert had not missed them. They seemed to know more about the life that was available. Their dancing was as much an expression of their exhibited superiority as it was a statement of their pleasure. They knew what the newest and the best were in the grand, sparkling, artsy outside of Savannah world. Ricky did not.

The music, the dancing, the singing came to an end only after the second side of the record was completed. The two entertainers sat themselves in the large cushioned French provincial chairs and resumed their consumption of what was announced to be "fine" cognac.

"It is a wonderful show. I saw it, you know," Hubert bragged.

"Yes? I did too. Last spring. Did you see it with Julie Andrews and Rex Harrison?" The challenge was on. Horace parried.

"She was there, but he was sick. A cold, I think."

"How sad. He was wonderful. Terribly droll. Wonderfully English. I really prefer the English in English plays, don't you?" Horace was winning.

"The substitute was an American. He did very well. I like Julie. She was terrific. I don't know. Are you one of those people who thinks only the English should play Shakespeare?" Hubert was moving closer. Ricky could hardly believe his ears. No one ever talked like this. He wondered what he was doing here. Everything was pretentious and phony. He began to fidget and think of a way to leave. He had thought he would enjoy himself, immersed in the heady air of intellectualism, but he found that he didn't like it this way. Where were they going with this conversation? The words seemed more a vehicle for them to exhibit themselves, a kind of mental preening. He felt a piercing nausea begin to snake up his gut.

"Well, I can't imagine Humphrey Bogart playing any Shakespearian role, can you?"

"Maybe Puck, ha, ha, ha, ha." They both laughed at Horace's response. Ricky really couldn't stand it anymore.

"Ah, I think I'm going to have to go. Fred, do you need a ride?"

"Yeah. It's late. I'd better get home." Wonderful Fred. Whatever his deficiencies, whatever he lacked in perspicacious wit, it was great having someone kind and supportive leave with him. Ricky was gratified.

Neither of the now seated dignitaries got up from their seats. Horace, the kindlier of the two, said good night. Hubert artfully refilled his glass. It was clear the two were going to continue their pomposity with each other for a while. As the door closed, separating them, Ricky signed inwardly in relief. He didn't know if he could suffer these two again. He could not believe they represented the city he wanted to discover and absorb. He refused to accept this cultural slob was what he dreamed of discovering. He would have to discover New York in his own way.

CHAPTER 12

Robin Allows Ricky to Take Her to a Party

"WHY DON'T YOU wear the white dress with the pink collar?" Mrs. Linkowitz queried Robin.

"I don't like the white dress. Besides, it lays flat. I can't wear my crinoline with it." Robin answered.

"But that dress goes nicely with the pink headband."

"Mom!" she answered, exasperated. "I know what I want to wear!"

Mrs. Linkowitz gave her daughter a resigned look and retreated from battle. She felt frightened that her Robin would not tolerate her presence and fell into an immediate silence. Subdued, she nevertheless refused to leave either the second floor of her house or her daughter's teenage girl's room. It was a large room with a single window looking out onto the street, walls painted a plain white and decorated with pictures of cats, dogs, and movie stars. The bed was cleanly made and had a lacy, frilled coverlet. Against the pillow was a large pink stuffed cat with equally large black whiskers. It was the favorite pet of the little family of two and, on this occasion, would soon find itself in Robin's mother's arms as protection.

cRobin sat at the dressing table combing her hair and looking into the mirror. Her mother stood behind her holding the dress over which she had lost this most recent war. She turned to put the dress back into the closet near the entrance to the room. These two women were the only people in the large, two-story house. There was no father, and there were no siblings.

They had just finished a light meal. Robin had half a hamburger. Mrs. Linkowitz had the other half plus an extra helping of carrots and string beans. Both decided to save the chocolate pudding for another time. Robin's mother didn't want to eat it by herself, and Robin believed she would eat something at Tanya Herstburg's party anyway.

The meal was pleasant. Mother and daughter liked each other; in fact, they had come to depend on each other. Mrs. Linkowitz had lost her husband to another woman, her best friend, six years ago when Robin was only eleven. She would never recover. She thought Roz was an ally. She had confided everything to her. All her disappointments with Alex were duly recorded by the woman that was now his wife. She never imagined Roz would betray her. Roz was so close. They were inseparable friends.

Robin now filled that role. But Robin was not an easy companion. Even more worrisome, she gave in terribly with the boys. Her mother knew the truth. Robin's toilet habits were not exemplary, and the evidence was there. The boys seemed to always attain exactly what they wanted. "I have to get along with her. She's all I've got." Robin was now her best and her only friend. Her daughter became the rare soul with whom she shared anything of herself.

Mrs. Selma Linkowitz tried hard not to fight with her daughter. She was afraid she might lose her. She heard that happened. The paper sometimes had stories about how teenagers left home, went up to Atlanta, and got into one kind of trouble or another. It was important to stay friendly. You never knew what could happen. Besides, the loneliness would be excruciating.

Robin did help with the dishes. Even in adolescent brashness, she valued her mother and tried hard not to create scenes between them. "She's not really a bad girl," her mother often encouraged herself to think. "I just hope she's careful. Her big problem with boys. Well, tonight she's going to Tanya's party. A lot of nice Jewish boys will be there. You never know what can happen. At least with a Jewish boy, there's a sense of responsibility. The goy run off. They don't care about anybody, especially a Jewish girl. Why did Alex leave me? My daughter's going to a party, and I'm going to listen to the radio. What kind of life is this for me?"

Mrs. Linkowitz shared none of these thoughts with Robin. She placed the white dress with the pink collar back into the closet and took out the blue print that Robin requested. She sat on the side of the bed holding the stuffed cat, repeating all of her woeful preoccupations in her mind while she adoringly watched her seventeen-year-old preen.

"Mom, you know I might be home late tonight."

"Why? It's only a party. What's late, Robin?"

"Well. I can't say. Sometimes the parties go past one. I just don't want you to worry." Robin was only telling a half truth. The whole truth was that she did not want her mother calling Tanya's house and embarrassing her. Once, her mother called a party and cried on the phone to Robin's friend. It was terrible. Her mother was so possessive. She let the word string out in her thought so that it lasted a long time—"Pohhsessssiiivvvvvve!," leaving its angry sense lingering.

"All right, Mom? Now don't call again like you did at Phyllis's party last month. All the girls laughed at me, and I was so ashamed. You've got to trust me, Mama. I'm not a little girl anymore. I can take care of myself. Besides, it's only a party."

"I promise not to call you. But don't come home too late," she answered meekly and submissively.

"I don't plan to, really!"

"How are you getting to the party and coming home?"

"Oh, Mama. I do wish you wouldn't bother. OK, I'll tell you. Don't get so upset!" Robin saw her mother had tears in her eyes. They were so visible she could even make them out in her mirror. She turned around to calm the parent. As she spun her head, her dark black hair twisted and fell back beautifully upon her shoulders. The blue headband was made almost invisible within the darkened strands. She could not help feeling a resentment toward the grieving person who had never recovered from her husband's abandonment. Robin saw her mother as weak. Robin was proud and prided herself on her strength. She was determined to let no man ever hurt her as her father had betrayed her mother.

The dour matron waited patiently for this small reply. "Who's taking her?" she thought. She sat upon the bed, her right hand wiping the unexpected tears from her somber eyes. Her own hair was mostly gray. She was only in her early fifties but had the countenance of an older woman who had given up her life to its unexpected events. Her face was still unwrinkled and smooth, and a man would certainly have found it beautiful; but it was placed upon an overweight body wearing a plain housedress decorated with fading red flowers that seemed to enhance its drabness.

"Richard Bateman borrowed his father's car. and he's driving me both ways."

"Richard Bateman?! I thought you didn't like him. He's been calling you for months for a date. and you keep turning him down. How come you're going with him now?"

"I'm not *going with him*, Mom. I'm just going to the party with him. It's convenient. Besides, he's not so bad. I'm not wild about him, but he's OK. I just wish he wasn't so serious. I really wanted George to take me, but his car's broke, and his parents are out of town. He said he didn't want to go to the party anyway. I think he's really with that shiksa Mary Sue Lane. I don't hate Rick. He's kind of cute. He's all right as a second choice." She laughed as she said this, pleased with her little joke. Her mother smiled too. It was one of those wonderful, shared, happy moments they rarely had. "He has asked me out so many times, I didn't feel like turning him down again. Maybe he just wore me out?" They both laughed again.

Robin completed her dressing. She and her mother talked about the print she was putting on, about its cost; they compared it to similar dresses her friends had, and the cost of those. Robin mentioned a slight she felt from a friend. She complained that she might never talk to the friend again, and her mother said she was being too severe. It was too easy to lose friends who later turned out to be important. In this way the two chattered, touched fabrics, gazed into the nothingness in each mind, and felt the illusion of being connected to their world.

To the two women, living was all a matter of momentary experiences, disconnected events that happened for a few seconds, deserved a reaction, and were then forgotten. They were completely at one within the context of the immediacy of the small town in which they lived. Even this town had no history for them, just as they themselves had no history worth investigating. Life consisted of the unreflective moment. You dealt with the moment. Tomorrow was a matter of that moment. Long-range consequences, past events that impinged on the present, simply did not enter their minds. If a topic arose from the past or toward the future, they would consider it, apply a speedy consideration, and quickly put it aside. Understanding anything was tedious and boring. It was as if the full tripartite scope of past, now, and future had been eliminated.

Robin had just finished dressing when the doorbell rang. Mrs. Linkowitz smiled.

"You stay here. That must be Rick. I'll tell him you're not ready. It's important not to let him think you're waiting for him. I'll talk to him for a few minutes and call you."

The women looked endearingly at each other. Robin turned to the mirror to adjust her eyeliner as her mother went down the stairs. Selma fixed her housedress, smoothed her hair, and opened the door.

"Well, hello, Richard. How arrre youuuu?"

Rick saw her broad, welcoming grin and felt pleasantly surprised at her warm Southern greeting. He expected something more formal, less receptive. Even though he had known Robin and her mother for his entire lifetime, he always found them somewhat distant. His surprise over the greeting was exceeded only by his amazement at Robin's accepting his invitation to take her to Tanya Herstberg's party.

"I'm fine, Mrs. Linkowitz."

"Well, come in, Rick. Come in and sit down."

Rick felt awkward but pleased to be in this house under these conditions. He fingered the edge of his new paisley tie in his nervousness. The two walked into the living room off the foyer, and Rick sat on the flower-patterned couch. He sank deep into the sofa and felt uncomfortable in his angulated position with his knees arched upward and his feet almost off the floor.

"Robin is going to be a few minutes. Is that all right?"

"Yes'm."

"Would you like a drink? I have some wonderful lemonade." The phrase "wonderful lemonade" was stretched out so long that its meaning was almost lost in the extended melody of it.

"Yes'm."

When she returned and placed the yellow drink in his hand, he felt more awkward than ever. He had to hold his elbows high to keep the cold wet glass from touching the sofa. He was afraid to move simply because he incorrectly believed this would make a bad impression on his hostess. Sitting in this ungainly state, he was barely able to carry on the conversation. He struggled to manage the slight sips of cold, sweet, ice-tinkling fruit drink and to be as debonair as he could.

"Where're you going to school next year, Rick? Have you decided yet?" Mrs. Linkowitz knew how to begin the conversation, even though she had no interest in what Rick was doing for school. She and Robin had long decided that Robin was going to Atlanta to work in her brother's clothing store. She had heard, though, that Rick did well in school, and she assumed the question to be appropriate to the occasion.

Rick did not sense her genuine lack of interest. He was more concerned with his posture, the lemonade, and making some kind of good impression. In his naivety, he began an extended explanation of his plans, the whys and wherefores. She listened with what seemed to be attentiveness, but in fact, as he continued, she was mainly considering a rescue from him by her now likely well-prepared daughter. She could not understand the ins and outs of academic concerns. Colleges, SAT scores, courses of study, and other school ambitions meant nothing to her. She only wanted to be polite and had no intention of paying attention to the reply to her question.

"I am not quite sure what I'll be doing. I applied to Emory, Oglethorpe, and Harvard. I don't really think I'll get into Harvard, but I figured I'd give it a try. I did pretty well in my overall grades, but my SAT scores were not impressive. Did you know this is the first year they gave SAT tests in the Savannah schools? We really didn't have time to prepare. In the North they take special courses to get ready for them. I may have a chance of being accepted to Emory. I have an interview at Oglethorpe in Atlanta. Did you hear of it?" Mrs. Linkowitz was barely able to shake her head before he continued. "Well, it's a liberal arts school in Atlanta. Small. Only about seven hundred students. I may get a full scholarship there. But if I get into Emory, I don't know if my family can send me. It's expensive."

Suddenly he felt like the complete fool he was. He could see he was being vain and self-centered. Mrs. Linkowitz looked uncomfortable. She had that all too familiar dazed expression that showed she had not the least interest in his college applications. He reddened with this awareness and tried to squirm out of the situation.

"But none of this is important, Mrs. Linkowitz. What is Robin going to do next year?"

Before the answer came, Robin, who could not stand her isolation in her room any longer, came down the stairs and was seen by both struggling conversationalists.

"Oh. Hello, Robin."

"Hello, Rick. I'm so glad you and my mother had a chance to get acquainted."

"Yes. We were just talking about next year, what Rick's going to do and all that."

"That's great, Mama. Well, I guess we'll be going."

All of this happened within seconds. Robin had taken control and was dealing successfully with both her mother and her ride. Her mother was happy to be dismissed and allowed herself to wonder why her daughter would even spend fifteen minutes with this stuffy boy. She thought how funny he looked with his zigzag shape, holding his lemonade while being almost consumed by the sofa. "And could he talk so!" she thought as she closed the door behind them. She asked herself how the evening would be for her daughter. "He's kind of cute, sort of a handsome boy, but he's too peculiar for Robin. Too much into his books. She needs a more regular boy." These thoughts lingered as she saw Ricky maneuver his car and her daughter out of the driveway, leaving her completely alone.

CHAPTER 13

The Party

RICKY COULD NOT help but smell Robin's perfume as it filled his father's Oldsmobile. The gripping, penetrating aroma, too great a quantity for this small space, affected his concentration on the road and increased his nervousness. He felt proud and satisfied. Here he was in the atmosphere of this girl, this special person, this person he had pursued with repeated disappointment, this estimable person who finally allowed him to spin around with joy in the sparkle of her radiance, in the starlit brilliance of her world. That he was here with her, absorbing her odor and her being, experiencing the same car ride with her, accompanying her to a party, was such an exquisite sensation, such a super event, nothing else for the moment could possess anything of comparable value.

Yet he felt dimly somewhere within himself what he may not have consciously accepted: he was where he was by fluke. He knew she was not enchanted by him. She had granted him this date because of some kind of unknown largesse, a probably self-serving generosity he could not fathom. But he wasn't going to talk himself out of the pleasure of it all. He had finally won the coveted prize of taking Robin Linkowitz out, and he was going to enjoy it even if it meant being less than sensible, less than completely truthful to himself.

Could he enjoy it? He was fidgeting in the driver's seat, wondering what to say. From the corner of his eye, he could see she was completely nonchalant, satisfied with herself, appearing convinced that she was in control of her present situation. She sat, both arms extended upon her lap, holding down the crinoline that was pushing up her print dress, looking for all the world like the princess in *Zenda* on the way to a ball with her erstwhile prisoner.

He wanted so much to make a good impression, to solidify their relationship during this opportunity so that he might obtain another date in the future. He had no idea what would please her. So far, he perceived that nothing he did made him particularly endearing. She seemed indifferent to him and treated him as little more than a chauffeur. He was livery, and livery has its proper place.

He brushed away his doubts and glanced over at her. She was so pretty. Her breasts threw him into passionate musings. The strapless bra shaped her two feminine punctuations into parallel intimidating points, extending the tantalizing mamma outward like dual buttressed cantilevers covering her torso with their shadows. The rest of her womanly surprises added intensity to the even greater enticing mysteries he imagined beneath her multilayered skirt.

He felt himself stiffening beneath his pants, hoping painfully that she wouldn't notice. His ardor was increasing with each of the darkened Savannah blocks he drove past. He assumed he would not be able to touch her tonight, he accepted his need to restrain himself, but his mind betrayed his wish, and he found himself immersed in erotic considerations beyond complete control. It suddenly occurred to him that he could wet himself. This anxiety rushed so fervently upon him that he impetuously put on the brakes to shake off the possibility.

"What's the matter?" she asked.

"Oh, nothing. I thought I saw a dog crossing," he answered quickly. He was delighted to note that the incident he created distracted his preoccupation well enough to lower his pelvic tension. He sighed with relief both at his physical improvement and his realization that Robin was accepting his flimsy explanation. There was no dog of any kind to be seen that night on Reynolds Street, but her lackadaisical manner, in this instance, worked to his advantage. She did not seem to care or notice.

"Those dogs are terrible when they run in front of the car," he continued.

"They are! My friend's father once hit a dog on Drayton," she offered with a kind of lilt at the end of the sentence as if she clearly wanted him to encourage her to continue her little story. What else could he do?

"Really?"

"Yehhsss," she articulated with that sweet Southern extra feeling that unfortunately made him begin to stiffen again. "She killed that poor critter. It was a spaaaniel, a cocker spaniel. It was sooo sad." The exaggeration was thick and pretentious. Ricky noticed this disingenuousness, but he was in the throes of controlling his barely checked sexual responses and could not be concerned with the excesses of her emotion. He drove still faster.

Suddenly, a car pulled out of a side street, screeched its wheels by accelerating its speed, and came within inches of hitting the Olds. It had clearly ignored the stop sign. Ricky put on the brakes again, but this time so hard that Robin was thrown against the dashboard.

"What is the matter with that man?" she cried, pushing herself back onto her seat. "I do declare, he is crazy. Blow your horn at him, Ricky. He needs to know he almost killed us." But Ricky did not. He simply started up the car again and turned the corner toward Tanya's house.

His mind left all thoughts of Robin, his sexual sensitivity, and his driving. Thoughts intruded effortlessly and uncontrollably, and they erupted onto the world of two weeks past, remembering what had happened then when he blew his horn at the car in front.

The sock in his face, the guy in jail, his dad's heroic behavior distracted him. He recalled the strange time, a dark, otherworldly time, a time that seemed to lose its boundaries and therefore to undermine all the conceptions he once took for granted. So many things had happened. There was the tall stranger socking him in the mouth, Horace and Hubert cavorting about Horace's apartment like albatrosses about to take flight, Fred looking on as if he were a perplexed prairie dog staring out of his hole at the incomprehensible meanderings upon the threatening desert around him, his father searching the Savannah darkness to find his assailant. It was all too much for his memory, certainly too much on which to focus in the car, with Robin, in this present moment. Besides, the heady smell of his very sexual seat partner brought him back from his momentary lapse to the here and now. Like Proust returning from his madeleine musings, he realized intuitively that all of life could not be anamnestic reflection. Anyway, he preferred to wander away from the dark German forests of recollections and engage himself, if he could, in the heady aroma of his semidate. Life memories, a witch's coven or Hecate's dancing night demons, could not have more held attraction for him than Robin did.

He turned into Tanya's driveway on live-oak-lined Washington Avenue. At that moment, he not only absorbed Robin's perfume but glanced at her breasts, her hair, again at her pelvis disappearing into the uncontained crinoline, and imagined an erotic scene that was obliterated by the sound of her voice.

"Well, we're here!"

They were indeed "here." The large brick house loomed before them as he nestled the car between the others on the spacious driveway.

He mused on how much of life was automatic. He unthinkingly turned off the car engine. He automatically opened his door and, half dizzy with sexual excitement, lifted himself from his car seat and into the brisk night air. Then, as if in a well-known ritual, he went around to the back of the car to come to her side. Robin waited, sitting in her front seat like an elegant debutante properly expecting all that was transpiring.

He opened the front door as expected, extended his hand, helped her out, and heard her say, "Thank you, Ricky," as she glided ahead of him toward the door of the party house. He, with animal instinct, in deft combination, swung the door closed in a slap-bang against the wall of the car. Continuing, then, equally without consciousness, without losing a step, fell behind her. Now side by side in stride with her, he walked toward their destination. The two were like two grebes in an instinctive mating dance as they skipped up the three steps to Tanya's house. Wrapped up together like a long-anticipated package, they ignored their surroundings. Their eyes did not take in the building, its large entrance, its impressive two and a half stories of mottled Savannah brick. They did not once lift their heads to see the grand American eagle over the door lintel.

Robin, empty of thought, stood with her gloved hands crossed in front of her pelvis, like an expectant chorus swan from the Tchaikovsky ballet. She remained still and poised. She was a Southern portrait in frame, paused in seemingly infinite patience The moment had come. Ricky, quite properly, raised his arm as expected and, as if rehearsed, pushed the little white button next to the door to make it ring.

The restless moment passed.

"Well, hel-*lo*, you all! Now Robin, don't you look just beautiful? And Ricky! C'mon in, you two."

Memories dispelled instantly. He was collecting himself in front of Tanya when Robin pulled at his arm and whispered, "Where are you? We're here, and you look miserable. Tonight should be special. It's our birthdays."

The thought of it being *their* birthdays had, surprisingly, never occurred to him. He snapped back into the moment just in time to collect himself and pay attention to his host. He began to feel the creeping oddity of the night.

Ricky knew that the speech meant nothing. It was the Southern style. He had lived seventeen years in this town—no, eighteen, now that tonight was his birthday. He had learned, as early as he could remember, that these superlatives and emphatic verbal gestures were a manner of social engagement, no more.

He could not help reflecting upon Tanya's "And Ricky!" Was she surprised to see him? Did she remember that she had invited him? Here he was at the outset of the party feeling alone, alienated. Was it his bias, his conviction of estrangement, his conviction that he was always the outsider; or was it real, real in the sense that the sentiment was being foisted upon him?

If she did remember inviting him, the problem was not over. Was she surprised that he landed Robin for the date? Maybe she was slighting Robin. His mind went on with the imagined thoughts of Tanya. "Why, Robin, dear," he thought she might have considered. "whatever brought you to my party with Ricky? He's such a drip. He's not really one of the regular boys. I thought you knew better, dear."

Maybe it was not as bad as all that. Perhaps Tanya knew he was coming all along and was just acting aloof, letting him know by implication that he was a fortunate addition to a party from which he might ordinarily be excluded. Did she think he was dressed poorly? Or was he dressed too well? He really couldn't figure the whole thing out. He became grateful for the noise and bustle that engulfed him as he entered through the doorway. He felt relieved to be taken from himself.

As they walked past the foyer, he observed the lavish decorations. Though the Herstbergs were thoroughly Jewish with strong European roots, they preferred to give the impression of being completely American.

The house was decorated with every bric-a-brac and antique imaginable. Most of it was from the Federal period. The walls were filled, edge to edge, top to bottom, with late-eighteenth-century primitive paintings, embroideries, muskets, documents (which he assumed must be famous), framed metal designs, or other discarded items that were drawn in the form of scenes from everyday life from the past.

Ricky had seen much of this before but was always amused by the large heads of the primitively painted figures atop the shrunken and poorly drawn bodies. Massed together on the eighteenth-century-style papered walls, the dense array of art gave an unruled quality to this pretentiously orderly period of American history.

Leaning in the corners and scattered about wherever space could be found were iron pots, pothooks, fire tongs, wooden buckets, warming pans, and spanking boards decorated with flowers and leaf patterns. On those specially designated wall spaces where there were no pictures, the honor of display was given to quilts, linens, and framed written letters with unknown revolutionaries' signatures at their bottom. It was a veritable museum of the time almost two hundred years earlier. It was a testimony to the boldly advertised pretension that the Herstbergs were not merely Jews. They were not the humble immigrants or the descendants of immigrants who knew nothing about muskets and Benedict Arnold. The paraphernalia said loudly that this family would not accept their designated roles as outcasts by the Protestant Southerners who more rightly deserved this exhibit. No. They were Southern people of importance who had to be taken seriously. They collected Americana, and the collection showed who they really were: Americans!

This view of the Herstberg self-defense "museum" could not long be savored. The artifacts, while dominating the foyer, festooned themselves along the spaces of the walls and floor into the adjoining room on the left. However, the artifacts did not at all extend to the other room on the right. Ricky saw Robin go in there, and he followed.

As he entered the room, he saw the floors, seats, even walls were populated by kids ages sixteen through eighteen. The room was actually an enclosed porch extending from the side of the house, its jalousies open to allow just enough cool air to enter. This mild breeze barely helped to purify the stale expirations of at least twenty people.

Everywhere the girls were chattering among themselves, while the silent chorus of males either looked on or consumed each other in a muttered verbal orgy over football, golf, or basketball. Continuous with this first room was yet another that served more as a real porch. It was not too hot a night in June, so seven or eight could comfortably sit in this room to play spin the bottle.

Robin left Ricky the moment they entered the house. He discovered her and Tanya huddled on a large cushioned couch with three other girls pressed around. He could not make out what they were saying but knew at once it was of little interest to him. He instantly dismissed the idea that came to mind, that they noticed him or even cared that he was there. He caught a few words that revealed they were somewhere in the worlds of clothes and other boys.

He was standing at the entrance with a glass of Pepsi in his right hand and a clump of potato chips in his left. His mouth was filled. He had just begun to swallow some of the chips and clear his throat with a swig of soda when one of the girls in the circle of bottle spinning called to him.

"C'mon, Ricky, play with us." Becky giggled a little.

Come play with them? They must be crazy. I'm seventeen. I'm not a baby. I played spin the bottle when I was eight. This is ridiculous. He hesitated, suspended between the attraction of sitting with girls playing a silly game and the fear of retreating ostentatiously from his aspiring adulthood.

"Yeah, come on." It was Alan, the lone male in the group. His presence made the possibility more appealing. Alan was known to be among the in kids. The girls liked him. He dressed well, was soft spoken, and had a soft, insouciant presence that charmed them. Ricky knew that this composure belied the fact he was an aggressive ping-pong player, someone impressed with his own popularity, and often quite insensitive to the feelings of others. More than once Ricky had been excluded from an activity with other guys because Alan made a gesture to them that Ricky was superfluous or unwanted. Despite this, Ricky was persuaded by Alan's newfound warmth and responded to his beckoning. It made him feel part of it all. The invitation made him feel, even, that he wanted to be a part of the party, an accepted soul among the Normals. His anxieties began to diminish.

What difference does it make? he thought. I'll play a little. The bottle will never stop at me anyway.

Becky saw him walking toward them and moved over a little, leaving a space for him. He did not sit completely on the floor but squatted in place, fearful of a full commitment. Pauline, a red-haired, skinny girl with a pink sweater and white dress, took the empty Pepsi bottle and twisted it with two hands. It spun wildly on the thin rug and bounced into feet and legs in the circle. Ricky had to pull himself back to avoid it. Despite its chaotic journey, it came to a stop in the circle, pointing at Becky.

"Since I'm a girl, it goes to Alan. He's the nearest. Alan, you must do whatever Pauline says. That's the rules." All the girls giggled. Though Ricky said nothing, he felt a vague excitement within. He had no idea what would happen if the bottle fell on him after a spin. He wished to continue and, at the same time, to leave the silly game.

Alan looked nonplussed by his position. He reluctantly got up and stood in front of Pauline. It was part of his pose as a popular guy that he played the situation in a friendly manner. In fact, he was beginning to feel as uncomfortable and foolish as Ricky. Pauline, on the other hand, was clearly delighted. She grasped her hands in front of her, tightly squeezing her own fingers, and looked as if she'd caught a wonderful prize.

"You have to come with me, Alan."

"Where are we going?"

"To the closet." All the girls giggled and laughed. Some of the boys standing as observers made grunting sounds that were unmistakably suggestive. Alan smiled as if he was being a good sport. "OK." Ricky felt more uncomfortable than ever.

Alan and Pauline went to the closet in the hall. There was a pause in the party as all awaited their return. Though everyone knew nothing very serious was going to happen, there was general excitement over even this mild expression of suppressed sexual appetites. Moments seemed suspended as the entire group in the game waited for Alan and Pauline to return. Alan returned first, swaggering, as if to mimic the conquering hero. Pauline followed close behind with both hands over her face, giggling again.

Becky called out, "OK. Who's next to Pauline? It's you, Lyla. You spin." The command was so emphatic that Lyla didn't hesitate to take the bottle. Gentle, sweet Lyla. Ricky had always liked her. She was so easy, unassuming, never hurtful. She was always pretty with her dark hair, almost black, surrounding her round, nearly North African face. The combination left her with unexpected mystery. It suddenly occurred to him to ask why he had not been pursuing her instead of Robin. He felt an unanticipated excitement as lovely Lyla caressed the bottle for its spin. It landed pointing straight at him. He was nervous and delighted at the same time.

Becky, the directress, spoke. "Hmmmm. What do you want Ricky to do, Lyla?"

Lyla twittered and extended her hand toward him. He was overwhelmed and couldn't believe his good luck. He knew there were not too many male places for the bottle to go, but Lyla's extended hand was a blessing he could not have dreamed of. He leaned over the human circle and clasped her offering. They both began to get up.

"I'm sorry, I have to go, Ricky!" It was the voice of Robin.

"What? Oh—yes. OK. I'm sorry, Lyla." She truly looked disappointed. He was ecstatic but tried to cover his disappointment. Why was Robin there so quickly? It was still pretty early. Nothing much had happened.

"Robin? Why do you have to leave so early?" Becky, the manager, imperiously pressed herself upon the disrupting force.

"Sure," Tanya chimed in, "we're just getting started."

"My mom asked me to bring her something from Luigi's. Some special ice cream. I forgot. Maybe we'll be back. I don't know. Also, I'm not feeling so well." She made a female gesture as if to suggest her period was giving her trouble. This gesture was the guarantee that no one would further pursue her decision with her lame-sounding excuse. All protesters became silent except to say good-bye. Tanya waved affectionately from the door as Ricky drove away.

"Where are you going?" Robin asked him.

"I'm going to Luigi's, like you said. They close at ten. We'd better hurry, or your mom won't get the ice cream."

"What ice cream? I don't really want any ice cream. Did you hear my mom ask for ice cream? Really, Ricky, you can be so silly sometimes."

"Do you want me to take you home?" He was convinced at this point that she wanted nothing more to do with him and that the date was a dud. He was glowing still from the very brief romance with Lyla and was not thinking much of Robin's behavior.

"Let's go to Thunderbolt."

CHAPTER 14

Thunderbolt

"THUNDERBOLT!?" HE COULDN'T figure Robin out. He was completely confused. She didn't want ice cream, she didn't want to go home. She wanted to go to the docks of the little town behind the Negro homes. Thunderbolt? There was nothing thunderous about the sleepy place. No one knew for sure where the name came from. (The story believed by the locals was that a long time ago a bolt of lightning had created a spring that emerged miraculously from the ground.)

It wasn't a town or a hamlet, though it was incorporated as a village. Truth be told, the place was really a suburban extension of Savannah. Once it was the focus of a thriving shrimp industry. Now, for some, it was a vacation spot, an outlet for those who had boats and wanted to use them on the meandering waterways. It was the perfect spot for those of limited means who wished more than anything to live near the water, any water.

These wetlands were fed by the Wilmington River. The old waterway that remembered the Sherman occupation during the Civil War, and the American Revolution before that. This seventeen-mile turbid tidal flow came off the Savannah River in the north, then continued southward past Thunderbolt and the Isle of Hope for the marshes and estuaries of Wassaw Sound. More waterways splintered into hundreds of divisions ultimately leading to their terminus in the Atlantic Ocean. This was the end of the greater river and the special place where all these demarcating waters completed their larger journey. The lesser streams finished by cutting and swirling and creating multiple small islands with names like Mud, Cabbage, White Marsh, Hope, and Skidaway.

At Thunderbolt, the beachfront whose shores were caressed by the Wilmington tributary, was one large store on stilts above the river. It was part of the single town dock. Ramshackle but serviceable, it housed a restaurant and a shop selling bait, tackle, and sea-themed bric-a-brac. It was never open this late at night.

Ricky was thinking. "Maybe we could take a walk outside. The mosquitoes wouldn't be so bad now." It was very early summer, with its unexpectedly mild, even slightly chilly night. What did Robin want? "What are we doing here?"

Unexpectedly, Robin spoke with no prodding from Ricky, who was looking for the right turnoff. He always found the drive to Thunderbolt a little confusing. "I was tired of that silly party. Nothing was happening. I just wanted to get out. It's a nice night. It's not too cold, kind of warm. You don't mind driving to Thunderbolt, do you?"

At this moment, she was looking at him with the most tender eyes he had ever seen on her. She was also not sitting all the way to the other side of the car but in the middle of the seat, quite close to him.

"Ah, no." And he maneuvered the car toward Savannah Stadium and Victory Drive, the most direct way to get to Thunderbolt.

As the ancient Olds made its way down Victory Drive, Ricky noticed the almost full moon hovering over the carefully placed double row of palm trees. Legend had it that beneath each tree was the body of a World War I veteran, the remains of a proud man who gave his full spirit to the cause of the Allied effort. Each palm tree seemed to stretch its fronds upward toward the brilliant lunar-lit sky, beckoning. The bright feminine orb resonated an implicit renewal of life.

It did not occur at all to Ricky that the cycles of this airless lunar satellite were similar to those of the woman next to him. He did not relate its power to sway tides and capture spirit to her. In this unreflective moment, he saw her as an inexplicable enticement, a compulsion, a complete mystery. Like the bolt that made the spring, she might somehow unfold herself for him and reveal what he had an unrelenting male passion to know.

The red light glowed, forcing him to stop the car and wait. He became impatient. He dared not think about it. He drove cautiously beyond the section where the streetlamps stopped; the night's darkness engulfed the car, and the pure moonlight began. He adjusted his eyes to the increasingly darkened streets. He began to form more clearly to himself the glimmer of a possibility of why she had insisted that they leave the party early.

He turned the steering wheel and left the larger highway, making a right just as they approached the first bridge, which would ordinarily take them toward the Tybee beach road. He avoided the turn to the bridge and continued driving straight. He passed barely visible, undistinguished houses. Then he saw the familiar tall white church steeple of the old Negro town. It was a town allowed to retain its unique and ethnic identity, even though the edges of white Savannah were beginning to encroach upon it.

Complete darkness enveloped them. A cloud most have passed overhead. No matter; he knew his way well. His father had often brought him here when he was younger. The docks were a frequent destiny when he had the car and didn't know where else to ride. This color of darkness combined in his mind with the colored people that lived here. He was now immersed in the penumbra of their secrets. He felt the cave of his uncertainty. There, inside him, was a dark power he hoped to reveal for himself. George McGregor seemed present.

Replacing this sobering association, sexual thoughts began to consume him. There was a struggle brewing where shadows had a dominance that fought with his craving for Robin. For a few moments, the ambiance won. He remembered another woman, a woman for whom he had, or thought he had, no sexual considerations: his mother's maid, Cory.

Cory did all the ironing for his mother. She must have done other things, but all he could remember was her leaning over an iron, pressing down on the old burnt cloth-covered board and looking at him with a sweet and gentle tenderness that always pacified even his rambunctious childhood spirit. At the age of eight, he sensed her sensual presence as a full-spirited woman. He always liked her and never forgot her. In those fleeting autodriving moments, he imagined her worrying over him as a little boy, making him a peanut butter and jelly sandwich and talking to him as if he were twenty-five and her equal.

"Life's not so easy, Ricky. You listen to yo' momma, and maybe you'll be allll right. I knows you don't like school, but you got to go. You get out of school, and you do better than yo' Cory."

Then, suddenly, she disappeared, stopped coming to work. He asked his mother why and was told in a quiet whisper that Cory's boyfriend had stabbed her. No, she wasn't dead, but she was hurt. She probably would not be coming back. He sensed in his mother a kind of disapproval. It was clear that, from

Margie's point of view, it was better to let gentle Cory go than to take any chances of trouble from her colored boyfriends.

After Cory was gone, Ricky was left with the painful feeling that he could not be sure of anything about the Negroes. He missed her terribly. He loved Cory. He really did. She left him. She didn't have to. She wasn't dead. She could come back and talk to him.

He couldn't understand this yearning for the Negro maid. It's never completely clear why some experiences stay vivid in the mind, attached to some powerful feeling, while others fly away. He knew nothing about the girl, and yet his image of himself standing beneath the ironing board, listening to her talk, stayed with him like a message that he should never forget her. He didn't know why, but he never would. He felt betrayal and yearning simultaneously.

And Ricky, the eighteen-year-old of this night, driving with a girl he had always wanted to date and who had turned him down, it seemed, more times than the fingers on his hands, found himself suddenly feeling a connection between Cory and Robin. Neither woman made sense. What's more, his own feelings about them made even less sense. Yet the two females seemed strangely together, coupled, related, part of his same world, under a moon he thought he understood as well.

The smell of the salt marsh entered his nostrils. The living and dead mussels, the clams, the crabs, the moist earth, the entire concatenation of the spirits of the wetlands were in the breeze. The broad beams of his headlights broke the spell of the darkened waterside road as he began to follow the continuing shadowed outlines of the Thunderbolt docks to his left. Occasionally he would catch the fleeting image of a fruit bat darting from one tree to another. It would swoop like a phantasmagoric creature of Styx giving an inexplicable warning.

He found the clearing he was looking for. It was beyond the few rich vacation houses, which, were it full summer, might have been filled with light and activity; but it was really the end of spring, and their unlit presence was known only from the familiarity of his memory. He parked the car next to a large sprawling oak. Its exposed roots extended far from its wide trunk, and its branches leaned far over, forming a circle. The old tree's branches almost completely blocked the now unclouded radiating moonlight. He placed the car so that through the windshield he and Robin could see the refulgent lunar light and its reflection in the marsh water below.

Neither of them said a word. Ricky was not even sure how the engine and headlights of the car were turned off. They sat in the darkness for a moment. Ricky's hands were on the wheel. He could feel Robin pressing against him, side to side. He could not believe what was happening. He felt her hand touch his on the wheel. He thought he heard a rustling sound outside the car that seemed to signal an event, and he made a little jump. He was careful not to speak. There was a sound. He did not want to move her hand or prevent her from continuing. "Probably an old coon," Robin seemed to whisper. Maybe her voice was only in his imagination. He couldn't be sure. Now she was rubbing his arm. It wasn't completely instinct that made him reach over. He wanted to do it, but he would swear to himself later that it was not voluntary.

She molded into his body. The seat was big enough for them to hold each other, but she opened the door with one of her hands and pulled him outside of the car. She then lay down between two of those large old oak roots that formed a natural bed upon the early summer grass. She pulled him after her. It was not as uncomfortable as he expected. He felt the leaves beneath his hands as he supported himself. She pressed against him, and he wondered if he were hurting her with his weight. Then he realized that he was being pulled, pulled toward her. He did not know what to do but held on. She was in command. It was clear to him that he was not making happen what was happening. He was not resisting, nor was she doing what was expected in a nice Southern girl. He wanted it to go on. He felt like the recipient. Her ardor was irresistible.

She opened his pants and exposed his wonderfully and unexpectedly elongated stiff self so deftly that he didn't realize it had happened until the cooler night air wrapped itself around him. He gasped as he realized she held it and was placing it between her legs. "Panties," he thought. "Where are her panties?"

In a moment a softness engulfed him. He slipped into the most natural of places. It was moist, a surprising new pleasure, and encompassing. It felt as if her entire body enveloped all of him. He let it happen, though there was little else he could do. He had no intention of resisting anyway. He knew he was in her, in her softness, in her essence, and he knew he should be happy. But he couldn't help himself. He considered his situation. "So, this is what it is?" he silently questioned himself.

The question hung unanswered as he felt her push up against him. He pushed back. Once taught how to begin, he knew, automatically, how to continue. In any case, her pushing left him little choice. Before he could consider further the philosophy or morality of his circumstance, he cried out and felt the rush of fluid escaping from himself. Nothing seemed to come from Robin. He felt himself pumping, accompanied by an exquisite concomitant sensation, this fluid into her, pulse by pulse; and she seemed to receive it like a large, limitless, waiting reservoir.

As his pulsating ebbed, he began to regain his sense of presence. He was inside Robin, whom he could barely see in the partly hidden moonlight. Her crinoline was covering most of her. He felt his weight upon her and tried to support himself with his arms so as not to be too heavy. He felt her breathing.

He was still large within her, and he didn't know what to do. She pushed against his chest. He gave way, and before he could do anything else, he was outside of her on his back on the leaves. She lay there in the night shadows. He found himself separated from her by the adjoining oak root. He listened to her breathing and also his, feeling the leaves underneath in the same way as he imagined she felt them. They lay together, side by side, amid the roots of the large tree, which formed a canopy. The branches barely allowed the rays of the waning moon to penetrate.

Ricky considered what had just happened. He felt surprise at the forces within his body and the little control he had over them. But more importantly there was an overwhelming sense of the banality of the whole thing.

"So, this is sex?" he thought to himself. From all the novels, movies, and hidden pictures, he had expected something grander, something that would overwhelm him more. Though his moment with Robin had been exciting in anticipation up to the instant when he entered her, this was not what he had imagined in his dreams. He wondered what Robin was thinking. "She really made this happen," he considered within himself. "Did she enjoy it? What does she expect from me now?"

He found himself thinking of women as a group rather than of Robin in particular. Never before had he considered their needs, and he wondered if they all would push themselves into sex with someone as Robin did. "Does this mean she expects me to love her?" He felt a quickening, a sense of danger and anxiety that told him that he had participated as a full partner in this sex and that there might be consequences. He wished Robin would talk. He broke the silence by zipping up his pants while remaining otherwise motionless on his back.

He felt Robin shift a little, and her hand glided down to his.

"That was nice," she said.

"Did you like it?"

"Yes. Look, between the branches. There's a full moon."

"No. I think that's a gibbous moon," he corrected.

"Oh. Anyway, it's the time of Pisces. The Gemini are in conjunction."

"They are?" He was completely taken by surprise. "Do you believe in astrology?"

"Of course. That's why I had sex with you."

"It is? You had sex with me because of astrology?"

"Yes. You know we were born on the same day?" Of course he knew this, but for some reason he did not think she knew it. Her matter-of-fact declaration caught him by complete surprise. He answered her affectionately, almost in a whisper, wondering what she would say next, wondering more how she viewed the entire night with him.

"Well. I really believe in astrology. When you asked me out for this party, I had just read that Gemini would join in the same constellation as Pisces tonight. It would be a great night to finally have a date with you. Imagine the power of two Geminis having sex under the moon during the time of Pisces!"

Ricky found himself becoming angry, but he was careful not to express what he was thinking. "That damn girl used me to match the power of constellations. It was her crazy ideas that made her do it. She didn't care for me one bit. I was used. I was merely the guy with the right birth date. She was seeking some kind of astrological power from sex, and I was necessary for the experiment. My first sexual experience, and it was a woman's experiment?"

This was a parody that in no way fulfilled his ideas of ideal love, the kind of love for which young Werther committed suicide, or the kind of love that destroyed Tristan and Isolde, or Romeo and Juliet. This was cheap, second rate, a level somewhere between antlered bucks in rutting season and prostitution. At least with a prostitute you knew what you are getting into.

He thought Robin at least liked him a little. But did he really have any right to complain? Why would any girl let him get into her pants so easily? What did he think was going on when he got into her? He knew it wasn't love, but he refused to think about what it was because he wanted her. His reasons were not much better than hers. Didn't he do it to satisfy his bodily needs? Yet he did like her. He hoped there would be something between them. He didn't do it just for biology. She meant something to him. What? Anyway, he didn't do it for astrological reasons.

Though the argument continued in his mind, he remained silent. Robin could not have known the mental turbulence of her lover. The two of them spent a few more minutes looking between the branches of the moss-covered tree at the now almost invisible moon traveling ineluctably about the earth. Slowly the satellite moved away from them. Occasionally, they could make out another large fruit bat crossing the remaining moonlight, swooping back and forth with its own internal mission.

Ricky was beginning to feel the chill but was afraid to move. Whatever his doubts, any gesture might change the air between them.

Then, with no announcement, Robin lifted herself up and ran to the Olds. She opened the door, took out her pocketbook, opened it, took out a wad of tissues, and placed it under her skirts, between her legs. She then sat down in the car and called to Ricky. Startled by what he saw, he did not respond at first.

"C'mon, Ricky. I'm cold. Please take me home." She pleaded with him in a singsong tone he had never heard or imagined hearing from her. He got up quickly and entered the car beside her. He was delighted to hear the engine catch, having for a worried flash the thought that it might not. He put the car back on the route home but directed it in another direction from where they had come, down Old Thunderbolt Road.

Old Thunderbolt Road completed a big elliptic connection with Savannah, running roughly parallel to Victory Drive but completely removed from the city and its lights. It was a narrow road, barely paved, almost a path, and on either side, two or three feet below, were the wet marshes. Ricky wondered why he decided to go back this way with the darkness due to the receding moon and his realization of the ease with which he could go off the road into the receptive swamp. His headlights were the only means he had of seeing which way the road went, and he realized that if he were not careful, he could have a disaster. He must have chosen this way, he mused, because it guaranteed there would be no light. He must have wanted to be unseen and alone in his thoughts as he took Robin home. The dark road afforded a kind of disguise to mask who he was and what he had done.

He felt shame, a sense that he had gone too far with himself. It was not guilt, he insisted, but shame. He had wanted to have sex, to no longer be a virgin, but he did not want it done the way Robin had him do it. The seeming unimportance of the entire act was sullied by Robin's using him selfishly with no concern for his feelings.

None of this was on Robin's mind. She talked all the way home with a confidence that made his considerations tedious and ridiculous; or at least that would be how she would see his thoughts were she to know them. It seemed the astrological event had gone to her head. She talked of nothing else, describing in detail what constellation went where at different times, and how this night had so many special qualities. Since it was so dark inside the car, she could not see his reaction She wouldn't have cared anyway. There would have been little to see, as his mind was in an alien world far from her concerns. In a sense the tables were turned. He imagined the many times females must have felt taken advantage of, maneuvered into a compromising situation, duped. He was now defensive as the girl might be, only into him himself. At the moment, he had no interest in her or her preoccupations. But the male-compared-to-female mystery lingered.

The two of them traveled down Old Thunderbolt Road, releasing into the darkness of outer Savannah their thoughts and their feelings. Wrapped up in their recent lovemaking, they had no interest in being part of the barely perceptible night sounds broken only by the car engine. They refused, in a silent mutual consent, to be affected by the natural world around them. They would not be taken in by the smells of the marsh grass, the night crabs, the salt air, or that special musty Southern night swamp sensation. Their immersion in the recent event would not allow them to embrace the beauty of the moss-laden trees shadowed by the remaining moonlight.

The two human creatures drove down the bumpy road in their own self-contained time travel. They traversed a space in which they were peculiar partners. They seemed to be in the same place, but neither had any awareness of this. If asked, each would have denied the reality. They were in nature, but apart from it, and refused to see how the estrangement they strove so hard to maintain had meaning only in their imaginations. There was, in fact, no way to disengage from the cycles of life within themselves or as part of themselves The were, like it or not, within the rest of the world, whether in darkness or in light.

As the dream night of the outer world of Savannah gave way to the emerging city lights, the contrast with where they had been, the change from darkness to light, made little difference to them. They were within their self-deceiving disguises and saw only the mask of their perceived self-contained existences. They felt alone, independent, but were not. They were part of a fabric that meshed with their beings.

C H A P T E R 15

Virginity Lost

THE MIST BEGAN to rise from the surrounding wetlands as Ricky drove the car away from the darkened dampness of Thunderbolt Road onto the now familiar city blocks punctuated by the hazy halos of the evenly spaced streetlamps. As he drove Robin the final distance to her house near his, he began to consider what had happened more clearly. He felt frightened, confused, and exhilarated. He was no longer a virgin. He had finally become a full member of the male fraternity— perhaps more than that, of the adult human world. He could hardly suppress a smile to himself as he now considered this as a kind of success.

He remembered that Byron Goldstein had teased him, more accurately horrified him, at Scout camp when he was twelve. Whatever age the adolescent Byron was, he loomed over Ricky and announced how babies were made: "Your mother and your father do it in the toilet together…like shit." Byron was tall, at least a head and a half more than Ricky, but what's more, he was huge. To Ricky he appeared like a standing bear with paws raised, menacing his chosen victim.

Ricky stood his ground: "I don't believe it." But he was not sure. He knew it had something to do with excretion. Now he knew what Byron meant. It amused Ricky to know that his old threatening adversary, the bully in his life, was partly right. Now he knew exactly how much.

The smile left his face. He considered the fact that Robin might become pregnant. In their haste, in their expressive impulsivity, neither had considered using a rubber. "Did she use something?" he wondered. He thought of his parents. "How else do you think she got pregnant?" he imagined them questioning him. "And now you will have to take the consequences!" The consequences? What were the consequences?

He convinced himself in a sudden moment of insight that he would marry her if he had to. At least she was Jewish. But he knew this would alter his life. He could not go to college with a baby. He would have to work. He would not move beyond his father's level, at best, managing a pawnshop. He would never be an educated man. Well, these were the consequences. It didn't matter that she had manipulated the entire evening. Even if she just wanted to use him because of this crazy astrology idea, the baby was still his. He had to take the responsibility. If the worst happened, he would have to pay for it. A sullen gloom encased him as he turned in to Robin's driveway.

He opened the door for Robin, who kept her legs together as she exited from the car and walked up the walk with a kind of scissor gate. He walked her to the door. She must have sensed his mood.

"Don't worry. Nothing's going to happen. It's the right time for me. Hey, you were pretty good."

"With your help," he confessed. He beamed with her singular gesture of kindness. Telling him he was pretty good was the nicest thing she had ever said to him, and he couldn't help but enjoy it.

But before the pleasure of the compliment was allowed to sink in, she followed it with, "OK, good night. Thanks for everything."

He couldn't believe the banality of that last comment. He had lost his virginity, become a man, satisfied an astrological requirement, maybe even become a father, and she saw it as if everything amounted to just another date. The night was simply over. "OK, good night. Thanks for everything." The words rolled through his mind again in complete disbelief. It was as if they had only gone to Luigi's for ice cream, nothing more. He wanted to complain, to ask her what was the matter with her. "Are you kind of crazy?" he wanted to throw at her in bitterness. But before he could react and destroy the little tea set atmosphere she tried to create, she put her key in the lock, turned it, opened her door, and disappeared inside.

Less than a moment passed. He was still standing in front of the door when the overhead night-light was turned off. She didn't even wait for him to get back to his car. He felt the darkness. He felt turned off by her, flicked out just like the night-light. He felt worse than ever.

Ricky drove home immersed in the same thoughts. He was repeating himself, but he couldn't help it. The power of his thoughts led him into predictions so all possessing that he didn't even realize he had reached home. He turned the car off. He stood before the door of his house gathering his wits before putting his key in the door.

He broke out of his self-absorption when he looked up to see his father in the foyer.

"Do you know what time it is?" his father asked.

"About two, I think."

"Two thirty, to be exact. Your mother is asleep, but we were worried. I thought we had an agreement for one o'clock." His father stood there, scowling, one hand holding a book on his hip, the other a fist clenched at the other hip.

Ricky was not in the mood for this now. He was afraid his father would see a stain on his trousers. He didn't dare look down to see if there was one. He had wanted end this night with no more events, take a shower, and go to bed. He was too filled with conflicted feelings to engage in another battle of biblical proportions.

Usually he would get very angry, and then the shouting match would begin. There were never physical blows, but furniture and walls might suffer. The father was having trouble allowing his son to grow up, making up rules that infantilized the boy. Ricky was unaware of this. All he knew was that his father could be infuriating. He was determined not to fight this battle tonight. He listened without responding as the man railed frustratedly at him for mere seconds. In his role as patriarch, Sam insisted on pointing to the failure of his son in the most intense words. These words released from the earth declared with baritone intonations how irresponsible the behavior was. Unexpectedly, in the face of Ricky's abject and unresponsive silence, he was moved to silence, his rage effectively spent. He pivoted, turned his back on his miscreant son, and stomped off to bed.

Ricky was relieved that it ended so quickly. If the teenager was in full rebellion, war could extend through the night. His father might have resorted to an already once-used maneuver and thrown him out of the house, screaming at him, "You're nothing but a bum!"

Instead, the new nonvirgin walked a few paces toward his room. He saw down the small hallway to the left, beneath his parents' door, that his father had turned out the light. That sealed his certainty. War was averted, no further encounters were on the horizon, and he was joyfully alone. He washed in the hall bathroom and went to bed.

Lying there staring toward an imagined sky, he was intensely preoccupied with what he had done. It was amazing, the power of sex with ejaculation. In a few ounces of liquid is a force that can change lives. It could stop him from going to college. It could create misery with his parents. He might be obligated to someone he never loved and perhaps never could love. His face screwed itself into a tightened mass of muscle. Then he began to relax. He would have been surprised, had he been able to observe himself, at how very tired he was and how easily his controlled thoughts turned into fantasy. Weariness took hold, and then he drifted into Sunday morning dreaming.

He is flying through the clouds on the back of Pegasus. With a push of his heels against the flank of the horse, he can swoop high or dive down. It is a marvelous ride, and his surprising confidence confines his natural fears. Suddenly he realizes his mission. He signals the wonderful steed to descend toward the buildings he can just make out on an island below. As the wings extend to brace the landing, he takes his shield and sword and starts off toward the structure before him. He notes an ominous cloud above, which would ordinarily signal it contained the threat of rain, but this time it merely hovers menacingly. He enters the building constructed of rounded columns, Doric capitals, and a tile roof with elaborately carved figures upon an underlying frieze. He is Perseus and has come to kill Medusa. He knows to not look directly at her and holds his shield in such a way that he can see the entire room with its reflection. He is feeling very clever about this. Suddenly, he sees her face in the shield. She is moving closer to him. Though she hasn't seen him, she knows he is there. He hides behind a column and waits for her. At the exact instant he believes she is near enough, he swings his sword and cuts off her head. He glances in the direction of his happy success only to catch the merest glimpse of her eyes in the severed head searching for him. This eye contact is not enough to turn him into stone. He is relieved that his flesh is still flesh, but he notices a hardening between his legs. His hand moves to his crotch and feels what his sensations tell him is there. His penis alone has turned to stone. At his touch it breaks off in his hand. He is aghast as he holds the piece of solidified phallus in front of his eyes. He stares. He begins to absorb the full meaning of what has happened, what he has lost.

A voice can be heard from the cloud overhead. He exits from the building to hear better. The voice sounds a good deal like that of his father.

"You have defied the laws. You have pursued the Gorgon Medusa. You have seen beauty where there is only ugliness. You believed too much in your power. You forgot your mortality. How dare you defy what is life? How dare you believe you can escape what no mortals escape? Punishment has been wrought. You live with your flesh, but none of your flesh shall live after you. Remember this. This is the lesson. You cannot defy the forces of life. You cannot defy the laws. You are mortal. You are mortal. *You are mortal!*"

Ricky awoke. His hands were clasping his penis. He shuddered. He was immediately relieved to realize his anxiety was due to a dream.

He decided to forget the dream and Robin. "I am not Perseus," he argued with himself. "I will not worry. The dream mirrors my worry, not the facts." This made him laugh. As for Robin, he would just put everything that scared him about her and what happened that night aside. He would tell no one. He would keep everything to himself. It was better that way.

It was ten o'clock Sunday morning. As his father and his brothers drove out to Gottlieb's for Savannah Jewry's own form of sweet rolls and Danish, he and his mother had their usual Sunday morning discussion over the kitchen table.

"What were you doing out until four in the morning?" she asked.

"I wasn't out that late," he replied with annoyance.

"What did you do out that late with Robin?"

He measured his reply. "Nothing. The party was late. Besides, it wasn't four, it was only two thirty."

If she sensed he was being evasive, she didn't let on. She must have felt this topic was pushed as far as she could push it with her touchy son, so she shifted gears. "Do you like her?" To this he nodded.

This marked the extent of her investigation. She felt satisfied, pleased that he was at least involved with a Jewish girl, though she would have been shocked to learn how much involved he was. She allowed his vagueness to stand and went on to ask questions about what everyone was wearing, who was at the party, et cetera. He answered diligently, trying to please her needs as much as he could. She should have suspected something. He always became irritated when she asked about such details. This time, he was happy for the diversion. She could not have been more delighted to live vicariously through his experience, at least as far as she questioned him.

Later, his father, who was not at all interested in what he did, but only attended to the subject of his late hour upon coming home, proclaimed in his Moses tone, "Don't ever do that again." Again, the two Titans did not fight. Ricky submitted. All became peaceful, and they finished their coffee and rolls together His father read the newspaper. His mother took a chance and asked him still more questions. His brothers felt bored with the conversations and went outside to play.

CHAPTER 16

Ricky, Wally, and Serious Musings on Life

RICKY WAS A soft misanthrope. He knew this, but he was not happy about it. He didn't revel in being a misanthrope the way Molière's wonderful eccentric did. He was struggling with the very idea of his irritability, his tendency toward sullen reflection, and his feeling that being alone was the most comfortable way to be. At the same moment, on a secondary consideration, he felt the other side of himself, the side that found pleasure in his own cantankerousness. Despite Molière's character's defeat, Ricky believed he held the higher truth, the truth that life was, at best, a difficult enterprise; he knew that most people hid behind the hypocrisy that life was supposed to be happy.

Happiness, happy—words of little meaning used as universally as air is breathed. Everywhere Ricky heard people wanted to be happy, but how would anyone know they were happy? Someone in severe pain appreciates it when the pain is gone. He becomes happier. Does the man in paradise know he is happy, or is he unable to see that he is only bored? Ricky knew that being a misanthrope wasn't making him popular. He felt the alienation such an attitude created. He wanted the opposite of this, and it seemed to him that this opposite was a kind of happiness.

Ricky pursued this illusion of happiness. Even at eighteen he believed friends would be a partial answer. He hated aloneness while feeling that it was the only natural state. He yearned for friends, but friends by his reckoning were sensitive, alert, there for you. They were intelligent but not foolishly pedantic, and they considered life in similar terms to himself. There was Fred. Even Hubert and Horace, despite their bellicosities and condescensions, never shunned him. He still felt their inadequacy keenly and realized there was no way to genuinely call either of them friend. They were insincere and shallow, seeing each day of life as an entertainment, perhaps a defense against an inner darkness they wanted to avoid. Ricky never saw any awareness in them of the complexity of life and the sadness that it contains. They might know of this intrinsic sadness, but their behavior was devoted to ignoring it or denying it. To them, life's meaning could be performed in a kind of adolescent show-and-tell, an exhibition of empty frivolity with a flavoring of intellect.

This was why Wally Streeter meant so much to him, despite his strangeness, his aloofness, his alienating Christianity. Wally never spoke of his religious beliefs, but his being a Christian seemed clear to Ricky, and it gave him pause. It was unfair, but the pause was created by his own experience with Christians. A sunny day a couple of years ago, he was walking toward a movie theater to buy tickets for a film he wanted to see. He passed a table with two boys in white shirts and ties who were clearly soliciting responses from passersby.

"Do you want to make Jesus your savior? He will deliver you from your sins. Embrace Jesus. Praise the Lord!"

Ricky was nonplussed. He stood in his tracks, not knowing what to say.

"We have all sinned. We are all brothers in sin. The righteous will be saved if they embrace Jesus."

One of the boys, who could not have been more than twenty, extended his hand with a pamphlet in it. Ricky took it out of politeness and began to read. The words repeated in bold caps what had already been said. Ricky remained silent and thought it best he smile politely and walk away.

"Praise Jesus and make him your savior!"

When Ricky did not respond, the other fellow realized something and said, "You're a Jew, aren't you?"

Ricky reflexively nodded, fully unaware of the situation he was in.

Suddenly, the taller boy moved from the back of the table so as to stand in front of Ricky. He put his hands on Ricky's head, seemed to feel around, and turned to his companion, saying, "No horns. I thought they all had horns."

Indignantly, Ricky said, "We don't have horns!" and rapidly walked away at the same time. In his wake he saw the slack-jawed white Christian boys in their intolerant ignorance, feeling superior in a peculiar way but never forgetting the memory assailing his sense of comfort in the Southern world of absolute belief.

There were Jews who would never set foot in a church. The harsh reality of anti-Semitism, especially after the war with Hitler and the concentration camps, left Jews with an acute sensitivity toward anti-Semitism coupled with a horror for the church. Even before Hitler, the Jews were often accused of blood rituals against Christian children, and this added to the aversion. Stepping into a Christian citadel representing all that the Jews have suffered through history was anathema to most who kept the Sabbath holy. By association, all Christians were to be avoided, shunned, never engaged socially. This prejudice, inculcated into Ricky's thinking when he was very young, left him with the feeling that even talking to Wally was breaking rules he barely remembered being given. He yearned for intellectual and emotional intimacy, yearned for a feeling of unity with another sentient being, a closeness of the mind. There were plenty of girls whom he found very attractive, but none who seemed to have the slightest intellectual interest. When that was present in another person, it was always in a male, mostly males like Horace and Hubert.

Well, that wasn't completely true. Lewis Jordane at first seemed like the kind of person Ricky wished for. He was a math and physics whiz. He and Ricky had some kind of mutual understanding. It happened after Ricky tied with him for a blue ribbon at the science fair. Ricky noticed that Lewis was observing him from time to time; because of this Ricky frequently sought him out in the cafeteria. They had high-flown conversations about where physics was leading, whether the moon would prove an economic boon to industry, and the misery of planned obsolescence in the American automobile. It was easy to get the impression that both were trying to top the other with their presumed keen intellects. Their relationship clearly was not going to work out. Lewis seemed one dimensional. If he couldn't discuss physics, astronomy, or some other recondite subject, then he was silent. He was not insincere and exhibitionistic like Horace or Hubert, but he seemed to lack soul, a feeling for daily life, a poetic concern for people. His world was the mechanical, the reproduceable of science, the quantifiable. Ricky looked for more than that. He wanted, at least, to understand the workings of his inner self, and Lewis had no interest in himself beyond that of a dispassionate investigator, a consumer of colorless facts. Ricky imagined him inventing a man such as the one Frankenstein created and having no concern for the moral consequences. He was the scientist to whom Mary Shelley had addressed her book. Ricky was sure he had never read a novel. His head seemed to operate fine, but the spirit was opaque, mechanical, distracted.

Ricky possessed a delicate sensitivity, which was proving more and more to be a handicap. He seemed to feel everything, and he felt everything powerfully. Implied sarcasms, friendly tones, gestures of indifference—nothing escaped him. When he looked about him, no one gave the slightest indication of having such insight. The kids who were his contemporaries walked through their lives as if oblivious of everyone around them. They dressed, dated, went to school, drove cars as if in a daze of unconcern for the meaning of anything. He felt a painful distance from all of them. He was alone and desperately did not want to be. The feeling of isolation threatened to overwhelm him. He eagerly sought relief, and the relief appeared to be in the form of Wally.

Wally had that special something. There was a poetry about him, the delicate, sought-for sensitivity that grabbed Ricky and made him feel sane, part of the real world beyond just his imagination and his hopes. Wally exhibited that contemplative, reflective aura. He left Ricky with the feeling that he knew the same feeling of being rare that Ricky felt. But could Ricky be sure? Was his perception of Wally accurate? He never wanted to put Wally to the test. He didn't want to provoke a situation that showed him that Wally was anything less than Ricky desired him to be. There was always that dreadful possibility that the more Wally came to know Ricky, the more likely he might find him undesirable. He didn't want to chance creating that tragedy. Yet again Ricky would be put aside by someone.

It had happened more than once before. Ricky had always had a problem with allergies and postnasal drip. He frequently sniffled despite himself. He knew it could be annoying and carefully tried hard not to let his nose be too obtrusive. He felt so much like the victim. "It isn't my fault I have a nose like this," he more than once lamented to himself.

On a camping trip years ago, at eleven or twelve, he remembered, he was assigned to share a tent with Alan Stanford. They were both in their sleeping bags when Ricky could not stifle a sniffle. He couldn't help himself. It was cold and damp. He tried to squeeze himself into the folds of the bag, covering his head completely so that the sound would be muffled. He was unsuccessful, and when it happened, he knew it was too late. Things couldn't have occurred more suddenly had a wild animal entered the tent. Alan jumped up and, in the process of almost knocking the tent down, scuffled out from his bag, declaring loudly to all within earshot, "I'm not going to stay in there with Ricky snorting!" It was terrible. Ricky felt the guilt of spoiling Alan's night. He wasn't angry; he was abashed, mortified. Without a murmur of reproach, without the slightest annoyance, and without saying a word, he, the pariah, gathered all his bedding, his clothes, his gear, and departed into the night cold. The scoutmaster, completely without a kind word, came out to him and helped him find another reject with whom to spend the night.

Wally would not react the way Alan had. Ricky really believed he wouldn't. He believed Wally would not turn out to be the crass, harsh, and uncaring person Alan was. But he wasn't going to take any chances. Wally had slowly taken on that special importance in Ricky's life, an importance almost equal to a sense for survival, and he wanted nothing to disturb the fragile relationship. "If it's going to be good, it's going to be good. I have to be myself. I can't control the universe. My sniffling or anything else will be what it is. I can only hope it shouldn't make a difference. I can only hope to be accepted for who I am," he thought. Yet he couldn't fight his anxieties. He felt immensely safer with Wally idealized than with Wally real.

Ricky was beginning to lose all his idealizations. Before this year of high school, he thought he had things figured out. The world was orderly. Things happened according to plans. If you planned carefully and had the right ideas, consequences would follow projections. Being a nice person, something with which he had the utmost difficulty, was all that was necessary. His mother would often say in her unerring simplicity, "Just be nice." Somehow that was going to guarantee friendship, comfort, and happiness.

He was nice to Robin, and she had used him. Whether it was because of the silly astrological ideas or because she was too free with her body and just wanted to have sex, he felt that he was certainly missing in her equation of wishes and wants. It came as a shock to him that girls could be that way. He knew nothing of promiscuity, prostitution, extramarital affairs. His naivety was incredible, or perhaps ordinary for a Southern boy of his age. He had seen girls as gentle, caring, yes, even motherly. He never before considered them any other way, certainly not as dangerous, not as harsh. Robin, in one brief, surprising night, introduced him, however vaguely, to all those terms and dispelled forever the notion that being nice or thoughtful to others, whether they be girls or boys, guaranteed his happiness. His mother was wrong. Being nice was certainly inadequate as a guide. Girls were much more complicated than he had thought. Everybody was more complicated than he had thought.

Is there a plan?

His father was proving to be no exception. Ricky believed for the longest time that his father was a bastard. He hated him. He saw him as a man devoted to earning money, to pleasing his boss, but not truly interested in Ricky. To Ricky the boisterous, cigar-smoking dictator was nothing more than an impediment to his happiness. It seemed that no matter what Ricky did, his father would have a complaint, a criticism. Ricky was too much into his books, too sloppy, too loud, eating too much, too quiet; everything and nothing was a subject for attack or a paternal expression of disappointment.

And now? He could not even hold on to the one prejudice about which he felt most confident. All his life his father fit a pattern. He felt a strange comfort in seeing him in the rough, difficult light he had shone upon him. The recent events impinged on his perception, altering the salutary presumptions of his younger years. He saw his father as a man searching through the night for his assailant, searching for someone who could prove dangerous to him, searching for someone who had dared to trespass upon his family's soil. His father seemed passionate, committed, sincerely concerned over what had happened to Ricky. This man who spent all of Ricky's childhood fighting with him, kicked him out of the house more than once, yelled at him in a crescendo of spitting rage that he should never return; this man with a terrifying temper, a temper that was famous among Sammy's own friends. It was even laughed about among these friends, how he had to be held, arms locked behind him, lest he do something, something that actually never happened. The father was not actually the uncontrolled beast. The man never hit anyone, never hurt anyone…physically. His only weapon was his acerbic mouth, the guttural, bellowing mouth that sounded like an animal making its severe threat of imminent destruction upon another animal on the primitive African plains. In fact he never beat Ricky, never laid a hand on him. Despite the fact that over the past few years he was increasingly tender, Ricky remembered his fear and couldn't trust the present.

This newly expressed tenderness left Ricky suspicious, but his father knew it was emerging, wanted it, and felt the pleasure of knowing it was replacing his previous behavior. Sammy was well aware that his son was leaving him. Ricky might think only that he was going off to college, but to Sammy Bateman the departure was evidence that he had lost an opportunity. He knew he had lost his grip on the boy, a chance to make it a close father-son relationship, and he felt sad. He felt regret that he had not been closer, more sympathetic to his son's growing pains. He wished he had been less temperamental, less prone to losing his temper, but he hadn't. On this penultimate moment of his son's leaving, there was little he could do but show whatever love opportunity allowed him.

Ricky saw his father become more reflective, softer, and felt confused. The night search stirred his thoughts immensely. What was his father? Was he good or bad? Ricky couldn't decide. There was the past and the emerging present. The puzzlement was beginning to possess him. He couldn't answer the question. He wanted to hate him, but he also found he wanted to love him. The loving him was just beginning to win out.

Ricky had not acquired the intellectual equipment to appreciate the fact that his usual sense of reality, the reality he confidently held dear throughout his development, was dissolving. He would never again be sure of anybody or anything. He would from now on feel a nagging, constant uncertainty. Was someone real based on their presentation, how they appeared, what they said? Or was someone real from how they behaved over time? Were all their actions to be believed, or only some? If Robin seemed pleasant at a party, made as if she wanted him, and then used him for her own peculiar purposes, what of her was really Robin? His father acted all his life as if Ricky was a pariah. Now he was being softer and genuinely caring. Who was his father? What was his father?

Wally was even more difficult to understand. He seemed interested in Ricky. He seemed to share a certain similarity of vision, and yet he remained distant, aloof. Ricky had telephoned him many times. Once he called to ask him if he wanted to go to the movies. In fact, it was the *Julius Caesar* film with Brando that was playing the night Ricky was hit. Ricky figured it was culture and Wally wouldn't refuse. He would not have dared ask him to see *Giant* with Elizabeth Taylor, or a musical, though it would have been enjoyed by Ricky. No, he felt Wally was too profound for the usual Hollywood production, even though it was Shakespeare, which was what had brought them together in the first place. Wally said, "I don't go to the movies."

Why didn't he go to the movies? Did he sense something crass in the movies that transcended the fact that this particular movie was Shakespeare? Ricky had been careful to say it was a "Shakespeare movie." It seemed to make little difference to Wally. He didn't go to the movies, and that was that. He was abrupt, to the point, and made little of the fact that Ricky had called in the first place. Ricky missed entirely the reality that Wally had brushed him off. Rather than face the possibility his friend didn't want to be with him, he hid behind the puzzlement of why Wally didn't like movies. He didn't allow himself to see a fault. He still hadn't developed sufficiently to see Wally as an uncertain personality, someone that might be insensitive to his feelings. There was too much to distract Ricky from this idea.

Once, Ricky saw him at school and tried to discuss something that had come up in class. Wally was standing alone.

"Hi, Wally."

"Hi." He smiled receptively.

"What did you think of *Heart of Darkness*?" referring to the discussion in history where the novel was used as an example of the mysteries of Africa. "I didn't think it was book that should be used for history, did you?" Having posed his question, Ricky smiled, affecting an attitude. This was a surefire question, calculated perfectly to start a conversation.

"I didn't think much about it."

That was that again. Ricky knew he did indeed think much about it. This time he caught the slight. It was clearly a put-off statement. Wally had actually had an argument with the teacher consisting of his belief that Africa was a pot-boiling continent. The problems Kurtz was having were indicative of the fact that white men shouldn't be there. It was quite a discussion, with whispers in the class suggesting Wally was a nigger lover. He had actually made his point in almost a whisper. His concern had nothing to do with racial preferences. The supersensitive Southern white, his antennae always tuned to the slightest leaning toward the Negro, expressed his barely suppressed prejudice against the implication of upsetting the status quo. It was a pregnant moment, and Ricky was stirred by it.

Now, here was his hero saying he didn't think much about it. Wally was one of the very few people in school Ricky felt was thinking and feeling about life in the same way he was. Ricky wanted so much to reach out to him, to share with him the turmoil of growing and developing, the uncertainty of his own opinions about things, the persistent feeling of intellectual isolation, and his inchoate friend was denying this to him. Why?

Wally was not consistently distant and indifferent. After a few of these estranged behaviors, Ricky began to back away and treated Wally with some hesitancy. It pained him to do so, but if that was what Wally wanted, he felt he had no choice. Ricky was not going to embarrass himself by pursuing a crushed ideal. Whether Wally was aware of himself much or not, he began to change, to soften, to be more responsive. He came up to Ricky several times and began chatting. He sat with Ricky at lunch. Once, when some friends at the table got up and left because the conversation was too intellectual for them, Wally and he had a good laugh together. "No. We're not phonies," they declared to each other simultaneously.

Their friendship warmed with no explanations. Ricky was well aware of this transformation and felt a reserve of fear that matters would dissolve and he would lose his thought companion.

Wally, Robin, his father, Uncle Remus were the changing, moving, unstable anchors. Anchors that were no more. Of overwhelming importance to himself, they helped even to define him. Their shifting, their unpredictability, was causing him to lose confidence. He could no longer trust his intuition. Everyone was more complex than they seemed, and the fluctuations of it all made him lose his sense of an underlying pattern, lose his sense that he could make out some meaning from what he was experiencing in his emerging life.

Sex was not simply sex, it was a sensual complexity, something between boys and girls that could take many forms. He could not any longer simply fall in love; he would have to assess love, see if it made sense, then maybe, assured that the girl was not, like Robin, using him, let it happen. Hate was not simply hate. The person you hated might suddenly do a kindness, and the hate could not be sustained. You could trust hate no more than you could trust sex or love. Friendship was no less chaotic. It could come and go according to the friend's moods. It seemed determined by forces as mysterious as those that managed the electron performing its orbit. Life, as he understood it, was losing its stability, its predictability, its clarity of meaning. Ricky's head, as he entered the last months of his high school career, was a buzz of uncertainty. He knew there were some guidelines, some patterns on which he could depend, but he wasn't sure why he knew that. He wasn't sure if these guidelines were only the illusion placed there by his brief life lived under the protection and influence of his parents. He felt there were these orienting posts, there must be, and he knew he would spend the rest of his life trying to identify them; but he wasn't sure that even his quest wouldn't dissolve into a miasma of mystery and uncertainty.

It was indeed a pregnant year, filled with the expectation of his ineffable birth into adulthood. It seemed that everything he believed, all his certainties, had been turned upside down. He wasn't even sure about himself, who he was, what he was.

In Alice's Wonderland, the caterpillar asked Alice the same question that now so much troubled Ricky.

"Who are you?"

"Why, I'm Ricky, of course."

"No! *Who* are you?"

CHAPTER 17

Ricky's Father's Story

SAMUEL ABRAHAM BATEMAN was a normal, for 1957, five foot eight. He was considered attractive by the married women with whom he and Margie socialized. To his dismay, he, early on, was slightly balding in the front; this was compensated somewhat by his broad shoulders and a large upper torso that made him appear more athletic than in fact he was. He would often brag of both his white hair and, more importantly, his baseball skills as a young boy. Once he impressed his admiring son with his ability to hit a triple in a pickup beach softball game. He had called out to Ricky, "Watch this!," gave a broad smile, and smashed the first pitch past the startled shortstop. It was a glowing moment for father and son.

Sammy had a winning smile, a keen wit for social propriety, and an engaging sense of humor when he wasn't angry. Despite these gregarious attributes, he tended to be alone, completely devoted to his family, never strayed in the direction of other women. Moreover, he had a singular intellectual passion for reading books on history. He bragged frequently that he forgot nothing. He was especially proud of the way he recalled his own immigration to the United States, insisting that though he was only three, he remembered walking through the formidable and forbidding gateway of Ellis Island, New York. He often said he could "see in my mind's eye" that he waved at the Statue of Liberty. He described in terms of vivid reality experiencing the tumult, the jostling people, a tall guard, bundles, noise, uncertainty. But really? Could a three-year-old who had only heard Russian, a little boy forbidden to express the natural devilment of his age and filled with the wonderment of a strange language and strange place, recall all this? Could a boy held tightly by his mother while his long-bearded, Russian-speaking father, wearing all the stereotyped, symbolic accoutrements of the religious Jew—the yarmulke, the frocked coat, the tallit—and his six older siblings, all charged together with the managing of all the details required to enter the cherished gate of the new world—this being beyond the full scope of anyone, as there really was too much to do—truly recall such a history? No one could tell the prideful Sammy no. He took pleasure in his insights, his recollections of this very special, never to be lost experience. He would always be that grand little immigrant boy of 1913.

He glowed as he told the story of the ship, how everyone but his family became seriously ill, and how he watched the crewman express their anti-Semitism. Even at that age, Sammy knew anti-Semitism. He was proud of his acute perceptiveness. He was pleased that he was so good at sensing the nuances in the attitudes of the crew as they went about their tasks, grumbling. His acuity was aided by his lifelong assumption that it was always present in the goyim. If, in fact, it wasn't there, it didn't matter. For him it was better to be paranoid, a little wrong, self-protective. It was the only way to survive in the Christian world. So he always believed he had to defend himself. He always warned his sons to be wary. This man who denied his personal Jewry, who revoked his father's traditions, could not eliminate from his mind that he was a Jew and that it was dangerous. So when he spoke of his anti-Semitic experiences, discrepancies or no discrepancies, no one wanted to burst his bubble. In a strange sort of upside-down way, he was enjoying himself as he railed against those real or imagined anti-Semites. His recollections of his hardships (rarely of his pleasures), and his special interpretation of his difficult development, became the essence of provoked angers against the world. No one wanted to interfere while he told his stories.

"Hard!? You don't know what hard is. Nothing could be harder than New York after Russia. All of us lived in a small room on Avenue A on the Lower East Side. There was no money. My father? He was a manikin maker. I don't know where he learned it. It was a craft. Around the corner were the Italians. See this?" He pulled up his right pant leg and pointed to the five-inch irregular scar on his outer thigh. "An Italian gave that to me because I wasn't afraid of him. I never told anyone in the family about this. I didn't go to a doctor, and I didn't go to the hospital. That was the way it was. You never told your parents anything. You took care of it yourself."

Sammy was the youngest and a rebel. He was smart. But he was caught up in the fast street life, the adaptation every Jewish kid needed during this time of immigration with its peculiar adjustments. The street had one set of laws, and the family, as led by his overbearing and strict religious father, an entirely different set. The two sets had to be balanced. In the middle of this struggle for equilibrium, he didn't always do the right things for himself. And one of these right things he later confessed that he didn't do was to finish high school. This became the tragedy of his life.

"There was no money. I had to go out and get work. The family needed money. Everyone worked. I remember the principal of Stuyvesant High School… that was a special high school, you know. Not everyone got in to Stuyvesant…I was in the eleventh grade. This principal sent a note for my father to come to the school. My father never went. He was afraid of the government. In his mind the school was like the government. At home he was like a tyrant, but with official things he was soft, scared.

"One night the principal came to the house. Can you believe it? He came to my parents' apartment, sat, had tea with my parents, and begged them not to let me quit school. He said I was gifted and that I had a talent for studies. My parents knew nothing of talent. I had already quit, even before they drank their tea. There was nothing they could do. I left school. In effect, I also left home to earn a living. I still lived at home, but it was just a place to stay. Besides giving my mother almost all the money I earned, I was never there. It was the biggest mistake of my life, not finishing school. Don't *you* make the same mistake. Where did it get me? Working in a pawn shop?"

His family was close and completely, reverently Jewish. "My father was very big in the synagogue. He was like a deacon. No, he was not the rabbi. He could not be a rabbi because he was a Cohen. Kohanim are the priests descendent from Aaron, Mose's brother, and can't be rabbis. But people came to him for advice. When it came to religion and the Torah, he was an expert. Zeder was also a difficult man. Yes, I admit it—my father, he was impossible. He yelled and screamed at his children. His rule was patriarchal, severe, brooking no opposition."

Sammy, the youngest of seven, naturally got away with the most. He was brought up mainly by his oldest sister, Frieda, and she doted on him with his peculiar white hair and swift, clever ways.

He fought his father. When he escaped from school, he also escaped from his home. He struggled to get odd jobs, running errands, selling papers, but jobs were scarce in 1927. He found himself occasionally bristling at the enforced dependency. There was no career, just a struggle. He and his father had an understanding, an unspoken moratorium. Though both were furious at the other, they kept their fury within, silent. Sammy complied on the surface with the religious family rituals, but both men knew his heart was not in it. Finally, in the early 1930s, Roosevelt's National Recovery Association, or the NRA of the time, began, and Sammy, as a young adult of twenty-three, with his brother Sye, left home for good to work in a Civilian Conservation Corps, or CCC camp.

"That was where I really learned about anti-Semitism. That was where I learned that being a Jew is equivalent to being hated by the goyim. Every day there was a fight. As we cut wood, the Christians would look at us in hate. There was no question of their feelings. In their minds we were intruders. They wanted to get rid of us. The Jewish boys used to stay close together. It gave us a feeling of strength. Yes, I fought one of the goyim. They had to pull me off of him. I was strong then. I knew how to fight. I hope you never have to know how to fight like that. You know how in the movies, when a man defends himself, he gains respect from the group? That never happened with the goyim. Their hate was so deep. It was fundamental to who they think they are. If they don't hate the Jews, they are something less than themselves. In their eyes, white was right, and Christian was the only normal. That's the way it was. I left there after a year. A year was enough. I'll never forget the CCC."

Sammy was tired of being footloose. He was twenty-four in 1934, and there were no jobs in New York. He contacted Frieda, and they talked in Yiddish about what to do.

"Sammy, you could go to Savannah."

"Savannah? Where's Savannah?"

Frieda looked at him adoringly. He was her favorite. "Remember Tushy, your half cousin? Papa's brother's wife's daughter from her first marriage? She's in Savannah staying with her brother, Henry Menzel. She's pretty. She's single. They know you there. They would welcome you with open arms. Why don't you go and see them? Maybe they can find something for you. Henry got a job with the water department, and he doesn't have half your *seykhl*. It's something to do. What are you going to do in New York, become a bum? At least you know Tushy, and she's a relative."

He went. He felt there was little else to do. But before he went, he followed his brother's example and changed his name. He had had enough of the anti-Semitism in the CCC camp. He wanted the same opportunities the non-Jews had. Berensky was a handicap. It not only sounded Jewish, it sounded foreign. His brother chose Bateman because his mother was called Bertha. At least, it was argued, the new name sounded a little like the mother's, it had the same beginning letter, and it kept a connection with the family. Seymour, Sammy's brother, didn't ask his father's permission. Neither did Sammy. Two Batemans left Berensky. The separation from the despotic father was nearly complete. It didn't go any further than Sammy Bateman's emancipation to Savannah.

"Thank God," Bertha was said to have exclaimed. She consoled herself that there was still something vaguely Jewish in the name. "Our name wasn't Berensky anyway."

Sammy told the story of his mother's reaction whenever he was answering questions about family history. "So, where did the name Berensky come from?" Ricky or his brothers would ask.

"We'll never know the true story," she'd say. "I can only tell you the one I know. Your great-grandfather was going to be conscripted into the Russian army. In those days, if you were Jewish and in the army, it was almost a certainty that you would be put on the front lines and die in the first battle. Somehow, your great-grandfather (my parents said his last name was Cohen) stole the papers off a dead Russian soldier. The name on the papers was Berensky. He became a Berensky. When he was inducted into the army, it was Berensky's papers he presented. As far as the Russians were concerned, he was a Russian. He was less likely to be in the frontal attack. Now the next part is even more unlikely, I admit, but he was, it was said, supposed to have become a general in the army. When the battles were over, he left the army and forgot altogether about being a general. He became an unknown poor Jew again, and General Berensky disappeared from the Russian records. He thought he would have an advantage if he did not go back to being a Cohen, so he continued to use the name Berensky. Your grandfather became a Berensky too. It was the Berenskys who came to this country, not the Cohens. The Cohens of our line disappeared somewhere in Russia."

The hard-knocks New York immigrant Jew joined the quietly Southern Jewish Menzel family in Savannah. They gave him a place to sleep, but he stayed a very short time. Tushy was reasonably attractive, somewhat short, brunette with a darkened skin that looked more Sephardic than Ashkenazi. She was not a bad figure, if not exactly a wit (he told himself); she was all right, but not his choice. Whatever attractiveness might have appealed to him, it was offset not only by what he perceived as her diminished intellect, but also by her slightly sarcastic side. He always felt she was making fun of him, even though her style to an outsider was nothing but seductive devotion.

No, he wanted the inaccessible prize, Margie Guttman. Margie lived on the top floor of a house on Henry Street that made Sammy's family's apartment on Avenue A look like a hovel. Her diminutive, reticent father had successfully started his own tailoring business. To Sammy's eyes she was terribly intelligent, and she found his sense of humor unbeatable. She had the beauty Tushy Menzel lacked, with a white, creamy skin, light-brown hair, and a delicate shapeliness. She was the perfect Jewish girl in the eyes of the new Sam Bateman. In his heart, despite his usual spirit of rebellion, he knew his family would not be disappointed in his choice.

Mrs. Guttman had other ideas. When Sammy would whistle from the street below to let Margie know he was there again to see her, Mrs. Guttman would push Margie away and slam the window down. Her Margie was going to marry a doctor, nothing less. She would not let her daughter marry a Jew with a name sounding suspiciously too Christian, a no-good who worked delivering laundry and lived in a tiny room with his cousin.

Margie's brother, fifteen-year-old Melvin, was officially appointed the spy. His job was to report to the mother whatever they were doing. It was comical. Melvin was easily spotted trailing them down the street, ducking behind trees as they solidified their tryst in defiance of all the good sense of Margie's mother. Finally, with few alternatives left them, they eloped. Her parents made them have a second official marriage later.

"We loved each other," Ricky's mother would reply when asked why she married his father.

"Are you sorry you didn't marry a doctor like Grandma wanted, Mom?"

"I would have had more money," she laughed, but it was obvious the irony of her reply was meant to explain all the thought she had on the matter.

Much later, Mrs. Guttman got her revenge. She lived to age sixty-five in

Sarah's house, daily exposing for all to view the remaining stump of her one leg, amputated because of her diabetes. Her cranky, complaining style had not changed since the day Sammy took her daughter away. Despite her son-in-law's beneficence, despite the fact that he never raised an angry word toward her, she never forgave him. He felt her scorn but managed to ignore it. Ricky knew none of the history of his parents' romance and loved his grandmother with a naivete only a child could retain toward such a difficult woman. Although he shuddered with dread every time he saw her stump, although the scene of his mother going into the room to change the dressings of her new hospital wound made him turn his head away in revulsion, he held on to his affection for this old woman who gave him quarters and repeatedly said in her Romanian accent, "Be a doctor. It's best. Listen to me, Ricky, be a doctor. You're going to be a doctor, yes?" He would answer her with a nod, barely appreciating the full implications of her pleading.

Her diabetes finally consumed her. He was eleven when she died. His feelings were mixed: there was relief at the expectation he would no longer have to give up his room to the ailing old lady and sleep next to his brother four years younger, but he also felt a deep loss he could barely understand. It was his first death, and he cried with the new awareness that life was never eternal, that people you love can disappear, and that there is no way to explain reasonably their disappearance.

Ricky's father and mother loved each other with a keen intensity. This was despite the fact that his father's rebellious spirit had cost him a number of jobs, and caused him to continue to fight unnecessary battles of words, threatening his fragile self-esteem, implied or otherwise. Margie often stood between him and his sons as he railed against their misbehaviors, overreacted, and presented a verbal violence that belied the tragic sensitivity he possessed. He was an angry man who only dimly knew what he was angry about. He never connected his rage to his own father, the man he knew he had disappointed. He never connected the personality that haunted him with his own bellicosity. He was certain of at least two things. The first was that he was Jewish, and this was an honorable identity he would never deny. The second was that religion, Judaism or otherwise, was ridiculous.

"See, Papa," Ricky's father said to his father in New York on a memorable visit. "He can do what he wants. Tell him, Ricky. You can tell your grandfather. I won't be mad. Tell him whatever you want. Do you want to be bar mitzvahed?"

"I don't know."

"But you have the choice, right? You can do what you want, right?"

The grandfather was very old even when Ricky was twelve. He had a long white beard and sad, sallow eyes sunken into his face. He had long given up fighting and his role of a father caterwauling at his angry son. His sense of life's unpredictable anguish must have increased as he was forced to tolerate his son's challenge. At this point of life, fighting with your most beloved and disappointing son seemed futile. The old man's religion was being attacked. No, it must be stated more severely: in a very real sense, it was falling apart. He must have watched it crumble with the same dismay the Greeks felt as they saw the Turkish shells almost destroy the Parthenon.

Ricky's father sat as the family icon on his daughter's couch. He was in his Frieda's New York apartment, and it was Christmas holidays. Seymour's family was running about. He witnessed the *kinderlich* filling the rooms with noise, the sounds of Yiddish. Mr. Wizard was on the fuzzy new television screen. The dominant sound was the bang and bang and chopping of Frieda preparing gefilte fish in the kitchen. The occasion must have felt like a tremendous success to the very old man. There was a pride in having achieved this much in the New World.

Sammy looked at his defeated father, aged, quiet, all the fight of the past painfully worked out of him. His son wasn't going to be regimented, he thought. He wasn't going to have to spend hours on the useless Talmud, on the useless Hebrew language. He was free to choose. Free to be himself. Free to be what Sammy never experienced, even when miles away from his papa.

Ricky had no idea what was going on in the patriarchs' heads. He had no thought as to whether he wanted to have a bar mitzvah or not. Hebrew school was boring. There seemed no sense to it. The stories in Sunday school were silly. They simply did not seem logical, even at thirteen. Certainly they were not superior to fairy tales he had already grown out of. Still, he didn't want to hurt his zeder either. It was the first time he'd met him in a way he could remember. The old man seemed so quiet, so reflective. Intuitively, Ricky felt his father was being harsh. He sensed his own anger that he was being put in the position of hurting this gut-felt metaphor of Jewish significance, wisdom, and kindness. He would never forgive his father for this moment of harshness. His father's need to rebel was felt as the Babylonian destruction of his zeder's temple.

His ire would never be transferred to his mother. She was a lenient, easy woman, completely, so it seemed, overshadowed by her powerful husband. Later, Ricky came to understand that she was impervious to his complexity, incapable of appreciating his emotional pain, unable to be empathic to any suffering outside her narrow worldview. But at this point in his life, she held the position of the family angel, an earth mother to her sons, always there to embrace them. When it came to her husband, she enjoyed his sense of humor, his earthy masculinity, and repeatedly told her oldest that he didn't understand his father. "He's not as bad as you think. What makes you think you're so wonderful?"

Ricky's father, the once New York Jew, became the Savannah heretic Jew. He made jokes against Jews, never went to Jewish functions, never went to synagogue, but never abandoned his Jewishness either. He pressured Ricky so much about the bar mitzvah that he finally talked him into not having one. His "you can have one if you really want one" became for Ricky the equivalent of "don't have one." He didn't. This created a year's worth of a social nightmare, since all the other kids had the parties, the ceremonies, and they invited Ricky.

It was in this way that Ricky grew up with no ordinary prejudices about religion. He had no opinions either. It all seemed like a mystery without a solution. He thought he would resolve the conundrum as he learned more. He imagined himself one day choosing to be a Christian or even a religious Jew. When he seriously considered what it would be like to be Christian, he felt frightened. He knew he would never be forgiven for such a transgression. It was one thing not to practice Judaism, but he could in no way revolt to the extreme of being Christian, whatever that was, whatever that entailed. He knew if he did that, he would never be able to talk to his father and mother again. It had not yet sunk in that he might choose to be nothing. Religion would become a point of view, something one scrutinized but never accepted. He became in this way, even if only in part, the son of his father. He was a Jew without being a Jew.

CHAPTER 18

Robin's Illness

THE BLEAK, PIERCING-WIND cold of winter gave way first to the gentler warm breezes of spring and then abated entirely to the increasing warmth of summer. A weather softness caressed the blossoms of pansies and azaleas and helped to begin the recrudescence of the wonderfully colorful vertical gladiolas. In the lanes behind Ricky's house, the honeysuckle proliferated. The Southern sun did not yet have that sultry, sweaty intensity that makes one feel the constant need for lemonade and ice. It assumed a guise more like a friend come to assuage the mordant uncertainty of the colorless time it helped to dispel. Movement became easier, softer and lighter, and the music of the Negro peddlers began to again fill the bright sunlit mornings.

Ricky hardly noticed that the seasons had changed, so preoccupied he was with his inner thoughts. He was possessed. He had an extreme need to understand himself and to place himself in the world he was barely beginning to know. How could he appreciate the newly budded azaleas decorating his hometown with red and white splashes of color when he barely noticed that they existed at all? He was all into his shadows, worrying about what had happened to Robin Linkowitz. She had not been in school for at least a week.

The familiar smell of the school hallway seemed somehow off today. It was two forty-five, and the crowded, plaster-lined passage was filled with students, teachers, janitors, the principal, the assistant principal, and even an errant dog being chased out of the building. Everyone was rushing to get out of the harshly textured structure into the summer light. The din was considerable, so Ricky didn't hear Becky Ekelstein call out to him. It had been months since he noticed her. Of course, she was in school every day, but his world hardly touched hers. She was in none of his classes. The last time he saw her was at Tanya Hershowitz's party. It was the same night he had first experienced the presummer passion of inchoate adulthood within the unexpected embraces of Robin.

Becky had a twisted smile on her face. It was the kind of smile that suggested pleasure at the troubles of someone else. It was an invidious look, one that Ricky had learned to recognize. It was the familiar look that went after him as if it were a grappling hook. He was to become its victim.

"Did you hear about Robin, Ricky?"

"No, what?" She was pregnant! He knew in a flash this was the truth that was about to change his life. His heart began to beat faster within a micron of a second. His breath stopped. He instantly decided to marry Robin. He would not abandon her. He knew what was right, and he would do it.

"She's in the hospital. Something's wrong with her. It's her kidneys, I think. Oh, I don't really know. Somebody said she had a convulsion or something. It's serious, but she's not going to die or anything like that. She's just sick, that's all."

"What hospital is she in?" Ricky's mind began to race. Why did this girl come up to tell him this? If Robin was only sick, what did it have to do with him? Becky knew something she wasn't telling, but Ricky felt too frightened to respond to the matter. He supposed he would at least find out where she was and go there to see her.

"She's at St. Joseph's. I saw her yesterday with Pauline and Lyla. She looked OK to me. She didn't even look sick."

"Oh…thanks, Becky."

"It's OK," she answered. Then that twisted smile returned. "Are you going to see her?"

What was going on here? Why was this girl pursuing him with this? Why did she tie him together with Robin's "illness"? He really couldn't understand the motives in Becky's behavior, felt mysteriously yet increasingly agitated, but still elected not to ask further questions. He played his role as insouciantly as he could.

"I don't know…maybe…as soon as I get the time. Thanks, Becky…for telling me."

Becky looked disappointed as she allowed herself to be dismissed. He could see her farther down the hall, squirreling herself into a group of four or five girls, which included Pauline and Tanya. She was laughing and talking quickly. He had no doubt that the topic of conversation was him.

The weight of the responsibility of Robin's illness, impossible yet for him to grasp or understand, seemed colossal in size compared to the now frequent daily questions he posed to himself about life and his future. Again, expectations had taken an unexpected twist. This major event, terribly threatening in implication, seemed without solution. Was she pregnant? Becky certainly would have said if she was. Would she not? She could not allow herself to miss the opportunity to watch him squirm. She would not. The gossip was too juicy. Wasn't it? If Robin was only sick, how was that connected to him? Time stopped. He felt bound to Robin for the rest of his life. He was already beginning to resign himself to the situation. He didn't know her father. He had left her, hadn't he? God! He thought about how he would be forced to marry a girl from a broken family. Her mother wasn't so bad. She was kind of simple, but at least she was kind. What if she was permanently sick? He would have to be big about it if it was his fault. But how could it be his fault. He didn't make her sick. Well, if it wasn't his fault, why was Becky coming up to him like this? Why did she feel the compulsion to tell him? "Dad? Oh my god, Dad! What will he say? I'll talk to Robin and tell her not to say anything. If I'm going to give up college to be honorable for her, the least she can do is help me with my father." His mother was no problem. She would understand, or at least comply. "What will I do? I'll have to stay in Savannah. Maybe I can take some courses at Armstrong Junior College. Robin can't help. They have no money. My whole life…changed in moments. In moments!"

Every one of these troubling thoughts passed through Ricky's mind in flashes. From the time of Becky's announcement on the second floor of the high school to Ricky's descent down one flight of stairs, to halfway to the exit door, the minutes passed before the neuronal awareness of his foreboding destiny could send their messages to his brain. He was unaware of Becky and her group as he passed them, he was unaware of the tens of students who accidentally banged into him in their rush to maneuver around him, and he was unaware of the sun streaming through the doors leading him outside. Finally, he was unaware that Wally Streeter was sitting on the stairs looking into nothing in particular as Ricky passed. Even the distant, aloof Wally noted the enormous concentration and glumness on the face of his erstwhile friend.

"Ricky," he called quietly but searchingly. "Ricky," he called again.

Ricky heard him the second time. His thoughts broken into, their morose patter interrupted, he turned to meet his interlocutor. His surprise that he was called from the sunless abyss by Wally helped more than anything else to dispel his self-concerns.

"Hi, Wally," he said in a somber voice clearly pushed to the extreme to pretend social receptivity.

"You look very serious. Is something wrong?"

Ricky could hardly believe his ears. Was Wally really trying to help? Was there really someone with whom he could share this thing, or was this entreaty merely an automatic gesture of false interest, a mechanical element of social propriety that even Wally Streeter managed to acquire?

"Yes, Wally. Thanks. Something is terribly wrong."

"C'mon, Ricky. Let's go to the cafeteria. Let's talk there."

Carried along by the feeling of warmth and solicitousness from his newly acquired comrade, he felt lighter at once. He eagerly accompanied him.

The cafeteria was left open after school for snacks and different extracurricular meetings. Except for an occasional group of raucous kids, it was generally quiet and a good place to go for a talk. It was almost empty because the day was so perfectly summerlike. What was unappealing for everyone else proved a haven for Ricky. He and Wally sat down at a large empty table, he on one side and Wally on the other. The room was dimly lit by the little light that managed to make its way through the high, dirty windows. Had they not just come from outside, there would be no way for them to know that it was even slightly sunny. The room had an insular, otherworldly quality that gave the conversation an atmosphere separated and apart from school and ordinary social reality. Their speech would have echoed in the cavernous meeting place had they not made a special effort to keep conversation down to a whisper. Except for the occasional student getting an ice cream pop or drink and then leaving, they were alone. They sat as if suspended in space, as if they were not contained in an earth rotating on its axis and simultaneously spinning around the sun. One was committed to helping the other as if only their joined existences, separate and apart from the orb on which they rested, had importance and relevance.

The gentle Christian spoke first, even though it was so uncharacteristic of him.

"What's going on, Ricky?"

"I'm not sure. Do you know Robin Linkowitz?" the agitated Jew answered.

"I think so."

"Well, I dated her about a month ago…more or less. Anyway, we did it. Now she's in the hospital."

"What did you do?" The Christian had no smile on his face as he asked the question. If he already knew the answer, his seriousness gave not a hint of it.

"You know. We had sex. It was all sorts of ridiculous. It was my first time. She actually pushed me into it. She believed, she said, that the stars were right for us to do it. You see, we were born on the same day. She felt the night we were together was the perfect time by the stars for us to do it. She had this crazy astrological idea that it would be good for her. Anyway, she came after me. I admit I wanted to do it. It's as much my fault as hers."

The Christian still looked very serious, as if he was weighing the affliction of the Jew's universe, hoping he could find something with which to help it.

"But Ricky, that was weeks ago. What is upsetting you today?"

"I just heard from a friend of Robin's, Becky Ekelstein, that Robin is in the hospital. Becky seemed mean about it, as if Robin being in the hospital had something to do with me. All I can think about is what we did that night. She must be pregnant. But if she is, why is she in the hospital? Becky said something about a convulsion. I'm scared out of my mind. I feel responsible." Now that the confession had been made, the Jew felt better and very grateful for the Christian's attentiveness, so he added, "Thanks so much for listening, Wally, I really appreciate it."

"Ricky, I think you're jumping to conclusions. You don't know what really happened. I can understand that you're upset and Becky made it seem Robin's being in the hospital is connected to you somehow, but all the evidence is not in. Listen, I have some time this afternoon. It's only three fifteen. Why don't we go to the hospital? I'll go with you. Talk to Robin yourself. At least you'll know the facts. Facts always beat fantasies. You're letting your imaginings get the better of you. This is making you suffer. Get the true story. Then you can see what you should do or decide how you feel."

Religious identities dissolved as Ricky thought for a moment. It was a generous offer, an offer beyond anything he could have ever expected. He was deeply grateful and a little choked by the warmth he felt from his friend. "Thanks very much, Wally. You don't mind?"

"Why should I mind? It's better for you to know firsthand what's going on with Robin. We can deal with that better than with your imagination. Maybe it's not as bad as you think."

This seemed entirely reasonable and calmed Ricky further. Though he had no wish to see Robin, the logic of Wally's argument was unassailable. "OK. We'll go to the hospital. I'll put my books in my locker and meet you in five minutes. Is that all right?"

"Sure." With that the two stood and broke the spell. They entered back into the manageable world of getting themselves from the cafeteria to St. Joseph's hospital by bus.

The two boys sat on a seat in the front of the bus. They gave no notice of the sign that directed the Negroes to the rear, nor did they register that they were the only whites present. All the colored people were grouped far down the aisle from them. Both accepted the rule without consideration. They might not have agreed with the social restriction had they been questioned. Their complicity remained, a totem to the power of accepted custom, however wrong.

This inequality was only an assumed part of the world in which they lived. It had not struck them as an issue of great concern because it wasn't personal. It didn't directly affect their lives. They were Southerners, and this was the way of the South. Neither felt uncomfortable, though later in life they would realize they should have.

How easy it is in time of anxiety and strife to deal with necessary mechanical tasks that have other implications; how facile, how much easier, in the matter of course, to get from one place to another when suffering a possible calamity than to attend to the long-range implications of a misery in society. The Negroes were in the back, and the two friends were in the front. This inequality did not impinge on Ricky's preoccupation with the matter of the moment. The personal and the societal were not so much at war as in separate worlds of immediate concern. What might be quickly dispelled by placing money in the bus's coin meter, sitting in the first available seat in the front of the bus, and keeping alert so as to get off at the right stop at Abercorn near Forsyth Park never registered as a calamity of wider social concern. The reality of social unfairness was nearly lost. If it were not for Ricky's surprise encounter with George McGregor, his sensitivities would have been entirely dulled. However, because of his lesson with George, he did take note of the seating arrangement and winced for an aware second. Nevertheless, what was registered at this white moment paled in comparison to solving the problem of Robin's hospitalization. Racial disparity would have to take a back seat to Ricky's dilemma.

"I don't think I'll go in. I'll wait for you here. Take your time, I'll read a little." Wally offered this at the door of the large white Queen Anne–style building. Its Greek columns in no way seemed beckoning to either of them. "This really is a personal matter. I think you and Robin can talk it over better if you're alone. Besides, she doesn't know me very well. I'm not even sure if she knows me at all. I might make things awkward."

Ricky was so grateful for Wally's help so far; he made no indication to protest. The two friends parted.

Ricky walked up the eight or ten wide steps into the large foyer. Immediately he noticed the hospital smell. Alcohol, formaldehyde, laundered and starched sheets, and other more mysterious solvents and drugs. The exotic environment overwhelmed him and threatened his sense of himself. He felt his confidence ebbing. "Grandma," he thought. He couldn't extinguish the image of his diabetic grandmother with her leg stump appearing beneath her dress as she sat on the large chair in his parents' living room. Again her words echoed: "Here's *ein bisl*, a quarter. Go, go buy yourself some ice cream." He remembered her thick Romanian Yiddish accent as easily as he remembered his most recent thought. She was present in the hospital with him. Her death floated through the large entrance hall. "Rickyleh," he recalled her saying, "be a doctor. You want to be a doctor, no? Yes, yes, of course. You will be a doctor. That's a good profession. That's honorable. It's good, heh? Here, here's a quarter. Go get some ice cream. And remember, be a doctor."

He did not know what he wanted to be. There was nothing appealing about being a doctor, or anything else. He just felt ashamed that he took the quarter and didn't look at her because her stump revolted him. And now that he stood amid the overwhelming ambiance of medical treatment, he realized the powerful impact she had had on his mind. Standing in the foyer of the hospital, he thought of her and knew that the last thing he would ever want to become would be a doctor, someone who would have to look at the stump of his grandmother's leg all the time.

Catholic sisters in habits walked officiously about, some pushing carts with medical supplies on them, others seemingly hurrying to some important meeting. There appeared to be few doctors; he assumed those few were the men in short white coats. He wasn't sure. At any moment he expected to be accosted and told he did not belong. "If you can't look at stumps, you can't be in the hospital!" he expected to hear. This ridiculous idea made him laugh for a moment and softened his anxiety, but nothing happened anyway. He saw a small desk to his right and, bravely exerting himself to go beyond his inhibiting feeling of apprehension and unworthiness, approached the sister sitting there.

"I'm visiting Miss Robin Linkowitz. Can you tell me where her room is?"

To his surprise, the sister did not tell him he was too young to visit nor suggest he could not come into a hospital unannounced. She simply looked up the name on a chart she had on her desk and gave him directions.

"Go up the stairs straight ahead of you. When you get to the top, turn left. It's room 234."

As Ricky followed the directions, pleased to be treated as a full adult, he wondered at the peculiarity of her room number, 234, and contemplated whether the chance of consecutive numbers fit in with Robin's ideas about astrology. He climbed the stairs, made the left turn, and walked only a small distance to find the right number. At the same moment that he knocked on the door, he considered how it was that a Jewish girl was placed in a Catholic hospital.

"Come in!" Robin's voice sounded light, cheerful, even carefree. In a moment it almost dispelled all of Ricky's worries. In that same moment, he entered the room and saw her in a flowered nightgown, hair tied up in a ponytail, propped on two pillows and holding *Life* magazine in her hands. She did not look sick at all. He felt an overwhelming perplexity. Upon seeing him, she immediately put the magazine down so that it lay on the white sheets upon her knees, and she looked at him with annoyance. There was a wrinkle to her mouth he had not seen before. She expressed a sinister and wicked face, contorted perhaps because of Ricky's presence. Her expression signaled her assumption that he would demand that she explain what she definitely wanted to forget.

"Oh. Hello, Ricky."

"Hi, Robin, how are you?"

"I'm fine. How did you know I was here?"

"Becky told me."

"Oh."

"Why are you in the hospital?" Ricky asked this in a pleading, gentle tone, almost as an apology attached to the abject feeling that he would be very grateful if she were to simply spill the whole story to him quickly and efficiently. If he could have anticipated her mood, which he did not comfortably interpret despite the clarity of her facial communication, he would have never asked such a question. He was too immersed in his own needs, his own passionate desire for absolution for his crime, to differentiate the character or the feeling of the other person before him lying in the hospital bed.

"Why do *you* want to know?"

The question completely confused him. "Well…I…ah…I care about you, Robin."

"You care about me? What are you talking about?"

"You know. We were together that night. I thought it meant something. Ah… anyway, I thought that you…in the hospital…there may be some connection."

"Well. Let me reassure you, Ricky Bateman. There is no connection."

"Just tell me what's the matter with you. Could you at least tell me that?"

"Ricky, I don't know what's the matter with me. The doctor said it's something called preeclampsia." She expected to dismiss him with the technical word, but it had only the effect of heightening his interest.

"Preeclampsia? What's that?" He was quizzical and defenseless like a kindergarten child. He was out of his element trying to relieve himself of guilt. She was in her element of anger and bitterness. She played along with him.

"*I* don't know what that is. Ask the doctor. Anyway, I'm better now. It's all gone. I don't even have to be on medicine. I'm leaving the hospital in two days. I'll be back in school on Monday."

She didn't tell him to get out. She seemed intrigued by his uncertainty, his extreme discomfort. She was watching him as the proverbial spider would watch a victim in her web. She was Lilith, entwined with a serpent, tired of her male while continuing to work upon him with her angry spells. The victim squirmed desperately, wanting release, but the demonic female knew there was no liberation. There was only the pleasure in watching the doomed one's desperate yearning.

Ricky was completely unaware that he was consorting with someone's alien nature far removed from himself. He never thought Robin was someone for whom a rational explanation of behavior might not be available. He was worrying rapidly, fretting that he would never find out the facts he so very much needed to share with Wally. In the face of this hurtful sorceress, he tried another ploy.

"What were your symptoms, Robin?"

The pleasure continued. "I felt just a little sick. My mom made me go to the doctor for a checkup. When he looked at me, he found my blood pressure was high. He said it was way up. He did some tests, and then he put me in the hospital."

"But," Ricky pressed forth, "why was your blood pressure up?" He saw the question transform her. She raised herself in the bed and stared at him. He saw her take a deep breath and blow the wind of her thought at him. The sound flew tumultuously through the air and entered his ears.

"OK, Ricky Bateman, I'll tell you." The hammer was about to fall. Ricky steadied himself for the verdict. "The doctor said I was pregnant. I didn't even know. I had no idea. I went to him for a little headache. He said I had sky-high blood pressure because I was pregnant. He called it preeclampsia. He said that if I hadn't come to him when I did, I would have had a convulsion, or a blood vessel could have burst in my head. Now are you satisfied? Now you know everything." She smiled a wicked smile.

Ricky was stunned. His worst fears had come true. He got Robin pregnant, and now he had to marry her. He would have to marry this rotten, mean girl who couldn't care less about him. He would have to give up his future, his unrealized life, for a miserable one with her. She had no care for him. Yet he had no right to criticize her either, he quickly told himself. She had had this whole burden to herself. She didn't even ask him for help. He didn't hear about it from her. She didn't say he would have to marry her. He heard it from gossipy Becky, who incorrectly told him Robin had already had a convulsion. He was being unkind. He was being mean too. He felt a sudden surge of self-effacing guilt.

"Oh, don't worry, Ricky. It's not from you. I know what you're thinking. Besides, even if it were from you, it's gone now. I lost it the day after I saw the doctor. That's right, I miscarried. I'm eighteen years old, and I've already been made pregnant, miscarried, and had preeclampsia. I might as well be an old lady." She laughed. It was a loud, intrusive, caustic laugh, a laugh that pretended no pain in life was to be taken seriously. It was a laugh designed to help her run from herself. It was the laugh of evil, Ricky thought. He stepped back from the bed as if in fear that the laugh would attack him. It was as if the laugh had material digestive power, and again, he felt caught in the abstract web, except this time he was being consumed.

She stopped laughing after what seemed like a very long time. She looked at him with this surprisingly silly stare that seemed to ask how it was that he was still standing there. Silence. Nothing but empty silence persisted between them. Finally, he broke the sterile spell.

"Robin, I don't understand you. Why are you so angry? I'm really sorry all this has happened to you. If I had known, I would have done anything to make it up to you. I feel partly responsible. I care for you."

"I said it was not your fault. It was not your baby. Do you think you are the only person in the world? You're not, Mr. Ricky. And even if you were the guy who did it to me, so what? It's my body. I can do what I want with my body. If I want to have sex, then I'll do it. I don't blame you or anybody else for what happens. What makes you think you owe me anything? You don't owe me anything. I don't really like you anyway. I take care of myself. No man is going to care for me if I don't want him to, and I don't want you to. Don't come in here with your worries. I don't want your worries. I'm OK, I said. It's over. Now go away."

Ricky took a deep breath. He felt disoriented. This Robin seemed completely without resemblance to the Robin he dreamed of in his mind. Lying there in her hospital bed with her magazine, her dark hair held in that cute ponytail by a ribbon, her darkness amid the whiteness of the sheets, amid the whiteness of the room, she all at once appeared not only unappealing but a mere shadow in his life. He wanted to dismiss her as he would the momentary presence of any undesirable stranger who might cast before him the unwanted obliteration of sunlight. But he could not dismiss her completely. She had meant something to him, and her abrupt destruction of this meaning jarred him, leaving him with an intense discomfort. She wanted to pretend what they had done was just an adventure, a passing fancy, a momentary whim. He could not allow himself to view it that way. It was true he didn't sit down and consider sex with her as would a philosopher. It wasn't a reasoned decision to enter her. But he couldn't see it as trivial either. Had those few minutes with her led to her almost having a cerebral hemorrhage? She was in the hospital because of what they had done. (Or she had done with somebody else, he quickly told himself.) If he looked at everything the way she did, everything would lose value. Life would be merely a trivial, moment-to-moment diversion. Consequences would lose their significance. He would be unimportant. He had to value what had happened to him and Robin. He couldn't simply dismiss it as she would. He found himself speaking without considering the effect his words might have.

"You think that all you have to tell me is that it's not my fault and I will leave. What do you think I am? We shared something, you and I. Yeah, it was only for a little time, but I felt it was something special. I thought it was important. You meant something to me. I guess I was stupid. I made us more important to each other than we were. I really didn't believe that silly stuff about astrology, stars crossing, and all that nonsense."

"Astrology is not stupid. It shows what you know. It shows why I don't like you," Robin interrupted him. No one could accuse her of not being agitated now. The star-crossing certainly was more important to her than Ricky's pain.

"You can believe in the stars if you want to. Let's leave that out of this. You can't really care about anyone. You were pregnant. It meant nothing to you. You were happy you lost it. My God, Robin, isn't there anything that means something to you besides your astrology?"

"I don't want to talk to you anymore. Get out. You don't understand anything." She turned away from him toward the window, opened the magazine fiercely, and began looking at it as if he wasn't there.

The situation turned suddenly ridiculous. He stood there for a minute watching her reading *Life* magazine, her mouth stern and unrelenting in its expression. The wall she had built between them was unassailable. He was gathering his forces together to leave. Despite his anger and disgust with her, going out of the room was not easy.

"OK, Robin, I'm leaving. I won't bother you anymore. I just want to say that I'm sorry you were sick, and I'm glad you are feeling better. I really don't understand you. I don't know why you would be so angry. I don't know if the baby was mine. Maybe not. I just need to say that I cared for you even if you didn't care for me. I came here to see you because I felt a part of your problem. Even if you don't like me, that is no reason to treat me like this. I really don't know why you have to be so mean." And with that final statement, more to himself than to her, he went out the door of her room with an enormous sense of heaviness and darkness.

He almost bumped into Mrs. Linkowitz as she was turning to enter 234 to see her daughter. Both were startled.

"Oh, hello, Ricky. How are you? How nice of you to come and see Robin."

"Hello, Mrs. Linkowitz. Ah…yes…thank you. I'm glad Robin is feeling better." He was thoroughly embarrassed. It was clear in a moment, however, that she knew of no important connection between him and Robin's illness. "Amazing," he thought, "Robin has told her nothing!" He was immediately relieved.

"Please come and see Robin again, won't you? She likes company very much." Her tone was lilting, cheery, and relaxed, almost as if her daughter had just had her tonsils removed. This woman completely missed the tragedy of Robin's situation. "Tragedy? That may be too strong a word. Does this Linkowitz family understand anything?" His thoughts swirled around his brain like gnats looking for a place to rest.

"Sure. I'll come back. Thank you," he lied and left her in the busy emptiness of the hospital corridor.

CHAPTER 19

A Serious Conversation with Wally

RICKY LEFT THE shadowed, white-walled, insular false sterility of the hospital and stepped into Savannah's blinding white early-summer sunlight. As he passed through the doorway, the brightness was so intense that he could not prevent himself from partially covering his eyes with his hand. In the blur of sun-white, Ricky could not see that Wally was waiting for him on the right side of the steps as promised. He did not notice that his friend had raised his eyes from his book to welcome his preoccupied companion.

Wally saw at once that Ricky was deeply moved by whatever had occurred inside the hospital. Ricky was always a little somber, but this did not account for the intense and gloomy presence he showed of himself on the hospital steps. His mind was filled with rambling considerations of his conversation with Robin. As his eyes adapted, he seemed surprised, but very pleased, that Wally was there.

"Oh. Sorry, Wally. I…um, did I take a long time?"

"It's OK. I was just reading." Wally saw his distress and spoke briefly to allow Ricky to lead the moment.

"Thanks for waiting. Ah…can we walk to Forsyth?"

Wally understood at once Ricky's need and, without answering, walked beside his friend toward the park only a block or so away.

The wind was gentle and cool. Red and pink azaleas were everywhere fully in bloom. The trees possessed that dark forest green that makes a startling contrast against an almost surprising cobalt blue and cloudless sky. The density of the foliage hid the gray moss still upon their branches. Yet neither boy could feel the natural beauty that was around them. They were immersed in each other. One was trying to help. The other was suffering.

As they crossed Drayton Street and entered the park, they saw five or six unknown boys about their age playing half-rubber. For a moment, Ricky was distracted. His thoughts turned to his satisfying feeling of past successes. He remembered his skill at using the broomless stick effectively. He would unfailingly swat the half of a solid rubber ball that was thrown at him by the pitcher, almost any pitcher. He was good at it, often won, making more solid hits than his opponents. It was so long since he played. Then he admonished himself. "Half-rubber?" he thought. "That's stupid. I've got more serious things to worry about." And he switched to his previous self.

The two found a bench on the wide swath of sidewalk that went down the middle of the park. As they sat next to each other, they could easily make out the Forsyth fountain with its maiden of the sea, nereids, and craning egrets. The fountain was off. It seemed that it was always off. The lack of water made the white figures seem tame and cold. It was as if Orpheus had indeed looked back. Not only had Eurydice been lost, but all the sprites and playful spirits were turned into their material tedium.

"What happened?" Wally finally asked. His right arm was on the top rung of the back of the bench as he looked at Ricky. Ricky's hands were clasped in front of him, his back was bent slightly, and he seemed to be staring at the sidewalk.

"I think I made her pregnant."

"Really?!" It was the most dramatic Wally had ever sounded to Ricky.

"She's not pregnant now. She lost it. She had something called preeclampsia. She almost had convulsions. Becky got it wrong. That gossip. She just wanted to make it sound dramatic. Damn her!" Wally didn't say anything. He simply looked at his friend and listened.

"I don't really know if it's mine. I mean, if it was mine. She said it wasn't. Maybe she said it was. I don't really know. She was a bitch." He didn't raise his head or change his posture. Wally spoke.

"What's getting to you so much, Ricky? You said it was over. She's not pregnant. You didn't even know if the baby was yours." There was this musical, questioning sound to Wally's voice. It was soothing and comforting yet probing for an answer, a genuine friend trying to help in the complete spirit of kindness. Ricky felt an immediate upswell of affection and gratitude. He spoke from his heart and did not restrain his feelings. It was as if the fountain had been turned on within himself.

"The only thing I really know, Wally, is that we did it that night in Thunderbolt. We had sex. It was my first time. I don't know about her. I was scared afterward. I even had this nightmare about it. I thought it was great that she let me do it, but afterward I was afraid. I thought she might get pregnant and I'd have to marry her. I knew it would mess up my life. I tried to put it out of mind. I forgot all about it until today. When Becky came up to me, I was shocked. I got scared. Everything seemed dark. That's when you saw me and we went to the cafeteria." Ricky had a way of rounding out his thoughts. Sometimes it meant he would repeat himself. Wally gave no indication that he was distracted or uncomfortable with this style. It was as if he had merged into Ricky's mind, was trying to feel Ricky's feelings, but was looking at it from his own perspective.

Ricky continued. "When I went to see her in the hospital, I expected the worst. I expected she would tell me she was pregnant and I would have to marry her. I was ready to do it, Wally. That's what I thought about: marrying her, changing my life, being fair about the situation. I wanted to do the right thing. God! was I worried. I couldn't believe how Robin acted. After she told me about preeclampsia, she turned into a bitch. It was incredible. It was incredible." Ricky paused and Wally took the opportunity to ask a question.

"What is preeclampsia, Ricky?"

"I don't really know. Robin said it had something to do with being pregnant and having high blood pressure with headaches. She said sometimes people get convulsions. That's why she was in the hospital. The doctor wanted to watch her. Would you believe it? She didn't even know she was pregnant. She went to the doctor for a tension headache." Ricky turned to look at Wally at this juncture and gave him a smile. The two enjoyed the diverting humor of the moment. Levity quickly spent, Ricky resumed his posture of misery. This was merely a punctuated diversion from Ricky's primary mood. He saw that Wally regained his attentiveness and went on.

"Anyway, she told me I was unimportant to her. I should not worry about her. I should only take care of myself. It was as if the whole thing was nothing. It wasn't nothing. It was serious. What if she had died? I can't believe that one fuck could cause so much trouble." Ricky nor Wally even flinched at the word almost never used in Southern propriety.

"But Ricky, I can't understand what upsets you so much."

"It's her attitude. I felt like I didn't matter. I was ready to marry her, and she's practically kicking me out of her room. I mean…why did she let me have sex with her anyway?"

"You said it was because of her belief in astrology." Wally made a wan smile.

"I guess I can't accept that. I can't believe that two lives were almost changed and that someone gets very dangerously sick because of a belief in astrology. It really bothers me that she doesn't matter to herself and that I don't matter to her."

Wally stiffened. It was clear he had been very moved by what Ricky had told him. He saw Ricky turn toward him as if feeling that Wally had something important to say, as if looking for that support and understanding so much desired, as if expecting confirmation of his pain.

"Why do you feel she should have had stronger feelings for you? Why do you feel she should have sex for better reasons than her ideas about astrology? Why can't you see her for what she is?"

These were not questions Ricky expected to hear. He was surprised but felt compelled to try to answer.

"What do you mean 'what she is'?"

"What she is. I think she's a shallow girl, not too bright, who follows her feelings. She doesn't think much of anybody else. You're not important to her. Nobody's important to her. She used you, Ricky. To her you were only something available. You gave her more significance than she should have had. Why do you feel bad about this?"

"What we did was important. I admit I didn't like her attitude that night, crossed stars and all that. But we did something together. Either what people do is important or it isn't. How can anybody live with her attitude?"

"Ricky, I know you are miserable about all this, but look at it another way. You think the world is supposed to fit a pattern. You expect that pattern. When it happens a different way, you're upset. Do you ever think that we make the patterns? I mean, the world is really not so terribly understandable or organized. Almost anything can happen. But we don't want to see it that way. We want everything to make sense, so we force patterns on it whether they're true or not. You want to make Robin fit some idea about what girls are like. You think that if you have sex with her, she's supposed to like you. Or you think she's supposed to feel close to you. Maybe the usual girl would feel that way, but Robin doesn't fit that idea. I think she's mixed up. I don't think she's put together too well, but that's not your concern. What makes you think everything is so clear and understandable? Maybe life is incomprehensible, and we live a kind of illusion that it makes sense when it doesn't."

Ricky was absolutely astounded by what he heard. "Life is incomprehensible? We make patterns?" This was completely new. What was his friend trying to say? But if he was wrong about Robin, what was he right about?

"You mean I can't be certain about anything? Life has no meaning?"

"It isn't that life has no meaning, Ricky. It's that the meaning may change when we change. The way people think about the world today is not the way the people of the world thought about themselves in the Middle Ages. What's real, the thinking of the Middle Ages or the thinking today? How do we know that in five hundred years our ideas about right, wrong, and real won't be completely different?

"But all this is not what I'm getting at. I think you're upset because you believed that having sex with Robin obligated you to her. Maybe with most girls that's true. With Robin it's not. You can't handle the idea that you were just used. In Robin's worldview you were only her tool. I think you feel as bad about that as anything. All your usual values were turned upside down by her. In her world your values are meaningless. I think you should just accept the fact that you did something with a kind of succubus, a sort of mean female sexual spirit who had no interest in you. It's not your fault. You shouldn't feel bad. Put it behind you."

"So, Wally, how am I supposed to live my life? I mean…what is real, what is significant, what deserves weight, what doesn't?" Ricky was becoming fascinated with his friend's unexpected ideas. "I had something with Robin. It felt important. I guess that happens in all the things we do with people that have some meaning to us. How do we know what's important, what's not, what's real, what's fake?"

"I don't know what's real. I know my senses tell me something. I try to believe them. I get some confirmation from the world and from others. I also know that what I anticipate influences what I sense. Everything changes. The world is in constant movement. Even if something seems to stand still and unchanging, the way we feel it and know it can change. With people we must do the best we can. If we get along and it feels right, we can only accept the feeling. If it doesn't feel right, then we should not blame ourselves. Our ideas of right and wrong are usually on target. It's rare they are never absolutely right, right by any criteria at any time by anybody.

"I think Robin is some kind of deviation from the normal, but it is only important to see her relative to the expected. Judging her is a biased enterprise. It is only important to know that you should not try to be close to her. You need to see that she is not for you. Don't get involved with people who are not for you. Also, face it, Ricky. You did not see her for weeks. Did you really want her? No. It's almost as if you feel guilty about avoiding and ignoring her. Anyway, try not to worry about Robin anymore. It's over."

Maybe the incident with Robin was over, but Ricky was deeply affected by what Wally had said. He was feeling better. He was impressed by the power of sex and what he had let it do to him; he was more impressed by Wally's ideas. Nothing was absolute, with the same values for all; everything was relative and uncertain. His own senses could deceive him. The world he saw was constantly changing, and he was the subject of it, and his body was affected by everything without being aware. He could never be completely in command and had to accept his own limitations. Even his responsibility to himself and others was relative and changing. He wondered if his friend fully realized the power of the ideas he had expressed.

He looked at his friend with endearment. "What makes two people come together?" he thought. "Whatever Wally said, this friendship feels right. I can trust him. He means something to me. I don't think I ever want it to disappear." He embraced the new closeness with Wally. It held him fast and gave him a burst of confidence and ease.

"I feel much better, Wally. Thanks." He did feel better about Robin, but as quickly as his bond with Wally formed, his sense of insecurity increased. This new state made him uneasy and peculiar. The two friends had had a dialogue well beyond their years mostly conducted by a quiet boy with an advanced sense of who he was and what the world was. Who was this profound blond-haired Protestant? How did he come to know these things, have these views? How did he live in this world thinking the way he did?

"Good! I'm glad I could help. You want to catch a bus back on Abercorn?"

"OK."

The two got up from the bench and walked with light steps out of the park and into the evening. As the sun dimmed, a sweet, musty odor filled the air. The Savannah streetlights came on and, like a Magritte painting, night and day seemed eternally and strangely one. The shadows were friendly as the two noticed that the Forsyth fountain had been turned on. Water sprayed across their paths as they walked. Orpheus did not look back.

CHAPTER 20

Oglethorpe and Tomochichi

IN 1833, JAMES Edward Oglethorpe, a soldier, a friend of Samuel Johnson, a good dinner companion, a rather dull speaker, a man given to clichés but a noble of good heart, finally settled on the bluff later called Savannah. His ship's lookout caught a view of this highest point in an otherwise flat, watery terrain. The captain saw there on the banks of the to-be-named Savannah River an ideal place to build his new colony. He was aided by good fortune, firm seas, and complete financial backing from his England, a country that, in a happy moment, was spurred by its wish to help unemployed debtors and poor people who might be willing to settle across the sea; as if blessed, he had the further luck to happen upon the welcoming hospitality of the local Indians. Tomochichi was their tribal leader. He was old, wizened, and eager to learn from his tall, distinguished white visitor, who acted respectfully. There was none of the arrogance the Indian had encountered with the tradesmen and hunters formerly crossing his paths. The two became good friends. The Indian shared a plight like many of the passengers of the good ship *Anne*: he, too, was a reject in his own land. Tomochichi had been forced to leave the Creek Indians some years before and become the leader of a small outcast group he called the Yamacraws. He was looking for a friend as much as were the esteemed general and the new settlers. Each leader saw the virtue in the other, and they were rewarded. Their friendship was genuine and heartfelt; and consequently, life for both was made easier through their mutual support. The relationship provided that added security that can be fully appreciated only by those who find themselves amid an unknown and threatening new country.

The story is told that, long after the settlement was first developed, the general was on an expedition up the Savannah River when he heard that his Indian compatriot was ill. He sent message after message to Tomochichi wishing him well. Sadly, however heartfelt, his messages had predictably no effect on the disintegrative elements of fate. He could not get back in time to see his sick leader again and, in the end, returned only for the funeral. At Oglethorpe's written request, the old Indian's body was kept in state until then. Oglethorpe helped carry the Yamacraw's remains to their final resting place. The sensitive, esteemed colonist led a formal state ceremony with full honors. Tomochichi was buried in Percival Square, an English-style park in the emerging municipality of southern Savannah. The great man was interred far from his own people but nearer to the soul of the colony founded with minimal strife and a better chance of surviving in part because of him. He died the way he lived, as an independent, intelligent, caring spirit estranged from the common world as he knew it.

Ricky new few details of this history, but he somehow knew that Tomochichi was viewed as a great man. He felt an unexplainable closeness to this Indian, more than to any other historical figure. He had often come across the large stone that marked his grave while riding his bicycle and more than once found himself leaning over the handlebars to read the inscription on a bronze plaque pressed into monolith resting heavily on the turf that covered the Indian's remains. He knew Tomochichi was a friend of the colony's founder, and he knew he was supposed to be very sensible. He felt a peculiar awe in the racially prejudiced South that an Indian would be given such an honor, even assuming the man must have been very special.

He was distracted, forgot about it, and rode his bike away. He incorporated unawares yet one more sensibility of his hometown. This lore, like two hundred years of other tales, become a part of his spirit, never to leave him. Tomochichi was another piece of persistent Savannah.

Savannah was mostly like this, an ineffable sensation of sadness, significance, and history. It extended its arms to enwrap him. It was an inner sensibility, a multitude of sensations divorced of geography. It wasn't the political boundaries, the statues, and the other memorabilia all together that affected Ricky. It was this slowly digested feeling that metabolically worked its way into him like Southern cooking, that became part of his skin and bones. He felt without seeing the hold it had on his imagination and opinions. The hold his history had on him frightened him; it was like the moss that accumulated on the trees. He had no thought how it got there. This was a merging of body and place. He felt the extended tendrils of the metaphorical moss reaching for him. Despite his struggle for full independence, the sinews of the city were holding him fast.

The encounter with Robin, too, had reached out to keep him in place; he felt from her that mosslike entwining, that aerophilic persisting capturing. He was complete in his hometown, feeding the growth of the place that needed nothing from him but a receptive, nutritive soil to survive. Savannah was a place to breathe and thrive. Soon she would send her memory spores attached to Ricky to another opportunistic place.

Though Robin rejected him, and he, with Wally's help, had rejected that part within him that contained her, the experience continued to have a partial hold. It was as if another selection, a female selection, an addition to Savannah's hundreds of tales of silent mystery, was inserted into him in a kind of unwanted pregnancy. New life was growing inside. This was the soul of the place. Born within him thus was an inchoate something that might even seem old at delivery. He struggled against the emerging life-form. He didn't want to be attached to this place, nor did he want to be attached by it, its spirits, or its people. He wanted to leave. The time was nearing. Graduation was a mere few days away.

CHAPTER 21

Conflict Resolution

RICKY WAS IN the Savannah courthouse across the square from the post of-fice not too far from Broad Street, downtown. He had just entered the auspicious lobby with its high Romanesque arches, giving him the presentiment of being turned into something small within a complex largeness. The law was a remote subject about which he had no comprehension, thinking about it only in the simplest terms of punishments for crimes. It was reassuring that he was in this austere building to deal with a wrong that had been done to him. It was inconceiv-able that the law could ever make him its victim. In this he was disingenuous but, as a result of his naivety about the larger world, reassured.

He immediately spied his father talking to a man dressed in a tie and sport coat, not especially well attired, not dressed to impress, but nevertheless possess-ing a kind of confidence to which Ricky's father was giving considerable respect. His father exhibited that serious expression that in the past Ricky had feared but that on this occasion was clearly designed to show obeisance to his conversant. Sam saw Ricky out of the corner of his eye and spoke to this man in a familiar way so that Ricky became incorporated into the discussion.

"Excuse me, Joe, here is Ricky. Ricky, this is Mr. Harris. He's a lawyer, and he's helping us with the case." It was hard to hear his father speak to him with such regard. Ricky always felt unimportant and dismissed by his father, more of a bothersome kid than a son. Once in the process of a huge father-son battle, Ricky's mother had taken him aside and told him to calm down. He told her that he knew his father didn't love him, so what difference did it make? She seemed especially pained by this and said that his father loved him very much, that he was especially important to him, and he shouldn't act like a fool. Ricky dismissed this out of hand but retained in a small recess of his mind the feeling of reassurance it gave him. The incident with his mother came to mind when he heard the respectful tone his father used toward him.

The lawyer looked at Ricky. "Hello, Ricky. How are you? I've been talking to your father about the case. You know you can put this young man in jail if you want to. Your father says he doesn't really want to do that. What do you think?" And there it was. Ricky was suddenly placed in a position to help decide what consequences might befall another person. He had gone to so much trouble to revenge himself on this man who hit him for blowing the horn. He had even taken pictures of his cut swollen lip by holding the camera at arm's length. The pictures had come out and showed clearly the tearing of skin and the swollen membranes of his lower lip. But now that Mr. Joseph Harris was asking him definitely to decide the issue of whether to prosecute. Ricky was having second thoughts. If his assailant went to jail, would it serve any purpose?

Lawyers passed with briefcases. A large door opened at the end of the hall, and he could see a courtroom in session. Everything appeared so powerful, so imposing. He considered himself for a moment in his assailant's position. All he had done was sock someone in the face. Should he go to jail for that? Ricky was feeling increasingly embarrassed. He wanted nothing to do with the prosecution. His enemy became the source of guilt, not the man who hit him. He could now do much more damage to his assailant than was ever done to him, and he did not want to make this kind of decision. He would have been happy to walk out of the courthouse and forget the whole thing.

"He wouldn't get away with it completely, Ricky." Mr. Harris clearly detected how overwhelming the situation was to him. He was trying to help Ricky and his father feel better about dropping the charges. He didn't know that Ricky was becoming quickly delighted at the prospect. "He was booked the night he hit you. I think that should stand." Ricky's father nodded. Ricky only trembled unnoticeably as he stood silent. "But if you drop the charges, that would be all that he would suffer. He has to learn that he can't go around hitting people just because he is annoyed at them. Well, what do you think, Ricky?"

"That would be fine with me." Ricky saw his father smile as he uttered the words. He realized quickly that he had played the role wished for him. Everyone was in agreement that enough had been done.

"Good. There is no need to seek blood, right?" The lawyer went on without pause. "Sammy, I'm going to tell the judge. Why don't you and Ricky come with me into the court? I think I can interrupt his honor. He'll be glad to put this aside. Graham is already here."

"Who's Graham?" Ricky asked.

"That's the guy who hit you. His name is Graham Bartlett."

The three of them walked down the wide hall, dodging rapidly-walking people, and made their way into the court. Ricky was surprised that the very large room was nearly empty, giving the atmosphere an eerie, manufactured quality. It reminded him of a synagogue and the procedures a kind of religious ritual. Graham Bartlett was sitting at the end of a bench itself identical in style to the pews at Agudath Achaim, the only Jewish temple Ricky knew. There was a man dressed better than Mr. Harris next to him. The formal demeanor he exhibited assured Ricky that it was his assailant's lawyer. No one from Graham's family seemed to be present. Ricky was glad his own father stood next to him.

Mr. Harris went to talk to Graham and his lawyer. Ricky saw Graham light up where his face had been quite glum. It never occurred to Ricky that his enemy might be frightened by the proceedings. He assumed the guy was cocky and unrepentant. Ricky's thoughts moved to presumption: "He must be a hard, insensitive person, someone who sees life as made up of daily hurdles, someone who denies pain." Only someone like that could have hit Ricky without warning. But here was Graham Bartlett looking better dressed than anyone, wearing a newly pressed suit, smiling with relief over what he had just been told and giving the impression of a regular person who had suffered before this ritualistic confrontation with his victim.

The judge had clearly put aside the preceding case. The people involved went outside for a recess. There were only eight people in the cavernous space. Mr. Harris, Graham Bartlett, and the other lawyer came toward the judge on the dais. Mr. Harris motioned to Ricky and his father to join him there. The five stood on the floor below the black-robed judge above them. The rabbi of secular law assumed an air of dignity, solemnity, power, and profound seriousness. No one smiled as he spoke.

"You understand, Mr. Bartlett, that what you did to this boy was an assault, do you not?"

"Yes, your honor."

"You understand that this boy and his father could put you in jail if I found their accusation to be justified, but that they have decided to drop the charges?"

"Yes, your honor."

"You are a very lucky man, Mr. Bartlett. If you had done this to my son, I don't think I would have let you go. You are dealing with fine people here. The next time you get angry, for whatever reason, you will consider the consequences of your act, will you not?"

"Yes, your honor, I will."

Graham Bartlett's manner completely disarmed Ricky. These past months Ricky had thought about him as a large, brutal man, a man with no fear. Ricky assumed there was no way to reason with him. He saw him as powerful, frightening, intransigent. Now, before the judge, he looked like a simple boy, only a few years older than Ricky, someone Ricky would not even notice on the street. His reasons for hitting him seemed even more puzzling. Most important, though, was Ricky's sense that the man had less strength of character, less confidence than even he had.

Ricky experienced a surge of pride in his own person and saw his assailant as a fragile, inconsequential person. He had the idea the guy would amount to little in life. First he felt a surge of superiority, then pride, and finally the return of embarrassment.

Look at the trouble Ricky had caused by blowing his horn. It was true he felt provoked, but he had stirred in another the kind of rage that might have killed. Then he'd entangled himself, however gently, within the intricacies of law. Finally, here he was bestowing, with his father, the gift of freedom to someone. That unnecessary act of social intercourse, the small act of blowing the car horn: both seemed like the tiny waft of air. It was the shift of wind that turns a giant's head and distracts him as David slings his stone. How weighty was it that in life such small acts could have such grand consequences?

"Remember today, Graham." The judge transformed into an avuncular advice giver. His tone lowered, the edge of his voice softened, he leaned over his desk and looked down. "This could have been a serious situation. You seem like a nice boy. I'm surprised you're in my court. Now go home, and be sure you've learned your lesson."

"Yes, your honor. Thank you, your honor."

The judge ceremoniously hit his hammer and said, "Case dismissed!"

The ritual was officially completed. Graham Bartlett and his lawyer quickly left the court. Graham not once looked at Ricky. As he left, Ricky saw only his back as the rest of his countenance disappeared forever. His figure would now exist for Ricky only in memory.

Ricky, his father, and their lawyer made to follow them. But Mr. Harris turned toward the judge and said, "Thanks, Bill. I appreciate it."

"It's OK, Joe. Glad to do it." The two men shook hands. The judge turned to the sergeant at arms and asked him to bring in the next case. The participants now finished with jurisprudence walked out of the courtroom, through the hall, and into the sunshine outside.

On the court steps, the three stopped. Ricky stood in the light, adjusting his eyes as the two older men spoke. Graham Bartlett and his lawyer were nowhere to be seen. Ricky was sure he would never see them again.

"I'd like to thank you too, Joe. That worked well. Thank you. What do I owe you? Ah…never mind. Please send me a bill." Ricky's father rapidly realized he was being indiscreet.

"It's all right, Sammy. I owe it to you. Forget it. How's your boy now? He looks good to me." Both men turned to look at Ricky, who smiled in spite of himself.

"I'd like to thank you too, Mr. Harris. I appreciate you helping us."

"Forget it, Ricky." He broke into a large grin. "Just don't go blowing your horn so much." With that he smiled and waved his hand as he walked down the steps into the Savannah streets.

Ricky and his father began descending the steps shoulder to shoulder. "Dad?" Ricky asked cautiously, partly expecting to be brushed aside and dealt with in a supercilious manner. "What did Mr. Harris mean when he said he owed it to you? Did he do this for nothing?"

"He did it as a favor for me. I've done some favors for him."

His tone was friendly and satisfied. Clearly, he was pleased that Graham Bartlett had come to justice. The Jew had triumphed over the goy. His son and his family had gained respect, even if only in his eyes, even if only privately.

"That was really good of him, wasn't it?"

"Yes, it was." Ricky couldn't imagine what favor his father had done for a lawyer, but he was also impressed with the regard the lawyer had for his father.

"Are you going back to school now? I have to go back to the pawn shop."

"I don't think I'll go back to school. It's not worth it. I'm going to meet Fred."

"Good. Well, see you later."

"Bye."

"Oh, ah…Ricky?" his father called out to him as he was walking away to his car.

"Yeah?"

"I thought you handled yourself really well in there."

"You did?"

But his father had already turned his back and started walking away at a brisk pace.

Ricky was alone. He was alone on the planet of himself, detached from everything he had ever believed in. His father was a person with a world outside of his own, a world of respect, regard, and appreciation. He was a complex person. Ricky was undeserving of him, he thought. All these years he had assumed the reality of his father was that of an uncaring screamer. The truth was far different, if ever there was a single truth. Ricky remembered his conversation in Forsyth Park with Wally. He realized that it might be impossible to know anyone completely. He found a new humility that would follow him for the rest of his days. He was emerging from childhood.

Ricky was alone. He was supposed to meet Fred at the hobby shop on Bull Street, a short walk from the courthouse. Fred wanted to get a car for his O-gauge train set. Ricky thought Fred's interest in trains, and his elaborate layout with houses, hills, and farms, was a little on the side of fanatical, but he enjoyed it too. He had agreed to meet him with the prospect of going to his house later and putting the purchase into action.

As he walked through the squares toward Bull Street, he ignored the squirrels on and around the benches in the tiny parks almost empty of people, the still-bright red azalea bushes, the relative tranquility of this garden oasis in what was mostly barren Georgia cotton lands with a nearby swamp. He thought again about what had transpired.

He felt for the first time the humanity of his father. His father was a person just like himself, not a tyrant as he had thought. Why had the man acted so harshly all those years? Look at the way the lawyer had treated him. The lawyer didn't see him as a tyrant. "It's OK, Sammy. I owe you one."

Ricky marveled at how he had only seen his father in the narrowest ways. He saw him only as a yelling, screaming, never satisfied man, a man whom Ricky could never please. Now here he was talking to Ricky as an adult, incorporating him into his world, being completely uncritical, quite sympathetic, there for him, respectful. Old thoughts can't just be extinguished. Ricky was having a battle within himself between the old opinion and the new. Maybe his father was softening because Ricky was graduating. Did that have an influence? But even if that were true, it would mean that he cared for him, that he wanted a good relationship with him, and that Ricky was important to him. Ricky's mother's words returned: "He loves you very much."

The world was not what it appeared to be. Ricky could not trust his senses. He could not be sure of his opinions. His mind fooled him. What was real? What could he trust? He thought about this a long time and concluded that because he depended so much on his senses and his mind, he could not be sure of anything. He lived in a world in which he was being seduced by the need to accept. This need was partly because the alternative was chaos and confusion. This did not mean the acceptable common-sense thing was real or right or true.

He had lived all of his young life with an absolute conviction that his father was uncaring and rotten to him. This was clearly no longer supportable. Ricky would have to change his mind, but what mind was he changing? What was the real truth about his father, about Robin, about Wally? Did other people feel this loss of faith in what they thought they knew? Ricky realized that if he followed this line of thinking, he could become hopelessly confused. He decided to put these considerations aside for now.

He had made his way to the hobby store. He was not going to be alone. Fred was inside. "Poor Fred," Ricky thought. "He never thinks about things like this. He has his trains. He is always talking about philosophers and physics. He uses large words whenever he is in Hubert's company, does he really know what he is talking about? Fred just wants to fit in—but to fit in to what? There he is doing something that looks quite real, buying his car for his train set. He seems to be in life, if not a part of it. Might as well go in and say hello." He smiled broadly at Fred as he entered the shop.

CHAPTER 22

Wally Drops a Bomb

Ricky's Worldview Is Altered Yet Again

SCHOOL HAD BECOME what the kids called a joke. The last week, the last few days, the end of a lifetime of developing and growing were upon Ricky and everyone else. Teachers had stopped teaching; exams had been completed; whatever wasn't covered in the class was simply put aside, knowledge, perhaps, never to be acquired; yet the schedule demanded that school continue. The students in the lower grades had to finish the year, so the graduating seniors were supposed to continue with their planned courses.

In fact, no one went to school, or if they did, they went only for homeroom to be counted present and then wandered the halls the rest of the day. They would see friends, talk to teachers, have their school Yearbook signed or leave completely. Everyone accepted this period of limbo, and it became part of the special though unplanned senior privilege. It was the gift, outside of usual rules of the school, to those leaving.

Ricky thoroughly hated this time. He found himself with nothing to do. Guys he knew went boating, played golf, or had little parties, but he was invited to none of these. He knew, in fact, that Robin, who seemed to have recovered completely, was a member of a group of ten going boating to St. Simons Island.

The group contained many of Ricky's old enemies, including Byron Goldstein, who, for some reason inexplicable to Ricky at this moment, no longer presented any threat. Byron had nothing to do with Ricky not being included. "It's probably for the better," he placated himself. He was pained when he first overheard their plans as the group left the crowded hallway together. He saw them get into their cars, which were waiting, against the usual rules, in front of the school. Clearly, this had been planned for some time. His rationalization had the soothing effect intended. He went up the stairs to the second floor, where he hoped to meet the librarian, a woman in her sixties who had become his friend because of their mutual interest in books.

The library room was a large, rudimentary rectangle with bookshelves in little compact units lining its walls. Except for the librarian, it seemed completely empty. It was always like this at the end of a school year, as most kids never came in when they didn't have to. There was the usual globe on a stand in the middle of the room and books in transit on the librarian's desk. Since the space was in the front of the building, one entire wall was taken up with windows, reducing the area for books.

Mrs. Boney was not in. Ricky was sincerely disappointed. He wasn't sure if he would get back to see her before graduation, so he wrote a note thanking her for their conversations and her help through the year. She was not a confidant but a kind and gentle person, a supportive mothering figure, someone he found easy to talk to. She always told Ricky how exceptional she thought he was and seemed cheered beyond expectation when he would discuss a book with her that he had recently read. Having written the note and folded it for the other librarian to give to her, he turned to leave. At the far end of the room, unnoticed before, he spied Wally sitting at a table in the corner, reading alone. Ricky hesitated a moment, giving consideration to whether his friend would be receptive to his interrupting him.

Ricky had not had any major contact with Wally since their discussion nearly a month earlier in Forsyth Park. It was not that they had not seen each other, nor that they had none of the light chats that easily transpire in a classroom or busy hallway; all of this had occurred. Both had very much, though, wanted to talk at length again. Now opportunity presented itself. Ricky took a breath and decided to brave the ever-present protective membrane that remained between him and his friend. He walked over and, without saying a word, quietly sat himself in front of Wally on the other side of the table.

The two faced each other in an otherwise empty room in which talking was implicitly allowed for this rare end-of-school moment. Wally reacted to Ricky's presence by raising his head and putting down his book. Ricky could see the title. It was *Moses and Monotheism*, by Sigmund Freud. He let his curiosity spur the beginning of the conversation.

"Sigmund Freud? I've never read anything by him. I mean…I've heard of him. He's a psychologist, right? Is it good?"

Wally smiled the smile of superior knowledge. Ricky thought he sounded ignorant and naive, but he realized that however important Freud was to his friend, not everyone knew about the famous psychoanalyst. Wally's natural humility took over when he answered, but Ricky saw the facial expression and correctly deciphered his friend's inward unexpressed criticism. Wincing, he remained silent as Wally said, "He's very important. He deals with the way we really are. He goes beyond accepting our pretending. But this book is about who Moses is."

"Who Moses is?" It had never occurred to Ricky that there was any question. Moses had always been one person, the man who led the Jews out of Egypt.

"Yes. You know, no one really knows if Moses existed. We have only the Bible to go on. Freud tries to show that Moses may have been an Egyptian who rebelled against his stepbrother, father, or stepfather. It's not clear who exactly Ramses II was."

"It sounds very interesting." Every time Ricky talked with Wally, his mind expanded. He found himself intensely curious about Moses. What Wally said meant to Ricky that the emancipator of the Jews, the man who supposedly gave them the laws they followed today, may have had other motivations, that he may not have really talked to God, that he may have been a man with his own personal reasons for leading the Jews to Canaan. Suddenly, Ricky felt very close to this Moses and felt his own rebellion. "But it's pretty far fetched, isn't it?"

"Well, it is Freud's point of view. It's just interesting to read. I don't know if it's true either. Anyway, how are you? I haven't seen you for a long time. Do you feel better about Robin?"

Ricky was grateful for the change in topic. He didn't really know how far to go on the subject of Moses. After all, Wally was Christian. Ricky didn't want to thicken the membrane barrier by getting into a religious discussion, even though that, in fact, would not have occurred. He was uncomfortable with religion in general and found the discussion unsettling. There was no reason to assume Wally had the same discomfort. He just thought he might. He quickly changed the subject.

"I just saw Robin leave with her friends. They're going to take a boat to St. Simons Island. I think she's all right. I haven't seen her since that day at the hospital."

"But how are you doing?"

"I'm fine." Ricky found Wally looking at him with an unexpected intensity. He had never had anyone stare at his eyes like this before. It made him feel more was expected from him. "I'm OK, really. I'm…still trying to put what happened in place. You know, it's like truth doesn't matter. I mean, it's like reality doesn't matter. Well, I said all that. It's just hard to get that intimate with a person and they toss you away. But I'm OK."

Wally got that smile again. "What is truth, Ricky? What does it really mean, truth?"

"It means that you say what's a fact. You tell what really happened. You don't try to say what happened or what somebody said without being accurate, without being close to what was real."

Ricky looked toward the substitute librarian, who might well have shut them up, but she was at the far other end of the room shelving books and didn't seem to want to summon the energy to tell two soft-spoken, whispering seniors to shut up just because it was a library.

The smile broadened. "What's real? How do you know an event is what it really seems to be and not a misinterpretation?"

Ricky felt completely ensnared, nervous, unsure, and thought of getting up to leave. His interest in his friend's questions reminded him a little of Socrates. At the moment he wasn't feeling very Greek. In fact, over the recent months, he was feeling less and less like the toga-clad philosophers he'd once admired.

"What's real? Ah…it's whatever happens in front of us. It's something you can describe in detail. You and me talking, that's real." Ricky felt he made a good stab at the question, a question he never thought of answering before. He looked at Wally and saw him getting animated, a quality he thought his friend would never exhibit.

"Ricky, you don't appreciate what a problem reality is. Remember how Robin finally went out with you? Well, it seemed real that she wanted to go out with you, didn't it?"

"Yes."

"But it turned out she had some kind of unusual idea in her head about the stars. She had no feelings for you especially, right?" It pained Ricky to have to agree to this, but he did. "Well, Robin was two kinds of reality: the kind inside her that believes in astrology, and the kind that made her answer the phone in a nice way. The second kind misled you into thinking she really liked you. They are both real. I mean they are both there, but you only could find out about them by dating her and going through the misery you went through."

"So," Ricky said, warming to the discussion, "we can only know what we experience. Are you saying that what is real is only what we know, what we experience for ourselves? What about reading textbooks on things that happen in space? We can't experience that, and it seems real to me."

"Right. But the textbook represents the world as people have explained it in terms of people's ideas. Look, Ricky, you know about the spectrum of light."

"Yeah." Ricky knew a little about it but was getting even more on edge. This discussion was going far from anything he felt confidently. What was the point, he wondered?

"Well, we can only see part of what's on that spectrum, and only a small part at that. We can't see ultraviolet waves, and we can't see X-rays. We can detect them with certain machines we've built, but we can't personally experience them when they are there. X-rays may show effects days later if they are intense enough, but we don't know them. We know their reality only indirectly. That's just one example. The world seems to be filled with things of that sort, things we cannot know directly, things we have to take on faith or through special instruments that reveal them. Our senses fool us. Our senses, including our minds, which read the books and digest what the books say, tell us what they can. But we can only sense a part of the world. The entire world of daily living becomes our interpretation."

"I think you're talking about God." Ricky had a flash of insight and threw it into the discussion. He took a chance, in spite of his earlier restraint. He waited to see how Wally would handle his comment.

"Not exactly. I was really talking about how much you suffered when Robin hurt you because you wouldn't admit that you saw her one way when she was just as much another way. You had created a reality of her that was only a piece of what was there. But now that you bring it up, the same idea is true of God."

"You mean God is something we create? He's not real?" Ricky responded excitedly.

"Yes, I think mankind makes up God. Did you know, Ricky, that the word God has many different meanings in different cultures? Not only that, it meant something different in 400 BC than it does today. It is a created word. It tries to solve a problem."

Ricky was astounded by all this. Here he was worrying whether he could talk freely with Wally because he was a Christian, and now he learned that he had no religion. If he saw God as only a word people made up, then no religion had special significance. All religions were the same in that they were creations of the people who had them and were sustained by the people who stayed with them. He sat in silence as his friend went on.

"This is just the tip of the iceberg. We humans are not only living a creation of our concept of the world, we are completely unable to have a completely real concept. This is because real has no meaning. It is always a self-reflective rationalization.

"I know this is confusing, but let me give another example. I don't know if you have read anything about quantum theory. I have only read a little. Quantum theory is about how forces operate in the atom. When scientists tried to examine the atom carefully, they found they could not predict the position and the speed of the electron at the same time, as we can do with regular things we see and touch. This led to the idea that the fundamental things of nature, the atoms, had unpredictable characteristics. If causes cannot be determined in the atom, how sure can we be sure of causes in our daily life? Worse, the electron became more than one kind of thing. It was seen as both a wave and a particle. No longer could something that we know is a part of electricity in a wire, something that affects the way chemicals form, be seen as a clear-cut thing. It was neither one nor the other. It could be a blur or a thing. Frankly, what it is depends completely on how it is examined."

Ricky was getting entangled by what had now become a speech. He could not say anything, since every idea was new to him. He felt a gnawing anxiety growing within himself. It was as if every thought he had ever had about the world was changing, and only a dark sense of insecurity was replacing them. His old ideas seemed simple in comparison to what he was hearing now. He tried hard to comprehend the argument. "So you're saying that everything is uncertain. We can't know anything. There is no reality?"

"Not quite, Ricky. There is reality, but it is merely a word we create to apply to what we feel and think we know. Knowledge becomes a kind of adapting to the world we are born into by using language, which our brains create. Everything we experience becomes an estimation of this world based on our senses, but nothing is certain. Constant interpretation is the way we have to live our lives. This interpreting is a fluid, social phenomenon and has no absolute truth behind it. There is no absolute truth, only human approximate interpretation."

"But Wally," Ricky replied, warming to the discussion, "if somebody shoots me, I will die. The bullet seems very real as my life disappears."

"It's not a matter that the bullet isn't real. In fact, using the invented human word, there are levels of reality, or levels of certainty about reality. Perhaps the bullet is on the highest level. It breaks the skin and kills you. But the real is still defined by the human perception of it. Many realities are much more of an interpretation than the bullet reality."

Ricky was very impressed. He was being convinced by his friend that there was no certainty in life. He saw that God was a social fabrication different in different periods of history and different cultures. The distinction between Christianity and Judaism was also a fabrication of history. The two camps drew different peoples into them, each people having their own reasons for being what they were. Both religions gave value in handling life. They were both right because they helped people. They were both wrong because they represented interpretations of the world that satisfied people, not guaranteed truths. There was no absolute way of living life. But there was also no rug to stand on. The rug of confidence was being pulled away.

"So, if we can't be sure of anything, Wally, how can we live? We have to wake up in the morning feeling we know something. You can't live with a complete sense of confusion."

"We live by the senses we have. We perceive our world as best we can and try to balance what the world demands and what we wish for ourselves. We absorb the perceptions we experience, willing to change them when other perceptions and learned facts demand it. We always admit we are part of a moment in history, part of a special social environment that probably will never come again. Of course, we have to hold to the values of our time and place, but we also should realize that these values are time and place bound and not absolute for all places and all time. We learn this from our parents, who give to us the world and its values as they know them. By the time we are able to think for ourselves, we've absorbed most of what we need from Mom and Dad.

"At first this gives us our childhood selves confidence. But it is a false confidence because it doesn't necessarily see the natural confusion around us. As we get older, we begin to add to the situation. If we're smart enough, we come to know how contrived was the worldview our parents put into us. Only then will we see that reality is a social product, a word applied by the society our parents taught us about."

Wally and Ricky became silent. The empty library seemed unusually large, and they felt more alone, though the librarian had returned to her desk, and the place was no more occupied than before. Wally had put out thoughts that Ricky could only partly digest. Even Wally himself was affected by what he had said.

"These ideas are not really mystical."

"Mystical?" Ricky questioned.

"Yes. Mysticism comes from the Far East. It's the belief that life is an illusion. That reality is something God or the gods give you. The idea of the mystics is that the truth comes only with a supreme mental effort, and the truth is some kind of abstraction. So my ideas are more mundane, more Western. I don't think life is an illusion but that it is an adaptation thrust upon us. Even the mystical idea believed in by Brahmins of the Hindus is the result of an adaptation to our world, the world of life and death, happiness and sadness."

"So what should a person do with his life if he wants to find the truth? I mean, what kind of life gives the truth the best? Is it better to be a philosopher, a doctor, a lawyer, or what?"

"There are probably many roads to wisdom. I'm still young like you. I'm not sure what is best. But it seems to be that art is closest to truth. Using creativity, trying to always make something new out of nothing, is what life seems to me to be about. Art is the discipline of making facsimile. It's ironic and interesting to think about it. Art is always illusion, always created to deceive the recipient—the viewer of a painting, the listener of a concert. If it's done sincerely, genuinely, and intelligently, art approaches nearest to the truth. We must use our intuition to tap the feelings and thoughts of an age. The creative human being behind the art probably shows reality as well as it can be shown."

"Do you live by these ideas, Wally?"

"I try to. I've thought a lot about them. I tried to put together everything I've read. I never tell anybody about them though. I don't think most kids would be interested. They might even think I'm strange. But I really don't think I am."

Both boys laughed when Wally used the word "really."

"I want to thank you, Ricky, for listening."

"Oh no, Wally. It was extremely interesting. I've never heard anything like it. I hope you don't mind if I take some time to digest what you said. You must be very lonely, Wally. I mean, these ideas are very unique. You must feel there is almost no one to talk to."

"It's OK. I think loneliness is the price you have to pay for thinking for yourself."

Ricky was overwhelmed by his friend, completely dazzled by what had been said. Yet he also felt a little uneasy. There was something eccentric and unexpected in someone who thought like Wally. Wally seemed older and more intellectual than anyone Ricky had ever known. He looked at him sitting across the table, and for the first time, Ricky noticed a slightly effeminate, soft quality.

When Wally talked, the quality disappeared. Once he grabbed the book in front of him with both hands and placed it dramatically on the table. Occasionally his head would become animated, and his flat blond strands of hair would fly about over his eyes. He would brush the hairs away with a fling of his hand.

The spontaneous lecture was now over. He sat sad and still, looking at Ricky with a kind of penetrating awareness. His eyes seemed wise, caring, and receptive, somewhat like a bright, devoted German shepherd. Ricky suddenly felt an intense curiosity that he knew he had to satisfy. He decided to ask something personal.

"Wally, I hope you don't mind my asking, but how did you get your interest in these ideas?"

He made a long pause and then a deep sigh. It was as if he agreed with himself by thinking, "Why not?" He then began, "I come from Ludowici. My father left my mother. The last few years, I've been living with my mother and sister. I spend a lot of time at home with them. Since high school began, I had nothing much to do. I never made friends in Savannah. So I've been reading books, trying to make sense out of what happened in my life and to my family. I just came to these conclusions after reading. That's where the ideas come from, reading."

Ricky was puzzled why Wally abruptly began telling of his family, as if he were a faucet whose handle had been turned. In the next few moments, Ricky learned how his father was living with a black woman in Savannah and never saw the family anymore, even though he continued to help support them. He couldn't believe that Wally's father was a car mechanic. It just didn't seem to jibe with the entire conversation. Wally told his brief story without explanation. It was hardly an answer for anything, and in fact, it increased the mystery Ricky discerned in his nature.

Ricky ventured one step further. "What do you plan to do after high school?" He anticipated a response including college and further studies.

Without changing expression, without moving his head, without seeking comments to explain his response, he looked at Ricky and, as if reciting another matter of fact, said, "I'm going to be a truck driver."

"A truck driver!?" Ricky exclaimed so loudly the single librarian looked over to them for the first time since their talk began. "How could you be a truck driver? I mean, after all this…I mean…Wally, truck drivers don't talk the way you do!"

Wally had a smile on his face. He obviously enjoyed shocking Ricky. At first Ricky thought what he said was meant as a joke, but Wally persisted.

"I always wanted to drive one of those big vans. It's big and powerful. With twelve tires. It feels great behind the wheel of a truck. Have you ever done that, Ricky?"

Ricky didn't know what to say. One minute he was listening to the most profound thoughts he had ever heard. He matched these thoughts to his notion of what he thought Wally was like. The next minute the truth came to him as if from an out-of-tune trumpet.

"Wally, how can you talk about philosophy, how can you be so sensitive, and then want to spend the hours of your day doing something as coarse and of little value as driving a truck? There is nothing intelligent or even self-examining about driving a big truck."

"It doesn't have to be intelligent, Ricky. I just want to do it. It's what feels real to me. Maybe I'll do it for a short while and then try something else. I don't know. Don't be so shocked. I can't fit into your neat ideas. It's what I am. Frankly, I don't have the money for college. I'm poor. Destiny is everything. My parents are loving, but they don't care about ideas or learning."

"My parents don't care about ideas either, but they still want me to get an education. They may want me to be a doctor or something, but they see it as a practical thing to make a living. You really want to be stuck in a low-paying, anti-intellectual job?"

"There's something truthful and real about putting your hands on a machine and becoming part of that machine. I feel powerful behind the wheel of a large and powerful engine. I feel peace and kind of like I'm being the master of something."

"Have you ever asked yourself why being the master of something is so important to you? What do your parents say?"

"My parents play a small role in my life. There's no money, Ricky. They seem to accept their limitations. I have to accept them too."

"I got a scholarship. It pays almost everything."

"And the rest? Room and board? Who's paying for that?"

"My parents said they could help with that."

"Exactly, Ricky, exactly. I don't think you know what poor is."

Ricky looked at his friend, a person with whom he felt very close. Someone who tried to fit the world together the way he did. He saw the gentleness in his eyes, the profound awareness, and thought about his friend's plans. The incongruence grabbed him, held him, and would not let go. He tried to be broad minded. "Well," he thought, "he has a right to do whatever he wants." Then he became argumentative with himself. "But truck driving leads nowhere. It will wipe out the brilliance. You can't drive over miles and miles of American highway and have deep considerations. Those guys are rough. Wally is gentle and sensitive. What will happen to him?" And it went on like this for some time after the two parted.

Once Wally announced his future intentions, the conversation reduced itself to trivial niceties. Ricky realized he had been stonewalled. He could not accept the narrow vision. He couldn't understand how far-seeing Wally did not perceive the entire environment of truck driving so that he saw it did not suit his intellectual questing. Ricky accepted. He pulled back. He allowed the small talk to take the place of the profound ideas that went before.

Wally told Ricky of some other books by Freud. Ricky told Wally that he was going to Oglethorpe, where he had received the scholarship. Both boys knew the spark had been lost, but neither could do anything about it. Wally seemed to feel the sadness that his announced truth created for him and retreated into his stoic style. Perhaps he felt Ricky fell into the very category of people he had always feared sharing himself with. Ricky was clearly awkward as his mind was occupied with both being pleasant to his friend and arguing with itself.

Finally, they got up from the library table and went out into the hallway together. Each announced he was going in the opposite direction. Ricky wished Wally well, asking if he would see him at graduation. Wally said he was thinking about going but wasn't sure. He did not return well wishes to Ricky, but this was nothing more than a reversion to his usual laconic behavior. Ricky did not view it as any kind of thoughtlessness.

Both friends waved to each other as they went their separate ways. Ricky felt the loosening of the bond between them as the distance increased in the almost empty hall. He felt they would never restore this relationship that had lasted a short time but seemed as profound and important to him as were it to have lasted all of his seventeen years. He would always hope to see Wally again but never knew if he would. He would think of him often in his plain clothes, friendly Protestant blond hair, and angular body. He would never forget his ideas and never forget his tenderness. Wally would remain forever, for Ricky, the representative of what he would hope to find in a friend.

The hallway became empty. He heard himself saunter down the steps to the main floor of the school. He wondered what would happen to this beloved fellow traveler. In time it would become obvious to him that together they would never have a friendship like this again, but they would always remember each other for the fact that each of them had allowed it to happen at a certain time in a certain space.

An End of a Beginning

THE NANCY HANKS, its silver streamlined casing giving forth the burning impression of the speed, the movement, the impetuosity, the barely restrained force of a Spanish bull in the arena. The beast seemed to be holding back his charge before some matador, red cape beckoning. The animal spewed and pawed at the Southern earth. It was ready on the railroad tracks, ready for the ultimate bull run for Atlanta, Georgia.

Ricky, his two insouciant brothers, his father, and his mother made their way along the platform, incapable of not being impressed with this mundane example of mankind's power, its being the terrestrial representative of all that humanity was capable of. Sputnik might soon dominate the sky, but the Nancy Hanks, the passenger train, the seemingly limitless tracks away from Savannah, gripped, fascinated, and continued to astound its witnesses. They felt the steam, smelled its oil, heard its rumblings as it awaited Ricky's boarding for his journey to school.

"Good-bye, son," his father said.

Ricky hugged his father with a sincerity and bittersweet feeling of regret that surprised him. He felt a choked tear swelling within, but he suppressed it. His eyes gazed downward, avoiding the sentiment he knew must be in his father's face. The new understanding and regard he had for the man were there within but not fully matured. The sting of years of conflict and the new awareness of his father's essential goodness and devotion would have to grow still more within.

He saw his brothers wandering about, uncaring of this monumental moment. He turned to his mother, who seemed to be waiting for proof that his loyalties were not lost to her. He held her gently, tendentiously, and kissed her on the cheek. She was satisfied by this and smiled.

"Good-bye, Dad…Mom." The words were peculiarly formal, but the emotion seemed real, truly meant, and they did not possess that stale quality of unfeeling ritual. With the last departing traditional "All aboard!" uttered by a Negro conductor working his way out of the oppressive history of his fellow slaves of the near past, Ricky turned from his family, repressed the lump in his throat, and boarded the seventh car of the train. He found his seat rather quickly, happily noting that it looked out upon the platform where his parents were still standing. He sat next to the window to watch them, considering it his good fortune that his car was relatively empty and that the seats were not reserved.

"All aboard!" The conductor again uttered those famous words, words Ricky had heard on countless radio programs, words he saw on the lips of like conductors in the movies, words that were the signals for a life changing. It would be but a few moments now. The gargantuan steel animal would be released. He, Ricky Bateman, like a mythic being in its belly, like a sinful Jonah, would be transported away from his parents, away from his childhood, away from Savannah. Like Jonah, he thought to himself in doleful realization, "I'm sorry."

It was entirely clear who he was speaking to. He knew he was sorry for being such a fool, for not understanding the world he lived in. He was deeply sorry for seeing people one-dimensionally, for refusing to acknowledge their complexity. All of this was not clear, but he knew he was abjectly, profoundly sorry.

His attention had been drawn by boarding passengers, people walking by him and making him hope they would sit anywhere but with him. He wanted this journey to be alone; he wanted only his thoughts as his companions, his unswerving and loyal friends. Preserving his solitude, feeling safe again with himself, he turned back to look out of the window. At that very moment, the beast began to move.

His father had come over to where he was and slapped gently on the glass. Ricky waved. He saw his mother wave back. As he began to move away from them, he felt a bond break, he felt a terrible loss, he felt the beginnings of a startling transformation. "I'm sorry."

He was leaving. On his father's face he saw tears and an expression of remorse for his loss, an expression that Ricky never thought could be possible. He and his father realized in that instant this was no mere trip to college, with its anticipated return; this was a major event in both their existences. Ricky was leaving, and his father was losing. His father was losing his youth, losing his missed opportunities for closeness with his son, losing the sharing of a life. Ricky knew at once that his father not only loved him to the depths of his being but also depended on Ricky for his sense for what life was worth. He and his father were in that spark of an instant completely aware of the tragedy. Both knew that matters could have been changed, that they could have been close, that they could have enjoyed each other better, but that life was where it was, and nothing could alter what had happened or what was being felt. The instant of this realization was upon them, dominated them. It would remain in their memories forever. Both were realizing what had been irrevocably lost as the train moved out of the station.

"I'm sorry."

Ricky cried. It was one of those deep, choking cries with large breaths in between. It would have been a loud cry, but he worked hard to muffle his sobs. His soul was in gyrations. He knew as he pushed his head between the seat and the window that he would always feel the terrible missing part of himself and that he would have to live with it, absorb it, accept it. He would always know what the meaning of tragedy was.

He also knew that he was, indeed, sorry. He regretted his ignorance of the movements of people's emotions. He felt he wanted to tell his father and mother how much he truly valued them, but he did not. He spent his last teenage years resenting them, criticizing them, wanting them to understand him while he could not understand them. His realized losing his narcissism was an entrance into wisdom, but the full importance of this realization was still not quite in place. Still the world moved, whether Ricky understood its meanings or not.

The massive grooved wheels of the Nancy Hanks held fast to the tracks, gripping them like huge ponderous claws pulling themselves along at increasing speed. The thunderous tonnage of the train swerved, twisted, and propelled itself through the Georgia countryside. Already Savannah was miles behind. The geography of the flat, field-fence-sliced landscape began to creep its way into Ricky's perception. He gradually turned his thoughts from his father, his parents, and began to consider the world he had come from. The countryside before him began to feel soothing and calming, allowing him to think more clearly, with less emotion.

He found himself thinking in and out of the rhythm of the train. The clackety clack, clackety clack of the train wheels passing over the railroad ties made a rhythmic meter in his mind. Words jumped in, matching the clackety clack, clackety clack. He let himself go with the motion of the sound. He found the vista, his metric mental verbiage, and the wheel music a harmonious whole, a kind of life sonata, and he began to merge with the multifaceted fugue, feeling a part of a larger theme beyond comprehension.

He was the fugal theme, but the other notes were increasingly becoming important. What's a melody without its chordal base?

Wally Streeter, Wally Streeter. Robin Linkowitz, Robin Linkowitz. Dad and Bartlett, Dad and Bartlett, George McGregor, George McGregor, McGregor, McGregor, Mom, Mom. Cotton fields unfolding, colored people picking cotton. Poor and dirty, poor and dirty. What life must be like for them? What a different life for them. Gasoline stations and the rough dirt road leading up. Broken-down trucks and tractors. The rednecks, sunburnt, rough, difficult people who always seem angry at something, with their thick Southern accents and beer-swilling football passions. What do the rednecks have besides their anger, a rage that says life is unfair and biased against them? The have their football. The Georgia Bulldogs, the Georgia Bulldogs. Sitting outside in his old beaten chair in the small towns, holding a beer and waiting for any stranger to come around so he can feel disgust at the stranger's daring to intrude on his turf, daring to feel that he, the stranger, could be a part of the dry, tedious, unendingly boring little piece of street world that the poor, ignorant, half-drunk, Sunday-only Baptist or Methodist calls his own.

Clackety clack, clackety clack. The flatland marsh completely disappearing. Moving into the innards of the Southern feeling. Immersed in the Bible belt, where the resurrection of Christ is truly believed. Where, incredible as it may sound, the good, God-fearing Christian, the person Ricky would trust because he'd learned to rely on these religious people's absolute devotion to Christian charity, would still ask, in a genuine moment of naive confidence and intimacy, to look at the top of your head just to see once and for all if there is any evidence that the Jews have horns. And, as he had done just a few days, weeks, months, years before, Ricky would, in the spirit of friendship, tolerance, and conviviality, wanting a good-spirited relationship with this basically fine person, say, "Sure!" and bend his head with a smile or maybe even a laugh and let him look.

The tough brown soil changes into the red clay of Georgia, and the beast of the train seems to move faster out of the world of origins, the world that must be left. The red clay, the red clay, clickety clack, clackety click, clackety clack. Apple orchards, peas, peanuts, cabbages, crops of things Ricky has forgotten. His father used to show him proudly, like a Yankee still not used to the fact that food can grow in the ground. "See, *that's* carrots!" And Ricky, in his youthful naivety, would ask if he could pick one. His dad would look around to be sure no one was around and say, "Why not?" The time remembered when a colored man came up when they weren't looking and gave them all the cotton they could want just for a smile and a handshake. They really are kind, a gentle, good people, the Negroes, Ricky thought. They often killed each other, or so his dad told him, but Ricky always would find them warm, caring, friendly. He felt a white man's sadness for the suffering they endured. For him, Joel Chandler Harris had created an iconic good man in the abused and aged Uncle Remus. Later *Song of the South* would be called racist. For Ricky, Uncle Remus was the embodiment of the caring, loving old man. George McGregor had showed him this was only one view. To the Negro, Harris was a racist, a man making fun of slaves, a man who thought a pickaninny was a funny child, not a long-suffering person that would grow up stunted because of a white man's need to be superior. Still, genealogy be damned. Fiction was fiction, and Ricky had a right to embrace it however he wanted. In spite of his better knowledge, he would not give up his avatar. Ricky was Brer Rabbit in his beloved briar patch.

It seemed the train was going up a slight rise. The sound changed; they were moving north. Ricky knew they were moving north. It was a little less South now, a little less yet of Savannah, a little more of Atlanta, more north. The hub of the business of the South, the place where roads lead, the Rome of the South. Some said so. Some said so. Clackety clack. Clackety clack.

He had been completely rejected by Harvard. He didn't feel bad about it. He really didn't expect to get in. He knew it was hubris to have even tried. There was a wild chance, a boy from the South. His grades weren't bad. But the SATs. He had been among the first to take them. Not so good. Not so good. Clackety clack. Emory had accepted him. "We don't have the money for Emory," his mother said. "Even if you get a scholarship that pays part, we can't do it." Strange, he wasn't too upset. He liked things about Oglethorpe. It was as he imagined a small Ivy League school to be: crenellated Gothic castle walls, as if the place might be besieged, exaggerated pointed Gothic windows, large gray stone construction, and of course, an adequate supply of ivy. Was it built like a manor house, a chateau, a castle? Ricky liked its exotic, pseudo medieval quality, its being somewhat outside of Atlanta, near Chamblee, its emphasis on the arts, literature, writing. He really had no idea what he wanted to do with himself. It was good, he thought, to go to a small school. Perhaps it was a rationalization. Oglethorpe University wasn't even really a university. It had no graduate school. It was once a university, founded by Sidney Lanier, the Georgia poet laureate, endowed by Franklin Roosevelt himself. But it was just a small liberal arts school with Ivy League–type professors looking for the good, quiet, uncompetitive Southern life. He was going, he almost admitted, because the school had offered him a complete scholarship. He would have to pay nothing. Nothing. His parents were enthusiastic. He accepted. Accepted. Clackety clack.

Wally? What would Wally do? Drive a truck? Would he really do that? It was a ridiculous waste. Ricky refused to allow himself to believe it was a worthwhile undertaking. He saw Wally as a spiritual brother, a soul mate, someone who was an extension of what he wanted to be. Maybe Wally knew everything Ricky was going to learn. Maybe Wally was right. Did he say it? Did he say that being was an end in itself? Ricky wasn't sure. Maybe Ricky assumed it. Was being just an end in itself? Then the xenophobe in the small one-street town was just as good as Ricky? The poor Negroes bending their backs in the cotton fields were as content (as his father claimed) as they he would ever be? No. He refused to believe this. He still clung to his love of the Greeks, even though their limitations were being felt. He no longer wanted to be a Greek; he could barely be himself. It was himself he wanted to find, whatever he was. He didn't want merely to copy the ideal of an ancient time. He remembered the sacrificed Socrates. It was the examined life that was worth living. Socrates died, took the hemlock, because he couldn't leave his town, his Athens. He couldn't leave, leave, leave, hemlock, town, town, clickity clack.

Wally was an enigma. Buddha? Buddha? Clickity clack. He felt it in his bones. Wally could not drive a truck. He would have to do something with his mind, to learn something that gave him a sense of meaning. How could such an idea-laden young soul go against his inclinations? Wally? Wally? "Am I missing something here? What am I missing here?"

Life was so difficult to understand. Reality was elusive. What was the best way to think? To be? Was everything, as Wally said, a chimera, a projection of our restricted perceptive apparatus, our body giving us a view of the world that was limited by what our body could know? Ricky now believed that people were not easy to understand. They were certainly not always what they appeared to be. Robin was not desirable. He had thought she was, but she turned out to have ideas about life he could never find acceptable. However beautiful she was, however much he wanted to make love to her, he could not be with her. It was good, that night. It was good, it was good. He smiled. Glad it's over. Glad it's over. She was so different than he thought.

Wally was a contradiction to Ricky. He was sensitive, intelligent, and knew so much more than Ricky; yet he seemed somehow attached to his past, trapped by the misery of his family. Ricky thought hard on it. Finally, he believed Wally wanted to be a truck driver because it was connected to his father. Wally was not just what he seemed to be, nor was he what he thought he was. Wally's self-trapped him just like his philosophy would trap everyone were it true, and he didn't seem to know it. Wally's father did not value books and ideas. Ricky's father did; he always regretted not finishing Stuyvesant. Wanted Ricky to do what he didn't do. Maybe that was the thread of difference between Wally and Ricky—the fathers.

Even Graham Bartlett, the man who hit him, was different than the assailant Ricky had thought about for those three months before the court appearance. The assailant came to look like another of life's victims, incapable of governing himself, vulnerable because of his passion and his frailty of character, a weakling before the power of the law and revenge.

My father. My father. Clackety clack, clickety clack. The speed of the train continued its accompanying hum to Ricky's thoughts. "My father is not mean, a frightening beast bent on hurting me. I can trust him to love me. He seemed so formidable, so huge, so threatening when I was small and vulnerable, but he is not. He is struggling with something inside of him, something that made him irritable, angry. He was the son of his father. He was the son of a tough man, a harsh man. My father had to solve the problem of his father. I have to do the same. I'm his son, close to him; I feel his struggle, his frustration, and I completely misinterpreted it. I never saw him as a person, a human being with his own problems, his own difficulties. He was harsh. He did scream, yell. Yell. Yell. But it was part of him, not the whole. He didn't learn enough to stop himself. He was the slave of his past. I will not be the slave of my past. I will not let history control me, make me completely vulnerable. I will learn everything and always be unsure. Unsure. Unsure." Clickity clack. The train whistle blew for a crossing.

And Mother? Soft, gentle, loving of her children; not a formidable mind, but an embracing one. Her spirit taught him to love, forgive. Important things were not important. Time passed. Things changed. Just live. No need to think. Mom, Mom, Mom. Clackety clack. Clackety clack.

The hum, the clackety clack, the screeching of the wheels gripping the tracks, the clatter and banging of steel against sturdy steel, the fabric of the train holding itself together, struggling to carry its load safely against the strain of entropic forces, forces threatening its capability. It fought them, determined to get to its proper destination, feeling its responsibility to itself and its passengers, extending itself beyond itself as the beast, feeling the transmogrification of itself as an angelic protector of the ignorant and the innocent, accepting its transformation and reveling in it, acknowledging its limitations within the world, demanding that it achieve what was within its power to achieve, the power and presumed integrity of the traveling man made machine. Ricky began to find peace within himself. He felt at one with the train. The person and the machine were both placed on the earth outside of will, outside of accepting the life contract. Both were limited but had power. This power could transform, could make be what was not before. The train could not think like Ricky, it needed a master to guide it, but in a way, so did Ricky. His master would be knowledge, learning, open mindedness, acceptance of life as close to reality as he could discern. He too would screech, hum, clack, swerve, twist, move, go north, looking for a wisdom perhaps beyond reach, but looking until death. And at the moment of leaving life itself, at the moment of his entropic loss of sense, he would hope wisdom would be his. Ricky trusted himself that at that time of vitality lost, he would not expire in useless despair but in more hope. In the last moment, he would be reaching, extending himself, aspiring. In the last breath, he would be trying to comprehend, to understand, to feel, to sing, to breathe, to hold on to the last gripped track of existence. And as that last breath left, leaving the earth itself, he would be extending his arm to the heavens and reaching for the meaning, the elusive meaning, of his own existence.

Savannah would always be a part of that comprehending. It is impossible to destroy the past, to make it trivial. However, Savannah may have disappointed, it would always be a part of Ricky. He would never fully like it, never feel the devotion of Socrates to Athens, but he would always think about it, try to make sense of it. He remembered how as a child he would ride his bike with friends to Percival Square, to the grave of Tomochichi. His friends had taught him a ritual, a game. They would get off their bikes, lay them on their sides, and make a circle around the great rock that marked the Indian's grave. There were never enough of them to hold hands; they would rather dance around the grave like mock Indians. They danced the mock Indian dance as well as they could, but instead of rapidly placing their palms over their open mouths and making the typical Indian sounds children do, they chanted the name of the great friend of Oglethorpe. "Tomochichi, Tomochichi, Tomochichi, Tomochichi." Ricky played this game with the same fervor as his friends. While doing the dance, he sometimes forgot the fun of it and began to imagine what the old Indian might have been like, how he would have looked, what he might have said. He remembered this now as the train moved toward Atlanta. He remembered this soul bearer of his hometown and his own essence. He remembered the wonderful Tomochichi, this wonderful friend of Oglethorpe, this personification of trust and devotion, whoever or whatever he was.

The great massive train plummeted toward Atlanta and the beginning of life for one of its passengers. The massive wheels could be heard as they revolved and screeched as they were held fast by the rails. They repeated in sound the mood of Ricky's life. Leaving. Leaving. Leaving the end of the river. Seeking its beginnings. In rough rail fashion following alongside against the streaming of the great Savannah water. The car made music in its motion and sound. It spoke for the present and forever. Its young passenger was mind singing the song, caught up in its melody. He was singing for everything and everybody. He was part of the universe of the Now, the Forever, and singing with it. Clackety clack, clackety clack, screech and swerve, moving and humming. Friend and care. Friend and care. Friend, father and family. What matters in life embodied in a spirit. The power of a friend. The power of meaning between people. The Indians name repeated itself in the s of the reverberations of the wonderfully over powering train. Tomochichi, Tomochichi, Tomochichi, Tomochichi.

Tomochichi